BANE
OF
TENEBRIS

BLAISE RAMSAY

Black Rose Writing | Texas

ISBN: 978-1-68433-550-3
PUBLISHED BY BLACK ROSE WRITING
www.blackrosewriting.com

Printed in the United States of America
Suggested Retail Price (SRP) $18.95

Bane of Tenebris is printed in Calluna

*As a planet-friendly publisher, Black Rose Writing does its best to eliminate unnecessary waste to reduce paper usage and energy costs, while never compromising the reading experience. As a result, the final word count vs. page count may not meet common expectations.

Cover illustration by Alisha Moore © 2018 Damonza

To my loyal readers,
Thank you for taking such good care of these pretty wolf boys.
My husband, John, for once again being such a powerful support system.
My kids for sharing mommy's attention for such intense deadlines.

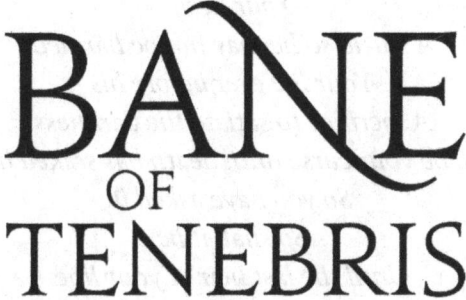

BANE
OF
TENEBRIS

"Your blood
Spilled so he might endure
Your flesh
A shield so he may not be harmed
Your life ever before his
A sacrifice to satiate the darkness
This will be your curse until death has staked his claim
So you have asked it
So shall it be
Until the last heir of your line
Takes his final breath."

CHAPTER ONE

The time of a hero is ever fleeting. They're born, their tales told, and they die with the hope those whose lives they impacted remembered their names.

To Alexander Kain, the term "hero" never sat well with him. He broke the laws of his people many times during his long life as a soldier in the Blood Wars.

The autumn moon shone in the night sky above Big Timber. Her light warm on Kain's chilled face. The sensation calmed him despite his inability to turn into the majestic wolf within due to the jagged scars across his copper skin. He inhaled, taking in the fresh scent of pine and the coolness of the night.

Beneath his boots, the leaves crunched on the forest floor. The small catches he pulled from the traps and river nets bounced against his shoulder.

The difficulty of the hike forced Kain to stop to catch his breath.

In his mind, a dark voice echoed. *"You are weakening, Kain. It will not be too long before your body fails. Why not surrender to me? I will take your pain and give you power."*

Barghast's arrival annoyed Kain. For weeks, the god offered him the same, only to be refused each time. If death was to be Kain's fate, he'd want to accept it with dignity.

He ignored the god, earning a snuff. *"So be it. Do me a favor. Die soon. I grow weary of tormenting a corpse."*

As he'd done with each visit, Barghast vanished as swiftly as he arrived. Grateful to be alone, Kain resumed his hike in silence to his cabin.

An hour had passed by the time Kain arrived at his intended destination. He took the catches to the shed where he prepared the meat to butcher and store it for future use. Once he finished, he returned to the main house to get a shower before dinner.

After removing his jacket and boots, Kain went up the wooden stairs to the master bathroom to turn on the shower. The heated water filled the room with steam.

Kain took off his shirt to see the many varieties of scars and gashes covering his back, legs, arms, chest and hips.

Sighing, eyes down-turned, Kain finished undressing and got in the shower. The warm water served as a relief against the ache of his sore muscles and the stinging of the scars.

Kain leaned against his forearm on the cold tile wall to support his weight, his chest heaving, sweat beading on his brow. A shudder ran down his spine, despite the warmth of the water. He could almost feel death running her cold fingers over his skin – beckoning him to her sweet, final embrace.

He clenched his jaw, slamming his forearm against the tile wall. Fear and resentment welled up inside him. He turned the water off after washing up, got out to dry off and dress.

Back downstairs, Kain began preparing some of the meat he brought in from the freezer in the shed in a bone broth. The smell of meat and fish filled the room, making Kain's mouth water in anticipation.

A soft creaking on the porch followed by a knock at the door caught Kain's attention.

Raising up from his haunches, he went to answer it, curious as to who could be visiting at such late hours.

Damien stood in the doorway. "Hey Kain, been a while. Mind if I come in?"

"Of course," Kain replied with a smile of delight to see his old friend. "It's good to see you, Damien."

Damien offered a crooked grin. "How have you been?"

"I won't lie, I could be better," Kain answered. His exhaustion betrayed his attempt to hide his weakened condition.

"How's Jillian? Howling has it, the two of you had the pups."

"We did. Three girls. Scared me to think about it at first. Jill wanted to come, but I told her not to."

Kain covered a laugh. He took Damien's coat and hung it on a metal hanger next to the door. "That sounds like Jillian. What about, Charlie?"

"Dad's fine. He moved out of the house and let Jill and I have it. He's actually dating! You know Sarah from the General store?" Damien settled on the couch in the living room.

Kain nodded, sitting in the lounge chair next to the fireplace.

"Well, that's who he's dating. From what he says, they're pretty serious."

"From what I remember, Sarah's a nice girl. She came into the bowling alley with her daughter a few times," Kain said.

A brief silence overtook the room.

"You don't look like you're feeling well at all. I've never seen it this bad. What's going on?" Damien shook his finger at his friend. His eyes held a sense of warning. "Oh and don't try to tell me not to be concerned."

"I just finished setting up for dinner. Would you like some?" Kain said, changing the subject.

"No thanks, I hunted before I got here. Wouldn't mind troubling you for some hot tea, though."

Kain departed to the kitchen, returning with a steaming cup of steeped tea. He handed it to Damien and made himself a plate of food before going upstairs to retrieve a leather book. His hand roamed over the cover, his brow creased at the memories it held.

It was time he told Damien about the cause of his scars. The reason he chose to seclude himself and why he looked so pitiful.

Inhaling a deep breath, Kain returned to the living room, setting the book down in front of Damien.

Damien looked at the book, then at Kain, his brow raising.

Kain exhaled through his nose. "Open it."

The pages cracked, their surface worn and yellowed. Words scrawled in ink lay coupled with etchings.

Kain watched while Damien looked through the pages. "My family is unlike any other of our people. We carry a heavy burden placed upon us countless centuries ago."

The tightening in Kain's chest forced him to stand. He stared into the fire. Ghosts of his past danced in the orange flames flickering in his emerald eyes. "It began long before my time. Vampires out-numbered us on almost every battlefield. Our royal line staggered on the brink of extinction. My ancestor knew if the genocide did not stop, we would lose our direct link to Tenebris.

"My father told me my ancestor cried out to the Night Father amongst the decay and rot of the battlefield. Tenebris met Velkin and despite his desire not to, struck a bargain with him." Kain's voice lowered. "My fate was sealed that day."

He grew silent, his thoughts drifting to a forlorn past.

"You're doing it again," Damien said, closing the book.

"Doing what?"

"Not telling me what you're thinking. You started this, now tell me everything."

Kain shook his head, trying not to snicker. "On my eighteenth birthday, my father told me what our family expected of me. We argued, and I ran from him. Truth is, I thought of ending my life. Dreamed of trying to run away. In the end, I decided to make the most of the life I was given."

Kain looked over his shoulder at Damien, eyes stern and emotionless. "I would fight until my time came. Not only to protect my chosen, but for my people. I became a mentor to many, adopted father to others."

"You're protecting someone? Is that why you have so many scars?" Damien asked.

"Yes. As long as I live, Barghast cannot attack the one I am protecting. I cannot say who. It is forbidden according to the terms of the bargain. What I can say is I want to live out the rest of the short time I have in peace."

Damien jumped from his seat and shouted, "You left to die alone! How the hell can you think I'd be okay with this? You disappeared for a fucking year without as much as a phone call!"

"I did. I knew you would be upset. That is why I left without letting anyone know."

Damien threw a fist only to have it caught right before it hit Kain's face. Kain shoved it aside. He grunted when Damien followed up with another hit at impressive speed, connecting with Kain's jaw making him stumble.

"You're a piece of work. You really are. You bastard," Damien said.

Kain wiped the back of his hand across his jaw. "Glad you think so." He laughed, embracing Damien. "It's good to see you, brother. Your skills have improved."

"Thank you." Damien held Kain tight. "Is there no way to stop it?"

Kain pulled away, shaking his head. "Only through my death can the chain be broken. I am sorry, Damien. Believe me, I wish there was another way."

Damien turned his back. His shoulders trembled, his knuckles popping the tighter he clenched his fists. "I'm not giving up. I'll keep looking for a way to fix this until you draw your last breath."

Kain sat back down in the chair and took a bite of his dinner. "How's Gabriel? Does he have any plans to restore his gym?"

Damien grumbled as he paced the floor, his hand on his hip. The other ran the length of his short, dark hair to the back of his neck. "Gabriel and I don't really talk. I'm not sure he actually likes me."

Kain stood and started collecting dishes. "Really? He seemed grateful to you following the battle with Lilith."

"Yeah, well, old habits die hard, I guess," Damien snapped, jerking his head to glare at the elder lycan.

Understanding the underlying meaning, Kain retired to the kitchen to place the dishes in the sink.

In the kitchen, the onset of a searing pain in his chest sent Kain to his knee. He squeezed his eyes closed as he reached to grip his chest. His lungs burned with each attempt to take in a breath.

"Kain!" Damien yelled and rushed into the kitchen. He fell to his knee next to his friend.

"I'm fine," Kain said, using the counter edge and Damien's body to stand.

"What the hell, Kain?" Damien asked, helping Kain sit down in one of the wooden chairs next to the round table in the kitchen.

Kain waved Damien off, cradling his forehead with his hand. "Damien, please. Do not push this. I need you to trust me."

Damien threw up his arms. "It's not you I don't trust, you idiot."

Kain looked up at him with his uncovered eye.

The young lycan tapped a finger to his head. "The time you entered my mind and drove out Barghast, remember? We're connected - mind and soul. We've both seen him. Felt what he can do."

Damien fell to his haunches in front of Kain. "I'm not letting that bastard get away with tormenting you anymore. He doesn't get to tear you to shreds and then your life on top of it."

Kain smirked, a slight 'tsk' came from between his teeth. "It's nice to know your heart and will are still so strong. Those are good qualities for an alpha."

Damien slammed a fisted hand the palm of the other with an "aha." "That's something else I needed to discuss with you," He sat down next to Kain. "I don't suppose you considered my offer?"

Using his thumb and forefinger, Kain rubbed the bridge of his nose. He knew where the conversation headed and lacked the mood to entertain it.

"Be my beta, Kain. You trained me; helped me grow into a strong leader. I'm the youngest lycan in all the packs around here. Please. I still need my mentor."

The younger lycan's pleading eyes started to melt Kain's resolve. "I will think about it, Damien. I do not know how I can be of any use. I no longer have the strength to change or to fight."

"You won't have to. Just think about it. That's all I can ask for now," Damien got up from the chair. "I guess now I know why I was called here."

Kain's brow raised, intrigued at what Damien could have meant.

"Luna came to see me when we trained at the Circle of Stones. She told me 'one we both love will need your help, as much as you needed theirs'. Now, I know she meant you. I'm going to save you, Kain. Somehow." Damien left the kitchen to go back into the living room.

Kain stood from his spot on the chair to stare out of the paned window above the sink. His hands rested on his fingertips on the cold granite cabinets. He dropped his head, eyes closed.

A dark and ominous feeling fell over Kain. It was a feeling he hadn't felt in years, and it angered him to find it once again began to surface. The demons of his past had returned, and he knew the time would come when he'd have to face them.

CHAPTER TWO

The following morning a soft snow whispered across the trees, blanketing the landscape with fresh white powder. A brisk wind shook the icicles, clanging them together to create a soft tinkling sound.

Kain lay on his side in bed listening to nature's calming music. A low rumble in his stomach reminded him he still needed to eat. With a groan, Kain forced himself to sit up and let his legs hang over the edge of the bed. He took a moment, gathering his will to get up, go downstairs and make breakfast.

The wounds on Kain's shoulders ached as he reached for the cast iron skillet in the cabinet above the stove.

Damien's words from the previous night echoed within Kain's mind. The idea of finding some way to escape his fate offered a flicker of hope. However, he pushed the thought away. Not one member of his family died in their beds or of old age.

Around mid-morning, Damien walked into the kitchen stumbling, half-drunk from sleep. He picked up the silver kettle on the counter next to the sink, rolling his eyes. "Really? Got a real coffee pot? Like a Keurig or something?"

Kain snickered as he gestured his head to the pantry. "Gabriel said the same thing. He and Spence got me one soon afterwards for Christmas. It's in the pantry on the floor. Help yourself."

Damien lifted the box at the bottom of the pantry and put it on the table. Freeing it from its cardboard prison, he set the Keurig on the counter and plugged it in. He put a pod into its maw and started the brewing before sitting in a wooden chair.

"See? How easy was that?" he commented, throwing his arms behind his head, a coy smirk on his face.

Kain enjoyed having Damien around despite his adolescence and inexperience. During their time together, not only had Kain grown to respect Damien, but to love him like a brother. The young lycan held an intelligence and wisdom of the world many lacked. His encounters with the vampires and his willingness to put others above himself were two qualities Kain admired most.

Kain set a plate of breakfast before his friend. "Damien, I have to check the traps in the woods. Would you like to come? I can teach you some basic survival skills."

"Actually, yeah. It would be nice. Thanks," Damien said.

That night the wind howled with an icy mix of sleet and snow. The small shards of ice struck the glass of the window. Branches scratched the panes of the window, their shadows taking the form of death's slender fingers.

Kain sat alone in the darkness of his room. His elbows sat on his thighs, hands hanging between his legs. The only source of light came from the gentle flicker of flames in a charcoal stove.

An evil presence filled the room, its arrival bringing about a stifling pressure. The scars on Kain's body began to feel hot, almost as though the evil within them rejoiced at the arrival of its master.

Kain sighed, his eyes directed to the floor. "I know you are here."

The sound of clicking talons accompanied the smell of burning wood as the new arrival made his way across the room. The nauseating scent of a wicked miasma mixed with ash spread throughout the room.

The dark god fell to a knee in front of Kain. He took Kain's jaw in his claws, raising Kain's head. *"Good evening, Alexander. I can see your life draining. The pain your soul endures as you battle the hate inside for your own existence is intoxicating. Forsake your gods. Serve me and I will lift you from this weakness. Free you from this fate."*

Kain hated himself for contemplating the Shadowed One's offer. He knew what the dark god asked of the mindless tools he bent to his will.

"Go to hell," Kain replied, jerking his jaw free of the claws, leaving a thin line of crimson.

The dark god snarled, raising his claw to slash Kain's face only to stop once their eyes met. He gritted his teeth and withdrew his hand. *"Tell me why. Why cast away your life to a shameful death?"*

Kane bared his fangs. "It is only shameful if I give in to temptation. You would not understand. You, who turned on your brother in a fit of blind jealousy!"

Barghast growled through clenched teeth. He raised his claws once again, but still hesitated.

Instead, he smiled. *"This is not over, Alexander. I will have what is mine. Time may have forgotten the laws you broke, the sins you committed in the name of your 'righteousness,' but I have not."*

In a rush of shadow and wind, the dark god disappeared, his laughter lingering in the darkness. The scorch marks on the floor vanished, leaving no trace of his presence.

A feeling of unease filled Kain. Whatever the god had planned for him, it wouldn't only affect him.

In the wee hours of the morning, Kain woke to find Damien already gone. A note lay folded on the bedside table. Kain opened it to read yet another reminder that Damien wouldn't give up on his efforts to save him.

Too weak from the fatigue, Kain stayed on his bed facing the window to see the moon through the curtains. The stars glowed bright against the still remaining blackness of the night.

His vision blurred as he fought death to do one last thing.

Gritting his teeth, Kain forced himself to slide off his bed to the floor. The simple action made him wince, gripping his chest as he tried to breathe.

Once he settled on his knees, he closed his eyes and took in a deep breath, allowing his mind to drift into a meditative state. His mind was swept into the celestial plane as he called upon Tenebris.

Kain looked up to see the Wolfgod standing above him, his fur white as snow, eyes radiating with the piercing light of the heavens.

"Alexander. It delights my heart to hear your voice again." Tenebris knelt before Kain, brushing his hair from his face. *"You are weakened and weary, my son. Will you not come home and rest beside your forefathers?"*

"I cannot," Kain replied.

Tenebris tilted his head in question, *"What is it I can do for you, most noble of knights?"*

Kain humbled himself, requesting to change the one he protected. He wanted to continue mentoring someone he thought needed his protection more than his current charge.

Tenebris lowered his head, exhaling crystals of ice. *"Alexander, are you sure? I would be unable to repair your body completely."*

Kain nodded.

Tenebris's eyes misted, his brow lowered in sadness. A soft whimper came from his throat. *"As much as it pains my soul to see you suffer so much only to begin again, I will honor your request."*

Tenebris raised his hand, his lips drew back over his fangs in a clenched snarl. He pulled his claws away from Kain's chest.

A glass orb filled with the last remnants of a red liquid emerged from Kain's sternum. The lycan looked on while it floated in his god's hands. The blood of his current chosen all but spent.

Pentacost had shown him drawings while he tried to explain how the "bane" worked. No matter how many times Kain saw it, the orb still seemed surreal.

Once Tenebris held the orb in his claws, Kain fell back to his knees. He gripped his chest, eyes wide and blurred, his heart pounding. *"I must collect the blood of your new chosen. Try to endure until I return."*

Tenebris disappeared into a burst of light.

Kain laid down in the fetal position to conserve energy for what seemed like hours.

When Tenebris returned, he knelt to take Kain's arm to help him sit up. *"I have what you need. I ask you again before I do this. Are you sure? You may choose to rest, my son."*

Panting, Kain refused the offer, not wanting to die before his duty was finished. As his ancestor did before him, Kain bade Tenebris to go through with his request.

The god held the orb, now full of the red liquid towards his servant. It melted back into Kain's chest, replacing the emptiness with the same warmth he'd experienced the first time he'd taken this blood.

Tenebris ordered Kain to kneel before him. *"Alexander Kain, last of the Kain line, as per the contract struck with your ancestor. Your blood to be spilled ever before his. Your flesh a shield against the darkness of death and pain. Your life a sacrifice in place of his own. This shall be the norm until death has staked its claim. So, you have asked it. So, shall it be."*

Kain woke up on his floor, gasping. The morning sun shone through the window. The warmth of its rays served as a comfort against the cold of the darkness shrouding his mind only a few hours ago.

Kain got up, dressed, and proceeded to begin the day's routine. He stepped outside, grinning brightly at the feeling of the warmth of the sun on his face.

When he reached the first of his traps, he could tell something was wrong. The woods around him seemed still compared to the previous day. No animals or birds could be heard, the wind didn't blow, the smell of the air stagnant and strange. It burned Kain's sensitive nostrils like the miasma of the Shadowed One.

The hair on the back of Kain's neck prickled. His body tensed. He whipped his head to the sound of a rustling bush, catching the brief hint of a shadow.

Something lingered in the protection of the forest's trees. However, for the moment, Kain could do nothing but return to his cabin. His instincts on high alert.

By moonrise, Kain had already turned in for the night, his body tired from his encounter with Tenebris the night before.

"Alexander," came a gentle whisper in Kain's ear.

Kain groaned in his sleep yet didn't budge.

"Alexander," the call came a bit louder.

He raised his head from his pillow to look around.

"Alexander," the voice came again.

Kain's eyes fell on the owl, stretching its wings on a branch outside his window. He left his bed, lumbering to the window to open it. "Forgive me, but do I know you?"

The owl flew into the room, coming to sit on the edge of the window sill. *"Does a son not recognize his mother?"*

Kain cursed under his breath. He held out his arm, allowing her to perch on it, raising her to feel the silky feathers on his cheek. "Forgive me, mother. I did not recognize you."

"It is alright, my dearest one. I worried for you. It has been too long since I have seen the handsome creature inside of you."

Kain averted his eyes. "I can no longer change. It feels like the wolf inside of me is gone."

"He is not gone, my love. Come. I know you can still run with me. I have something to show you," Luna used her wingtip to brush a single strand of hair from Kain's face.

She leapt from his arm and took flight out of the window.

Determined not to lose her, Kain rushed downstairs. Taking his jacket from the coat rack by the door, he threw open of the front door and looked around, trying to spot Luna.

The snowy owl fluttered above him, releasing a melodious cry before flying away.

Some time passed since Kain had the strength to run. He shook the stiffness from his body, his lycan blood heating his muscles against the cold.

Eager to feel the freedom running offered, Kain took off through the trees. As he did so, his body started to remember what it felt like to have the wind rushing through his hair. His spirit revived with each leap, each dodge of a tree branch.

At the end of the trail, Kain found Luna perched on a branch just outside a patch of thorny rose bushes. She almost appeared to smile when he greeted her.

"You ran beautifully. In time your body will remember. Walk forward. I will meet you on the other side," she said prior to taking to the sky over the menacing thorns.

Kain pushed his way through the bush, wincing at each jab of the thorns against his skin. When he broke through, Kain's eyes fell on a naked young woman lying on the ground.

In human form, Luna sat on her knees next to her, running slender fingers through the dark red strands of the woman's long hair.

From the looks of the bruises and the scratches all over her body, it appeared the woman got attacked.

"What happened?" Kain asked, stopping just before the two women, "Who is she?"

"Her name is Tala. Take her with you, Alexander. Care for her. We will tell you more when the time comes." Luna smiled, vanishing into a mist.

Luna's instructions confused him, but he did as she ordered. He covered the woman with his jacket, picked her up and took her with him.

CHAPTER THREE

Tala's chest hurt from running. Unfamiliar screams filled her ears, shifting into angry snarls and growls. Something rammed her hard enough to knock her down, but she quickly recovered and continued to run. Black shapes surrounded her, lashing out with their claws, leaving painful bites across her skin.

Exhausted, Tala collapsed. As she lay on the ground, her vision blurred and faded from the dark images to one of an angelic-faced man with dirty blonde hair.

Tala opened her eyes, free from the fractured memories, finding she no longer lay on the ground in the woods. Groaning, she tried to push herself onto her elbows to take in her surroundings and her condition.

She looked down to find herself naked, half covered in thick blankets, and her wounds cleaned and wrapped.

Lifting her eyes to the rest of the room, she saw a round, black wood-burning stove in the corner. In its maw an orange fire glowed.

When the door opened, Tala jerked her attention towards the noise of the creaking hinges. The same man she thought she only dreamed of walked in carrying a plate of food and extra bandages.

Polished, sculpted muscles lay scarcely hidden beneath the white undershirt he wore. The faded, dark blue jeans sat low on his hips. Soft features, worn by time, defined his face.

She felt her cheeks heat the longer she stared. The only imperfections were the jagged scars covering the copper skin of his arms.

"Oh, you're awake. I'm glad. I began to wonder if you would wake at all," the strange man said as he set the plate on the table next to the bedside and grabbed the bandages.

Tala backed away so quickly she underestimated the distance and fell over the bed's edge, landing to the floor with a *THUD*.

The man clenched one eye closed, hissing through his teeth. "I'm sorry. That looked rather unpleasant."

The man strode around the other side of the bed and took a knee in front of her. His gentle eyes met hers. In a tender voice, he said. "I'm not going to hurt you. My name is Alexander Kain. May I ask your name?"

Kain held out his hand to help her up.

"Tala. My name is Tala," Tala replied, taking Kain's hand. "Where am I and how did I get here?

"You're in my home. I found you injured in the woods not far from here. You've been unconscious for almost a week now," Kain said. He took the food from the bedside table and set it down in front of her. He followed with his own question, "Do you know how you came to be in the woods?"

Tala rubbed her head, groaning. The images from the dream returned to her, causing her to tremble. "I ... I remember running. There were black shapes. I don't remember anything before that."

Kain helped Tala sit back down on the bed. "These black shapes. Do you recall something strange about them?"

"They moved fast. I remember the stings of pain each time they got close."

Kain sat down next to her on the bed. "It's okay. It may take time for your memories to return. I'm not sure how long you were out there. Try to get some food and rest. I will come back later to check on your injuries."

"Wait. Where am I? What city?"

"Big Timber. About a mile outside of it to be specific," Kain replied.

"Big Timber?" Tala's eyes widened. "I was trying to get here."

"Get some rest and eat. We can talk more later." Kain departed the room without saying another word.

Kain leaned against the wooden railing of his covered porch, his eyes focused on the line of trees around the perimeter of his cabin. In the shadows, he made out glowing eyes staring from beyond the gloom. Snarls could be heard above the silence.

The lights of a black Mustang could be seen driving up the gravel road towards the cabin.

He soon recognized it, grinning. "Well, well, well. It seems I'm suddenly very popular."

Kain waited for the car to stop and the engine to turn off before descending the wooden stairs.

Gabriel stepped out of the driver's side, running a hand through shoulder length, curly dark hair. "It's good to see you, old friend." He commented in a thick European voice, embracing Kain.

"You as well. What brings you so far out of your pack's territory?" Kain asked, his eyes never leaving the trees.

Gabriel followed Kain's line of sight. "You see them as well?"

"Yes. As of yet, they have not ventured any closer. I cannot be sure of how long that will last. Come, we can talk inside." Kain motioned Gabriel towards the front door.

When they got inside, Tala sat in the living room in front of the fire with a cup of water in her hands, wrapped in a borrowed blanket. She jumped when Kain came in with Gabriel.

Gabriel whistled at seeing how pretty the young woman was. "Who's this?"

Kain shook his head, sighing and reaching the heel of his hand to the side of his head, eyes turned towards the ceiling. "Honestly, Gabriel, must you really?"

Gabriel shrugged, holding his hands up as he approached Tala. "I won't hurt you. My name is Gabriel Locke. I'm Kain's friend." Gabriel held out his hand. Tala waited for a nod from Kain before she reached to shake it. "There, see? What's your name?"

Tala told him.

"It's nice to meet you," Gabriel kissed her hand before addressing Kain. "Kain, I wish I came here to catch up, but I'm afraid that isn't the case."

"I imagined it wouldn't be. You rarely come to make a social call. What is it?" Kain sat down in the recliner while Gabriel chose to sit on the floor.

"Ramona contacted me," Gabriel said. A low rumble in the back of his throat. "Stoker survived the battle at the Stones and slithered to the

Cardozas in Great Falls. He's informed Anthony of the events that happened here. So far, it doesn't appear to Ramona that Anthony even cares."

Kain listened to Gabriel go into the details about how Anthony Cardoza, the Don of Great Falls, began to search for an item of unknown origin. His escapades caused horrendous damages to the lycan packs surrounding the city.

During the conversation, Kain's eyes never left Tala. Her actions indicated signs of familiarity with the situation.

"What is the damage so far, Gabriel?" Kain asked.

Tears began to fall down Tala's face. Out of the blue, she commented on how the Don began slaughtering the pack, recalling instances of smells of smoke and copper. Black shapes ripped and tore flesh from bone amidst crumbling cinders of houses where lycans used to live in peace.

Gabriel pushed his legs underneath himself to stand. "That about sums it up. Ramona says Desdemona is trying to reign Anthony in, but her efforts are going unheard. Whatever he's looking for, he wants it enough to commit genocide."

Kain shoved himself up from his chair so strongly, the force sent the legs skidding across the wood floors. "We will not let this go unchallenged. Gabriel, give me two days and I will return to the battlefield. For now, considering our unwanted guests, you should stay for the night. Return to your pack in the morning. They will need you."

Gabriel nodded, retiring to one of the guest rooms Kain often let him use when he visited.

After Gabriel left the room, Tala watched Kain walk into the kitchen. Curious, she got up to follow him and peeked around the doorframe to find Kain staring out of the window above the sink.

"You don't have to hide. Come in," he said in the same tender voice he used in the room upstairs.

Tala walked into the kitchen, sitting in the chair closest to Kain. She stared at his arms, taking in every jagged scar tarnishing his skin. She wanted to ask where he got them but held herself back.

"You said your last name is Kain? I'm not sure where, but I've heard it before."

Kain pulled up a chair and sat in front of her, his elbows resting on his thighs. "Have you? It's an unusual name around here."

"Yes. I heard stories about someone named Kain from the elders of my pack. They called him Penta-something," she closed her eyes trying to remember.

"Pentacost."

When their eyes met, Tala could see how sad he looked. "I think so. Did you know him?"

Kain closed his eyes. A remorseful sigh blew through his nose as he rose from the chair. "It does not matter. Be ready. In two days, I take you to Big Timber."

The following morning, Gabriel left after having coffee and talking with Kain over breakfast. He hadn't been gone long before a rustling and clanging from outside made Kain focus on the window overlooking the shed he usually prepared his catches in.

"They have finally come closer."

"They?" Tala asked. She glanced around, her brows lowered in fear, scooting closer to Kain.

As he headed to the front door, Kain spoke of the black shapes Tala mentioned, labeling them as werewolves and being sure they followed the commands of someone. He put on his jacket and went outside to confront the monsters tearing his supply shed apart.

Kain stayed close to the side of the cabin and snuck around the perimeter until his shed came into view.

Werewolves ripped and tore at the wooden walls of the shed, tearing meat from drying racks and fighting over meat they took from the overturned freezer.

A slight rustle in the tree line behind him brought Kain's attention to the new visitor. The large wolf form identified him as a lycan, not a werewolf.

Whites overtook Kain's eyes at the realization of the familiar black fur. *No, it cannot be.*

The lycan grinned, his fangs dripping with saliva over dark gums. Triangular ears stiffened towards the sky, deep orange eyes the color of a burning sunset thinned with satisfaction. Something about him seemed distorted; defiled as though he were bathed in Barghast's shadow. In a flash of fur and shadows, the lycan vanished into the trees.

A moment in his past flashed in his mind. The howling of a lycan in pain, the taste of blood, an angry promise of vengeance. Rage filled gales of wind and rain whipped, stinging with the icy knives of winter. *Those eyes. I remember those eyes.*

Tala jumped as Kain burst through the door, slamming it shut. He ran up the stairs only to return with what appeared to be a camper's bag. He ordered Tala to be prepared to go, his words laced with urgency.

"What's going on?"

"There's no time. We need to go." Kain rustled through a drawer, grabbing the keys to his car. Handing Tala some clothes to borrow, Kain told her to wait for him to call to her.

Tala wanted to argue but resigned to getting dressed and waiting until she heard Kain call to her from outside before following him.

Kain stood next to the open driver's side door, focusing his eyes on the surrounding area. He waved his hand, beckoning her towards the car.

Tala ran down the stairs, brushing her hair away from her face to keep it from hindering her sight.

She got into the car as the first werewolf jumped towards her, snarling. Tala raised her arms to her face, prepared to be struck with its claws. When no attack came, she opened her eyes to see Kain restraining the flailing monster, his strong arms around its ribs.

Kain growled as he tightened his forearm around the thrashing monster's neck. A sickening snap made the monster fall limp, its tongue lulling out of its mouth.

Kain threw the body aside before he got into the driver's side of the car, closing and locking the door. His breath heaved.

"It's been a while since I've done that," He smirked. Shifting the car into reverse, Kain slammed his foot on the accelerator making the tires shriek in protest.

When they reached the main road, Tala saw the werewolves running alongside the car in the trees. "What do they want?"

Kain didn't answer. The arrival of the lycan made him second guess his original theory as to why the werewolves stalked his cabin.

A werewolf slammed its body against the driver's side door of the car, jarring it.

In response, Kain used the body of the vehicle and the guardrails of the highway to pin the werewolf between them. It whimpered and howled in pain as its flesh was severed from its side in a storm of sparks and grinding metal.

Another werewolf took a flying leap into the windshield from the middle of the road, claws outstretched, fangs bared. The impact cracked the glass. It grasped at the hood with its claws, sending sparks where steel met bone.

"Hang on!" Kain said, slamming on the brakes, sending the creature flying down the pavement.

There were too many of them to outmaneuver, especially when Kain couldn't change and had Tala to contend with. He began to wonder if he could get either of them out of this encounter alive.

A howl above the wind made the werewolves freeze.

"What is that?" Tala asked.

Kain smirked, stopping the car. Just beyond the tree line, he saw Gabriel skidding down the side of the hill.

Lune followed behind him while an obsidian wolf Kain recognized as Jillian, sprinted ahead of them. Scott and Nathaniel followed close on her flanks.

The werewolves remained still. Another howl, like the shriek of a banshee, forced them to retreat into the woods.

Kain got out of the car to greet his friends.

Gabriel walked to the head of the pack, shaking his head side to side, snuffing.

"It's good to see you. How did you know?" Kain asked.

Gabriel turned his head. Kain followed his gaze to see a pure white wolf with black markings on his paws, chest, ear tips and tail walking towards them.

Kain grinned, offering a slight bow of his head. Damien broke into a canter until he reached Kain, whimpering. He lowered his ears, nuzzling his friend's stomach.

Tala got out of the car, her eyes locked on the white wolf Kain petted. "Lycans."

Kain rose up to look at her.

"My mother is a lycan. She's the one who told me to come here," Tala replied, remembering the voice of her mother begging her to run.

Damien looked at Kain, tilting his head, whimpering.

"I will tell you more when we get to your house." Kain turned on his heel to walk back to his car.

CHAPTER FOUR

At Damien's house, Jill told her mate she would take Tala upstairs to take care of her children while Damien spoke with the pack members present. With a quick kiss, Damien nodded, and the two women went to the pups' nursery.

"Spill it, Kain. What was that all about?" Damien asked, sitting down on the sofa in the small living room.

"I am still unsure as to what their exact reasons were. They were unlike any werewolves I have come across. They followed orders, calculated and weighed their options, even scouted before moving in close," Kain replied from his spot on the floor.

From his spot against the wall, Gabriel chimed in. "I went to talk to Kain about Anthony Cardoza's recent genocide of the local packs around Great Falls. It can't be a coincidence. These monsters have to be following Anthony's orders or someone who works for him."

A 'tsk' sound came from Lune who leaned against the wall opposite Gabriel, "Of course it isn't, think about it. Kain finds this mystery woman with no memory of who she is, yet, seems to recall her pack getting attacked by the same werewolves?"

Kain glared at Lune, silencing him. "Tala is not responsible for this. They chased her from Great Falls, tore her apart and left her for dead in the woods. Whatever it is she was sent to do, they do not want her to do it."

Damien's arms crossed over his chest, his weight shifting to his left leg. "Whatever's going on, it doesn't appear to be good. Great Falls isn't far from here. Who's this Anthony, anyway?"

Gabriel replied. "Right, you haven't encountered him before. He's Desdemona's son, the Don of Great Falls. Ramona says he's looking for something. Desdemona's doing what she can to get him to back off but so far, it hasn't worked."

"Okay, another psycho vampire, great." Damien turned his attention to Kain. "Does Tala remember anything about why she was sent here?"

Kain shook his head. "The only thing she remembers is the carnage and the voice of a woman telling her to come here."

Damien scrubbed his hand down his face. "Well, do your best to try and get her to remember. We're flying blind. Obviously, these new werewolves aren't afraid of your reputation or Gabriel's. When our meeting's over, we need to talk."

Kain nodded.

Following their meeting in the living room, Lune and Gabriel left with Nathaniel to return to their packs. Damien led Kain to the wrap-around porch in the back of the house.

Damien leaned against the wood railing. His arms spread, hands gripping the wood, eyes staring out into the yard. "Have you considered my offer?"

Kain sighed. "Damien, now is not the time."

"It's the perfect time. Look around you. Another war is on our doorstep and from the sounds of it, it's going to be worse than the last one. You can't run from this, Kain. Like it or not, we need you. You're a soldier and a damn good one."

Kain turned his attention to the backyard, following Damien's line of sight.

The cool breeze made the leaves in the trees rustle. The smell of pine hung thick in the air as the fog began to dissipate in the morning sun.

"I will be your beta, Damien, but only until this fight is over. However, I'm still unable to change."

Damien set his hand on his friend's shoulder, the look in eyes showing relief. "I'm sure in time you'll remember. Thank you for accepting. I'll take what I can get, for now. I'm going to need you."

Kain's eyes met Damien's. Inside, it felt nice to be needed again, even on the eve of war.

Tala giggled at the pup in arms suckling the bottle she held. To the eyes of others, she looked like nothing more than a normal human baby.

Jill smiled as she placed her first daughter into the crib. "You're great with children. Have you had any of your own?"

Tala rose from the chair, taking the second pup over to her mother. "No. I want them, but I haven't found a mate."

Jill chuckled. "I can see you have one in mind."

Tala's cheeks heated. She looked away from Jill. "What do you mean?"

"You have the same look in your eyes I had when I first saw Damien."

"Maybe." Tala sighed. "I'm just not sure if he could feel the same. I care about him, but I don't know how to tell him or talk to him."

"It's Kain, isn't it?" Jill asked.

Tala mumbled. Had she really made it so obvious?

A light snigger left Jill's throat. "Kain can appear intimidating to someone who doesn't know or understand him. Inside though, he's very gentle and one Sun's hell of a lover. Trust me, I've made out with him a couple of times. Get to know him, Tala. He's a protector. He's a perfect mate for someone as shy and reserved as you are."

Tala's cheeks grew hotter. She grumbled as she pictured Kain making out with Jill. "Open conversation may work for someone as forward as you. My words just choke in my throat."

"Then approach him as you would. I don't expect everyone to be like me. Some women turn as red as beets when they meet a man they fall for. It's not uncommon," Jill patted Tala's shoulder. "Imagine yourself together and let your instincts take over."

Jill left the room, leaving Tala alone.

Just approach him? How can I even hope to do something like that? I'm not like Jill. I'm not a soldier or a leader. What would someone like Kain even see in someone like me?

Tala left the nursery to the bathroom in the hall. She sniffled, her chest aching.

Kain sat on the front porch stairs reading when his ears perked at the scent of his dear friend. "Good evening, Jillian."

"Hey," Jill said and sat down next to Kain, leaning against his shoulder. "What are you reading?"

"It's a fantasy. Something I've had on my reading list for some time now," Kain replied. He took off his reading glasses, setting them beside him. "It's good to see you again, old friend."

"You too," Jill said. "Damien told me about his visit with you."

Kain sighed. "It doesn't surprise me."

"Why did you leave after your recovery, Kain? You didn't tell anyone, you just vanished."

Kain didn't reply. He set his book down beside him and stared into the night.

"I think you may have an admirer. She's quite taken with you." Jill said to break the silence.

Kain rolled his eyes. "If you mean Astrid, I'm already aware. She has been less than reserved in her attempts at courting. I have refused her multiple times."

Jill scoffed. "Please. Astrid is a self-centered bitch. I wouldn't wish her on any male. I was talking about someone a little newer to the area."

Despite being relieved to find that he wasn't the only one constantly annoyed by Astrid's behavior, Kain still wanted to know who Jill spoke of.

She winked at him, elbowing him in the ribs. "Sorry, that's for you to find out. I know why you haven't chosen a mate or allowed anyone to court you. It terrifies you."

"I cannot have an heir. I cannot wish this on anyone else, especially my flesh and blood. I know you know this."

Jill rested her hand on Kain's arm. "You can't let fear keep you from living. From loving another. It isn't what the gods want."

Kain watched as Jill stood.

"Think about what I've said. You're wise but you're allowing yourself to suffer and it hurts my heart." She kissed his cheek and went back inside.

Sighing, Kain picked up his book and glasses to head back into the house.

Kain went upstairs to the room Damien offered him earlier that morning. It surprised him to find Tala walking out of the bathroom into the hallway. Had he not looked up when he did, he might've run into her.

Red rims showed around her eyes. Her wet hair hung over her shoulder.

"Are you alright?" Kain asked.

Tala wiped her face with the sleeve of the sweatshirt. "I'm fine. Just borrowing the shower and thinking."

Kain raised her face to look at him. "Did you remember something else?"

"No. I wish I could."

"Then what is bothering you? Be honest."

Tala bit her trembling lip. The words she wanted to say stuck in her throat the longer her brown eyes stared into his longing pools of evergreen.

Squeezing her eyes closed, she shoved passed Kain to run down the hall into her room, slamming the door.

Tala leaned against the door, sinking to the ground. Once again, Kain's beauty froze the words in her throat. The longing in his eyes made her heart flutter.

She wrapped her arms around her knees. *He'd never accept me once he learned the truth. He'd probably kill me.*

A knock on her door startled Tala. She wiped her tears away, got up and moved away from the door to the lean against the dresser.

"May I come in?" Kain asked.

"Go ahead," Tala replied. Her words came out more like a sigh than actual words.

Kain came into the room and took a seat on the bed. "Are you afraid of me?"

"No!" She snapped.

"Then why do you take every opportunity to avoid me?"

Tala tried to think of something to say. She didn't want to hurt Kain.

Kain sighed, rising from the bed. "I won't force you to tell me. I only hope you will come to me in your own time."

"I don't know how."

Kain stopped, surprised, watching Tala clench trembling fists at her sides. She bit her lower lip, nose crinkled up.

"Gods dammit, I don't know how to talk to you! To someone so strong and wise, I must seem pathetic!" Tala yelled.

Kain grinned, his hand resting on his hip. His eyes lingered on the young woman in front of him. For the first time since they'd been together, Kain took the time to take in every detail of her body.

Well-defined muscles ran the length of long legs despite her petite size. The soft, voluminous deep red hair she pulled over her shoulder would fall to at least the middle of her back.

Her fair skin held the gentle kiss of the sun. Deep chocolate eyes full of confusion stared back at Kain. Her lips held the muted color of strawberry; full and perfect for kissing.

Kain reached his hand out, slowing his advance when Tala looked away. He brushed the back of his knuckles across her cheek, cupping her face and guiding her to look at him.

"You are not pathetic. Lacking confidence, maybe. Your memories will return to you. For now, try to make some friends. I will see you in the morning." Kain withdrew his hand.

Tala's heart sped like a racehorse. Kain's hand was so warm on her face. The comfort in his voice brought about a new sensation inside of her. Something she hoped would continue to grow the longer she spent with him.

After leaving Tala, Kain proceeded to his room and closed the door. Something he believed he wouldn't allow himself to feel ever again rose in his chest.

Kain dropped to his back on the bed. The heels of his hands rubbed his eyes, his teeth clenched.

Dammit, he thought.

He gasped when the floor around him gave way to another celestial plane. He fell through the sky, his arms flailing until he landed with a *thud* on his stomach.

Coughing, Kain pushed himself up from the ground. This plane didn't belong to Luna and Tenebris. The sun shone so bright that it forced him to shield his eyes with his arm.

"Alexander Kain," a booming voice called.

Beneath his arm, Kain made out the shape of a woman. Her main features hid themselves behind the intensity of the sun. He could tell she wore armor and possessed three sets of massive white wings.

Kain tried to stand. The presence of the goddess held such strength, he found it hard to rise. "Who are you?"

The goddess held out her hand, her deep voice resonating in the space around them. *"Alexander, I have come to claim you as mine. No longer do you serve the night. From this day forward, you are my soldier. Be my servant's guardian and I will save you the Shadowed One's wrath."*

"I don't understand!" Kain called out.

The woman didn't answer, she raised her extended hand, taking Kain from the ground. A comforting heat filled his body, returning his strength. The brand of a tribal sun burned across his shoulder. The once faded ink of his family's crest renewed, becoming vibrant.

Once it ended, Kain fell back to the ground.

"I have returned the wolf to your soul. He is stronger and bears the golden fur of sunlight. I was not able to return your full strength, for that I am sorry. The damage is too great. In time you will know me. Go, my soldier. Uphold the bargain we have made."

After the encounter, Kain woke up naked on the floor. An overwhelming sense of joy filled his heart at the begging of the freedom from the wolf. He walked over to the windows, threw them open, and jumped to the ground landing on all fours. His head raised in a howl that rang throughout the night before he took off running, relishing his renewed sense of freedom.

CHAPTER FIVE

The sound of a wolf howling made Tala lurch in her bed. She whipped her head, gasping at the thought the werewolves might've returned to finish her off.

Unable to go back to sleep, Tala got out of the bed and went to stick her head out into the hallway. When she didn't hear anything, she crept into the thin corridor, not getting very far after running into Damien.

The force of their collision made Tala lose her balance. She nearly fell until Damien reached out and caught her by the arm.

"Woah, I'm sorry. I didn't mean to scare you. I was on my way to the girls' room to take care of Maggie. She started whimpering."

Tala rubbed the sore, throbbing muscle in her arm where he grabbed her. She reassured him she was okay and thought she heard the howl of a werewolf.

Damien laughed, "That wasn't a werewolf call. Theirs sounds more demented and scratchier than ours. That's definitely a lycan. If my memory is correct, it's Kain's. I guess he remembered how to change, finally."

Damien patted Tala's shoulder. Keeping his voice quiet and gentle, he said, "You should get some rest. Those wounds look like they still hurt."

Tala watched Damien walk to the pups' nursery at the end of the hall. After he closed the door, she lowered her eyes to the floor, clamping her teeth together.

She fled to her room, closing and locking the door, then to stare in the mirror. Sweat covered her face. Her fangs ached from denying the wicked need growing inside of her.

The fear of rejection and underlying possibility she could be killed kept her from sharing her dark secret with her new friends.

During the early morning hours, Tala's dreams became a jumbled mess. She tossed and turned under her bed sheets, crying out in her sleep.

All around her, Tala could only watch as her family was slaughtered. The putrid smell of blood mixed with smoke and decay. Tears streamed from Tala's eyes, her stomach sick at the screams of mothers, pups, fathers and the elderly. She heard a desperate woman's voice call out to her amidst the screams of the dying members of her pack, telling her to go to Big Timber, find the Purifier and ask him for help.

Tala shot up from her pillow to find both it and her sheets soaked with sweat. She gasped, looking around the room to make sure what she'd experienced truly was a dream.

Needing to see Damien as soon as possible, Tala hurried from her bed to get dressed and head out into the hallway.

She wasn't paying attention to where she was going and nearly ran into Kain coming out of the bathroom. To avoid plowing into him, she slipped, hitting her butt on the hard floor. She rubbed it, uttering a silent "ow."

Kain looked down at the small woman. With regret in his voice, he knelt and asked her if she'd been hurt during their collision. He offered his hand to help her get up.

Tala told him she was fine, taking his hand and rubbing her sore rump with her free hand.

"Where in Luna's name were you going in such a hurry? It's not even dawn," he asked.

"I remembered why I was sent here! I need to speak to Damien. Please, it's urgent!" Tala replied.

With a steely look in his eyes, he told her to come with him downstairs.

The two of them arrived in the kitchen to find Damien sitting with a cup of coffee in his hand. His head lulled over the back of the chair, eyes covered with his forearm. On one of his shoulders, a burp rag hung limp, yellowed from where a pup spit up on it.

Tala felt bad for what she needed to do. She left Kain's side to stand in front of Damien, letting him know she needed to speak with him.

Damien raised his head, groaning. The wood of the chair popped and whined as he sat up. His dark hair looked more tousled than Tala ever saw it. His usually bright amethyst eyes appeared dull, likely from his lack of sleep.

Tala felt horrible for bothering him in such a state. "I'm so sorry for waking you but I remember why I came here. It's important I speak with you."

Damien stretched his arms over his head followed by a quick rubbing of his eyes. He hauled himself to his feet, grumbling. "Give me a few minutes then I'll meet you in the living room. Gabriel's going to love hearing from me this early in the morning."

Kain led Tala into the living room to wait for Damien. Gesturing his hand toward the couch, he let Tala sit down before joining her. The two of them sat in an awkward silence.

Tala cleared her throat, twiddling her thumbs in her lap.

Kain looked at her in his peripheral. During his run the night before, he found a place he thought she might like and wanted to ask if she'd join him. Her slamming into him and needing to talk to Damien interrupted his attempt to ask.

To calm her, Kain set his hand on hers. The action brought about a gasp. "I wanted to ask you if you would give me the honor of accompanying me tonight after your story. I found a place I know you will like."

Tala looked up at Kain, her eyes wide, smiling. The manner in which she answered 'yes' to him made her sound like a teenager who got asked out by her secret crush.

Kain returned her smile. "I believe this is the first time I have seen you smile."

Tala's face turned a bright red. She opened her mouth to say something until the sound of the front door hitting the wall made her jump.

Kain turned his attention to see Gabriel sizing up Damien and complaining.

Sighing, Kain got up from the couch to go and try to stop the ensuing fight.

"You better have a damn good reason for getting me up this early, Damien, you self-centered dick," Gabriel snapped.

Kain shoved his way between the two of them, his hands firm on the alphas' chests. His chastising eyes fell on Gabriel. "Gabriel, I warned you about respecting another alpha's territory. Do not make me repeat myself."

Gabriel scoffed, staying silent and shouldering his way into the living room to sit on the floor.

Lune came in shortly after, taking a seat next to Gabriel. His presence intimidated Tala who averted her eyes to the floor. She didn't understand why but Lune appeared cold and emotionless.

Kain took his hand off Damien's chest. The young alpha looked like he wanted to say something but the glare from Kain silenced him.

Surprisingly, the ruckus didn't wake Jill who lay sleeping in her wolf skin next to Damien's lounge chair. He shoved it aside, sat on the floor and positioned himself to lean against her large form.

Kain returned to his spot next to Tala on the couch.

"Glad you all made it," Damien said. "I wouldn't ask you here unless it was important."

Gabriel scoffed, earning him a glare from Kain.

Damien's brow twitched with annoyance.

After a roll of his eyes at Damien and Gabriel's antics, Kain nodded to Tala, giving her the chance to speak.

Tala took a deep breath against the anxiety of speaking to such important lycans. "I come from a pack who lived in Great Falls. Out of nowhere, werewolves tore our homes apart and killed everyone they came across. My mother and I hid but when they found us, she told me to run, to find Damien. The werewolves followed and attacked me. I must've passed out because Kain found me naked in the woods."

"You're a lycan then?" Gabriel asked out of curiosity.

Tala nodded. "The werewolves took orders from a lycan. Something about him didn't seem right. My brother drew his attention so I could escape."

Gabriel's eyes met Kain's, their brows drawn downward, and deep scowls on their faces. The death of Gabriel's brother, Azazel and Pentacost both occurred due to the betrayal of one of their kind.

"Do you know why they attacked you?" Damien asked.

Tala shook her head. "I don't know exactly but they appeared to be looking for something. The lycan screamed at them to search everywhere to see if they could find it."

Damien glanced at Kain. "What do you think?"

Kain didn't answer right away. He processed what Tala said in his mind. He asked Tala what it was she needed from them to get an idea on how they could help her.

Tears dripped down Tala's face. "I want to see if anyone survived. My brother sent a howl right before I passed out from my injuries. My mom had been killed. I just want to know if I'm the only one left."

A tense silence fell across the room. Each leader looked at the other. If they decided to see if anyone from Tala's pack survived, they could walk into a trap. However, if they neglected her plight, they risked losing her family to starvation, exposure, sickness and injury.

Damien leaned back, staring at the ceiling, his arms resting over Jill's black form. "And here I thought the quiet was boring. So, what do we think? Trap or death?"

Kain placed his hand on Tala's knee. "The choice is difficult. Tala was not spared without reason. The lycan had to have known we would be the ones to get the message. If I had to venture a guess, her pack is already dead."

Gabriel jumped from the floor, his hands outstretched in disbelief. "What're we saying here? Are we actually abandoning a pack in need? What if some did survive?"

Kain rose slowly from the couch. "The risk is too great. I have no idea how long Tala was in the woods. Her family could have been dead for days before I found her."

From behind Damien, Jill raised her head.

"No," he snapped. "There's no way I'm letting you go alone, Jill. Don't you dare ask it of me."

Kain turned his disbelieving eyes at Jill. The glare in the icy green orbs told him she'd made up her mind.

Damien took his mate's elongated face in his hands. "Don't ask me to do this. Please, don't ask me to let you take such a huge risk again."

Jill pulled away and barked at him followed by less than quiet growling.

Damien lowered his eyes, his brows pinched together. He didn't say anything out loud, but Jill's licking of his face told Kain plenty.

Kain didn't like his childhood friend taking such huge risks, but he knew once Jillian Styles made up her mind, no one could change it.

Gabriel sighed. "Here we go again with the suicide missions. If there's nothing else, I'm going to head back to my pack. Kain, send me a howling call when you can. I'd like to know what's going on."

Kain assured Gabriel he'd keep him updated. Once the alpha left the room, Kain glanced briefly at Jill and Damien, then departed to give them some privacy.

Tala followed Kain through the back door of the house. She saw him lean against the wood railing, the muscles of his back tense, his fingers gripping the wood so hard she heard it creaking.

She wanted to tell him she was sorry, how she knew he cared about Jill but she remained quiet.

Instead, she joined him in leaning against the railing. Her fluttering heart gave her the courage to lean against his arm, finding his bicep firm and warm beneath her cheek.

Kain relaxed his muscles. The touch of Tala's skin against his offered him a sense of comfort. "Did you still want to accompany me this afternoon?"

Tala took his hand whispering "yes" in his ear.

Kain offered his arm, a coy grin formed across his face. Tala took it, thanking him.

As they walked together, Tala took in every facet of Kain's beauty. She could imagine his short, dirty-blonde hair spiked if he chose to style it.

When Kain caught her gawking at him, she turned her head away to avoid embarrassing herself. He responded with a coy grin since he'd been stealing glances at her as well.

From what he could tell, Tala's inexperience with a male led him to believe she didn't know how to interact with one more intimately. In lycan years, she was of age to choose a mate but her timid personality appeared to make courting a challenge.

He had no doubt that males found her attractive. Her soft hair, gentle face and tender eyes gave Kain signs she'd be a perfect mother to pups. Her fair skin held a tint of tan. Her curiosity and admiration were two qualities Kain found endearing.

Tala's sudden gasp took Kain out of his thoughts.

In front of them, a field laced with golden flowers bloomed in the warmth of the new spring sun. Bees buzzed about collecting pollen from the sweet-smelling marigolds and buttercups. New leaves rustled in the gentle breeze.

The bright smile on Tala's face pleased Kain. "I thought this might appeal to you. You've been so stressed, I assumed you might want some time to relax. Stop and smell the flowers, I believe is the saying."

Kain sat on a stone beneath the trees and watched Tala walk through the flowers. She sat down and proceeded to pick one and smell it. He didn't know when it happened, but he dozed off.

The scent of one of the flowers close to him made him open his eyes to see Tala extending a flower towards him, her cheeks red.

Tala swallowed a knot in her throat. "I know men don't usually like flowers, but I wanted to give this to you."

Kain blinked, surprised at the gift. He reached to take it, an outstretched hand took his, cradling the flower between the two of them.

Tala's radiant smile beamed above him. "Come into the light with me. The sun feels great."

Kain's eyes grew wider, his heart full for the first time in centuries. A strange sensation of heat fell across his face. The emotion felt so welcome yet scared him because of what it could become. He discarded the unease and joined Tala in the warmth of the sun, sitting down amidst the flowers.

Tala dancing took Kain back to the days before the Blood Wars. Her melodious voice drove away the howling demons in his mind.

For this moment, he wanted to allow himself to be something other than a cursed soldier. He wanted to feel alive, to remember what life was like before the bane. Back to a time when he ran with his brothers and sisters across the mountain plains.

No blood, no cries of pain. Just his people running in the night, singing to their mother.

Tala joined him in sitting in the flowers. Her breath hard from dancing and singing.

"It's been a while since I could enjoy the warmth of the sun. It's a nice change," Kain said. He turned his chin to the sky, grinning, the breeze catching his hair.

Tala looked at the scars on Kain's arms. New, angry gashes crossed over faded pink scars. She wanted to ask about them but kept her mouth shut.

She watched Kain fall back into the flowers, his arms crossed behind his head, falling asleep in a matter of minutes.

The urge to touch Kain niggled in the back of Tala's mind. His biceps bulged at the crook between his elbow and forearm. The smell of him mixing with the flowers drove her crazy with want.

Her heightened senses brought forth the darker need inside. She covered her mouth willing the despicable urge away. Kain's blood whispered to her, the need prodding her to take some of it while he slept.

Tears began to fall from her eyes at the idea such an evil thing kept her from revealing her feelings to Kain.

Kain woke to find Tala sitting beside him. From the light in the sky, it had to be early evening. He sat up and stretched to alleviate the stiffness from sleeping on the ground.

"Good evening," Tala said.

"Good evening. How long have I slept?" Kain replied.

"About two or three hours. Did you sleep well?"

Kain nodded. From the ground, he plucked a flower and pushed Tala's hair behind her ear to place the flower there. The yearning he saw in her eyes made him curious about what she might be thinking.

Tala began to lean forward, her eyes half-closed. Her mouth got so close to his, Kain could've kissed her. He closed the distance, bringing their mouths together in a sweet kiss.

The taste of Tala's mouth reminded Kain of the sweetness of honey with a hint of heat from a red pepper. She moaned into his mouth, moving closer to his body.

Inside, Kain wanted nothing more than to keep her close. His lack of the intimacy so normal for his kind threatened to overwhelm his control.

To a lycan, companionship wasn't just a want, it was a need. Kain had gone many years without it. He pulled away from Tala, sad and aching.

When he saw the disappointed look on her face, Kain thanked Tala for not running and coming with him. He glanced at the moon and the sky, suggesting they head back.

CHAPTER SIX

Tala sat on the nook in the windowsill looking out at the moon. The afternoon she spent with Kain brought about a dreamy sigh as she leaned back against the wall. His smile at the flower she'd given him made her believe a future with him might be possible.

Kain showed trust when he'd fallen asleep beside her. His gentle breathing almost lulled her to sleep.

In her heart, she wondered what it would be like to hunt with him beneath the moon's light. It'd been so long since she'd changed.

She desired to forget the part of her that could drive a wedge between them, focusing on the majestic wolves they both harbored within them.

To satiate her need to change, Tala removed her clothes, leaving her naked. Her hourglass body illuminated by Luna's glow. She tilted her head up, closing her eyes and taking in a deep breath.

She jumped from the window to the ground, shifting into her wolf form. Her heightened senses captured the sound of a deer padding through the woods. The musky scent of its fur traveled through the pine and cool of the night to fill her nostrils.

With great speed, Tala took off to find the source of the smell. When she found her prey, she crouched close to the ground, keeping silent while stalking through the brush.

Once she got close enough, Tala lowered in preparation to pounce. Snarling, she leapt, her fangs digging into the doe's throat. Her size forced it to the ground so she could lap up the crimson fluid of its life.

It made her nauseous at how good it felt. Fearful thoughts of what Kain would think if he saw her infiltrated her mind, bringing about a sorrowful whimper. *I don't want him to see me as a monster.* She thought closing her eyes tightly and raising her head to release a mournful howl.

Following her short hunt, Tala shifted from wolf to woman, the feeling exhilarating. She forgot how good changing from one form to another felt.

Using the tree beside the house, Tala jumped into her room through the window. The soft beginnings of a warm spring rain brought about the scent of fresh grass and newly reborn tree leaves.

Tala gathered some of the new clothes Jill let her borrow from the drawers and went to take a shower. The idea of being naked didn't occur to her since she remembered lycans considered the body something not to be ashamed of.

She walked out into the hallway, surprised at how quiet the house was. The only sound she heard sounded like a gentle humming coming from the pups' nursery.

On her way to the shower, she stopped by Kain's door, leaning her forehead against it. The scent of him made her heart flutter. She thought about how badly she wanted to go in and tell him the truth. To throw caution to the wind and share the bond of blood so common for lycan pairs.

Tala raised her hand to knock but hesitated. If Kain was asleep, she didn't want to wake him. Her eyes lowered, she decided to continue to the bathroom.

The room gradually filled with a thick steam as the shower heated.

With a dejected sigh, Tala dropped the fresh clothes into the sink and stepped into the shower. The water was so hot, she yelped in pain, turning down the temperature.

Sheets of the heated water gave Tala dreams of Kain's warm, hard body pressed against hers. Images of him naked played in her mind. Memories of his fingers caressing her skin made her desire surge.

Moaning, Tala leaned against the tile. Her back arched as she imagined Kain's strong hands holding her hips still against his sculpted stomach.

She purred his name, whispering how she loved him, how she wanted him so bad it ached.

Daydreams of him making love to her led her to spread the wet folds between her legs to find the tender nub already beginning to harden. She gasped as her fingers rubbed against it.

Tala groaned as she imagined Kain's lips placing kisses on her back and shoulders. She could almost feel Kain's hot breath in her ear, his hand holding her throat while his tongue tasted her skin.

Whimpers escaped her throat the higher her pleasure grew.

The carnal hunger of her darker side wanted nothing more than to take Kain. The possession of the vampire threatened to cloud her mind with thoughts of wanting to fight him. It wanted to take his blood and make him hers.

Tala shoved the darkness away, reaching her climax. She fought to keep quiet while her orgasm ravaged her body with pure, sexual pleasure. Shaking legs left her panting while she came down from her experience.

Tala hurried to turn off the water, struggling to keep her legs from going out from under her while she dried her hair and got dressed.

Kain finished readying himself to go on a morning run when the pattering of feet on the wooden stairs brought his attention to Tala.

She stood before him in a loose-fitting grey t-shirt and pastel pink pants. The high cut of the shirt allowed a peek at her flawless, muscular belly. The deep cut of the collar revealed her lack of a bra.

Kain grinned as he admired her body, betraying his need for affection. "Good morning. I thought you might still be asleep."

Tala looked up at him, her cheeks red when she saw his hungry eyes. "Morning."

A short silence ensued.

"I should be going," Kain said, almost disappointed. He opened the door, ready to head out.

"Wait!" Tala exclaimed. Her hand reached out to grab the black muscle shirt Kain wore.

Her sudden burst of confidence shocked Kain. The warmth of her against his back coupled with the firm grip she held on his shirt froze him in his steps.

"I need to tell you something," she said in a low, almost trembling voice.

Kain didn't reply. He enjoyed the feeling of being touched, of her in a moment where she didn't appear afraid of him. "Is this something you want to tell me right now?"

Tala shook her head against his back. "It can be later, but it has to be tonight. Please."

Kain didn't know whether to feel relieved or concerned at what Tala had to tell him. He promised her they'd speak later and kissed her forehead before leaving on his run.

Kain chose a trail close to Damien's house known as the "Wood's Edge" to go for his run. It was a place many lycans knew since they tended to hold their First Moon events there, where pups who learned to shift presented themselves to the alphas of their packs.

The farther Kain ran down the trail, the higher his sense of caution rose. Around him, nothing moved, the lifeless woods reminding him of the day the werewolves arrived at his cabin.

He stopped, closing his eyes to reach his senses into the space around him. A malevolent presence filled the air.

Kain opened his eyes, his brows crunched into a scowl. "You can stop cowering in the shadows."

A cackle erupted from the branches above Kain, echoing in the emptiness of the forest.

From somewhere above, the lycan from before dropped to the ground in front of him. "After such a long time, your skills are still so impressive. How've you been, my old friend?"

Kain's frown deepened. "We are not friends, Bard. To what do I owe the displeasure of your company?"

Bard shoved his hands in his jacket pockets. He wore blue jeans, black work boots and a shirt with the skull of a dragon on it. His long, dark hair lay drawn back in the middle of his head in a tight ponytail. Five o'clock shadow darkened his face.

"Oh, come on, is that anyway to greet someone who hasn't seen you in 200 years?"

Kain remained silent.

A deep grimace distorted Bard's face. "I guess you wouldn't reply. How could you after what you did to me!"

"You deserved execution for your treachery. Be grateful all you lost was your forearm," Kain replied without emotion.

Bard laughed a wicked laugh. "You're still such a self-righteous prick. Enjoy it. You have no idea what's coming. I can't wait to see you shatter and fall to your knees. You and that pathetic pup of a Purifier you care so much about."

Kain moved with a speed so fast, Bard couldn't respond. He pinned the lycan against the base of a tree. Bard struggled to try and get free. "You will never speak Damien's name. Someone who lacks loyalty has no right. Now get out of my sight before I tear your throat from your body."

Bard fell to the ground, snickering between gasps. "Like I said, I can't wait to see you broken."

Kain watched Bard shift and flee into the woods.

Concerned, Kain shifted into his full lycan form and sprinted as hard as he could back to Damien's house.

Kain arrived home to see Tala holding a pup, humming to her as she rocked the porch swing back and forth. The smile on her face made Kain's heart pound. One side of her neck lay exposed, silently pleading for him to pepper it with kisses.

He glanced at the rose bush, deciding to pick one and sneak around the house to his room so he could shower and put some new clothes on. The last thing he wanted was to gag her with a strong smell of sweat and a foreign lycan.

It took so long to get cleaned to the point it satisfied Kain, he arrived in the hallway in time to see Tala backing slowly out of the pups' room. In her hand she held a baby monitor.

The timing couldn't have been more perfect to give her the flower he picked.

He stopped Tala on her way to her room, greeting her warmly and asking if he could join her.

Tala smiled, offering for him to come into her room.

Kain sat on her bed, keeping the flower hidden until the right moment. "You mentioned you had something to tell me?"

Time seemed to slink by while Tala tried to find the perfect words to use. What she had to say could be the end of any chance to be with Kain.

Beside her, Kain waited, his eyes never leaving her. His posture showed he didn't intend to rush her but was concerned about what she needed to tell him.

"I haven't been completely honest with you or anyone for that matter," Tala began, her voice barely above mumbling.

Kain said nothing, remaining emotionless.

"What I told you about my mother was true. She is a lycan but--" Tala sniffled.

"You are a hybrid, aren't you?" Kain asked, only half-surprised. He'd developed suspicions, but Tala never gave him any direct signs to show the vampire side of her.

Tears began to fall down Tala's face. She nodded, her stomach sick at what Kain might be thinking. "Not all vampires are blood-thirsty monsters. My father loved my mother. He died protecting us from Anthony."

Tala turned her body towards Kain. She searched for any sign in his eyes that he might try to kill her. When their eyes met, fear gripped her. She couldn't see what his emotions were through his eyes.

When Kain reached out his hand, Tala prepared for his claws to tear her to shreds.

Instead she saw a red rose, its thorns removed.

"You have nothing to fear from me," Kain said in a comforting voice. "Hybrid or not, I do not kill the innocent."

Relieved, Tala took the rose, cradled it in her hands and sniffed it.

Kain's fingers guided her face to meet his. His touch light. "I wish to court you, Tala."

Tala's eyes widened. She didn't understand why.

Seeing her confusion, Kain continued, "There's more to a mate than just strength. I have watched you care for Damien's children. You are going to be a wonderful mother and a caring mate. That is what I desire in my partner."

Kain withdrew his hand, his eyes searching Tala's as he waited for a reply. It came in a form Kain didn't expect. Tala closed the distance between the two of them, her lips meeting Kain's in a passionate kiss.

Kain's eyes closed, his arms wrapping around Tala's body, his hand gripping her hair. The other ran down her side. His need for closeness, for companionship ignited a flame inside of him the more he explored her.

Damien's voice in the back of his mind frustrated Kain at being interrupted. He pulled away from Tala, cursing under his breath.

He stood from the bed, his eyes wide at what he was being told.

Damien stood on the front lawn, his hand on his hip, the other scrubbing over his neck. His ears perked when Kain and Tala joined him on the wet, green grass.

"Hey, I wish I didn't have to interrupt you, but Jill should be arriving any moment," Damien said. His sullen eyes turned towards Tala.

Kain moved the conversation between him and Damien to avoid alerting Tala. *Is it as bad as you say?*

Damien nodded. *Jill said they were all gone by the time she got there. I'm supposed to be the fucking Purifier, Kain! What kind of savior can't stop the bloodshed he was sent to stop?*

Kain put his hand on Damien's shoulder. *It is a lesson we all must learn. Remember what I taught you about the nature of our world. We lose loved ones but do what we can to find reasons to keep living.*

Damien growled behind his teeth.

Jill came sauntering up the drive, her head lowered, tongue panting. She stopped in front of Damien, sitting down, ears lowered and whimpering.

Tala drew closer, her breath hastening. She shook her head, tears streaming down her face.

Kain took her in an embrace whispering "I'm sorry" into her ear.

A few hours after Jill's delivery of the news, Gabriel arrived following a text from Kain.

The alpha greeted Kain, the look on his face grim. "I'm sorry, my friend. How is she?"

Kain shook his head, sighing. His eyes ventured to Tala's closed door at the top of the stairs.

"Well, what do you propose we do now?" Gabriel asked.

Kain didn't reply. The roaring sound of a sports car engine caught his attention.

"Were we expecting someone?" Gabriel inquired, suspiciously.

Kain shook his head. His sense of caution peaked following his encounter with Bard in the woods. Nudging Damien in his mind, Kain walked back out onto the front lawn.

Lune sat on the front porch. His triangular ears turned towards the road, his watchful gaze focused on the vehicle.

As it drew closer, Kain saw the crest on the front of the car. Its design familiar and foreboding, yet different from the other few times he'd seen it. For one, the car was white, not the midnight black he'd seen at Lillith's coven. For another, the wings of the fallen angel were broken, its eyes bound.

Beside him, Lune started to get anxious. Kain knew the lycan had a history with the unwelcome guests.

"Easy," Kain said to comfort the jittery lycan.

Damien came out into the porch, taking his spot in front of Kain, next to Gabriel. "What crest is that? It's pretty creepy."

"The Cardoza family but it has been modified," Kain replied, agitated.

The car came to a grinding halt, almost hitting Damien's motorcycle next to Kain's car.

When the driver's side opened, Kain's eyes widened and he sent Lune away as fast as he could. The grey lycan tore around the house out of sight.

A tall woman with stark black hair cascading down her back got out of the driver's side. She wore a black leather corset, black pants, a blood-red shirt and knee-high leather boots. The woman's eyes met Kain's, a saccharine smirk over her lips.

In many ways, she resembled Lilith.

"Who's the Lilith clone?" Damien asked.

Kain could tell Damien did his best to hide the small trembles in his body. The young lycan's experience with vampires nearly resulted in his getting killed multiple times. The coven's queen, Lilith, attempted to force him to become hers or kill him if he refused.

To reassure him, Kain moved closer to Damien, his presence calming his friend. "Emeline Auberts, Anthony's current lover."

Damien scoffed. "That's vague. Annoyingly vague."

Kain half-snickered.

From the other side of the car, appeared a young man with equally dark hair and a cigarette in his mouth. From the way he held himself, Kain could tell he cared less to be in the lycans' presence.

"And the jerk off with the cigarette?" Damien snarled. The young man reminded him of Nathaniel before Damien kicked his ass in a fight.

Kain covered a chuckle upon seeing Damien's reaction despite the intense situation. "Jared Auberts, Emeline's younger brother."

Jared's arrival brought about a grumble from Gabriel.

Damien glanced at the alpha then back at Kain. "There's a history there, isn't there?"

Kain sighed, his shoulders dropped. "Unfortunately. Damien, stay close to Gabriel and I. These vampires are stronger than even Lillith."

Damien swallowed, nodding.

Kain turned his attention to Emeline, his glare stopping her in her tracks.

Emeline snickered. "It's good to see you too, Alexander."

"Enough," Kain snapped. "What do you want?"

Emeline moved her eyes to Damien. "Lillith's letters did little to describe your beauty, Mr. Pierce. You're welcome to come with me. I can show you what you can do with that gorgeous body of yours."

Jill snapped, calling the vampire a bitch and trying to lunge only to have Damien catch and start petting her.

Emeline burst out laughing. "Ah yes, the immortal lycan. I've heard of you in passing. Not as impressive in person. I'm surprised Lilith had such trouble taking Damien from you. I doubt I would have the same problem."

Damien snarled, "Okay, that's it. I've had enough of overly possessive vampire chicks to last me a fucking lifetime."

Kain held his arm out in front of Damien and warned, "You are treading dangerous ground, vampire. What do you want?"

Jared threw down his cigarette, stomping it out. "Stop toying with them. We're here to deliver a message, not so you can hang around with an old flame or shop for your next sex toy."

Emeline's eyes glowed a rage-filled red. She whipped her head around, glaring at her brother.

The younger vampire shrugged, averting his eyes to Gabriel. "Still hanging out with your boyfriend, Locke?"

Gabriel bowed up his shoulders, his fangs elongated. "Fang off, you bloodsucking bastard. I still owe you for Tulsa."

Kain stepped in front of Gabriel, glaring at him. The gesture enough to silence the lycan alpha.

Jared mocked Gabriel, earning him his own glare from Kain. "Keep your fangs behind your lips. I will tolerate no further disrespect. For the last time, what do you want?"

Kain knew the tactic the vampires used well. They claim neutrality, rile up their opponents and then attempt to strike them down.

Emeline held up her hands. "We haven't come to fight. You have something we want, Alexander. Anthony wants you to hand it over or we keep killing the worthless dogs of Great Falls. Should you still refuse, we come after you and all you love."

Kain didn't know what he could possess that would mean anything to a vampire of Anthony's status. Following the unfortunate and unwanted meeting, he'd go back to the cabin and find out.

With what appeared to be partially saddened eyes, Emeline blew a kiss to Kain, got into the driver's side of the car and closed the door. Jared flipped Gabriel off and got into the passenger's side.

Jill, Scott and Gabriel went inside after the vampires left.

Damien remained with Kain.

Kain leaned against the railing of the porch. He glanced at Damien exhaling through his nose and preparing himself for the question he saw in Damien's eyes. "Alright, Damien, what's on your mind?"

Damien scratched the back of his head. He glanced around, eventually staring at Kain. "Emeline acted like she knew you. What's the story between you and the vampire bitch?"

"It was a lifetime ago. Let us say I did all I could to rebel against my father. I would rather not talk about it," Kain replied with a regretful sigh.

Kain knew Damien would quiz the Sun's hell out of him if given the chance, so he didn't offer one. He requested to be left alone, waiting for Lune to return.

At moonrise, Lune appeared from around the house. He shifted back and climbed over the railing. Kain handed him a spare set of clothes.

"Forgive me, Master, but I can't get involved with this fight," Lune said. He dropped his saddened eyes to the ground.

Kain put his hand on Lune's shoulder, his reply understanding. "There is nothing to forgive. I remember what happened to you. You shouldn't feel obligated to call me 'Master'."

Lune didn't say anything.

Kain remembered when he first met Lune. The lycan was so scared and injured, he tried to fight Kain despite his weakness. Had Kain not been in the area, Lune could've died. "I have to go, my friend. Tomorrow evening, I leave for the cabin. Hopefully, I can find some information on what the vampires want."

Lune nodded. "I'll give Cade a howling call to see if he'd be willing to offer aid."

Kain thanked Lune, chuckling to himself at the thought of the "Silent Soldier" back in the battlefield.

CHAPTER SEVEN

Kain had begun preparing dinner after being chosen to take Jill's place. Apparently, the pack grew tired of Jill's constantly burnt meals, and when Damien got Kain alone, he begged the older lycan, asking him to keep the secret between them. It made him laugh as he cut the carrots in preparation for the scratch beef stew.

Tala still hadn't come down from her room. It began to worry Kain that she might not recover from the trauma she suffered for days, if not weeks or months.

The smell of bubbling stew brought about a sense of satisfaction for Kain. He hadn't been able to cook for anyone but himself for so long. In the days of Solstice, Gabriel's gym, Kain prepared breakfast for whomever decided to stay.

Kain's ears perked when the creaking of the wood floors announced the new arrival. He glanced over his shoulder in time to feel Tala's hand grip his shirt, her forehead placed against the middle of his back. Her presence comforting.

Kain stopped what he was doing so he wouldn't burn himself to allow Tala to nuzzle against him. "I'm relieved to see you finally out of your room."

Small whimpers escaped Tala. "I feel so alone. If only I'd remembered sooner."

The small woman's cries brought about a great anger in Kain. He turned to take her in an embrace, leaning against the cabinet for support and pulled Tala into his body.

Tears soaked the fabric of his shirt. He bent to lay his cheek against her hair, his arms cradling her against him.

"You are not alone, sweetheart," Kain murmured. "I will take care of you, protect you as long as I live."

Tala brought her arms up around Kain's waist. Her love for him made her chest feel light despite the ache in her heart. She raised her head, her bedroom eyes pleading for him to kiss her.

Their lips met in a deep kiss. Kain's hands splayed over the cheeks of her butt, exerting just enough force to push her into his body.

When they separated, Tala raised her hand to rub Kain's face. Burying his cheek in her hand tested his control, his chest heaving from wanting more.

"When you come back, would you go on a hunt with me?" Tala asked in a dreamy, almost longing voice.

Kain kissed her wrist. "I would love to. I have not been able to see you change yet."

Damien arrived in the kitchen. "We're ready to leave when you are." He took a quick sniff. "Damn, can't wait to have some delicious food."

A growl could be heard from the living room.

To avoid embarrassing Damien, Tala and Kain held back a laugh.

"Uh, right," Damien continued, swallowing hard. "So, whenever you're willing and ready to go, Kain."

Kain offered a nod and requested a moment. Damien turned on his heel to leave the two of them alone.

When he was ready, Kain joined Gabriel, Damien, Jill and Scott on the front lawn. He'd pleaded with Tala to stay with the pups so Jill could come with them. The group elected to take Kain's car to avoid any surprise attacks in the woods and keep from getting wet in the rain.

On the way, they planned on what they'd do if the cabin was being watched or in case of an ambush.

"We will have to deal with that when the time comes," Kain said. His eyes never left the road considering the limited visibility of the hastily falling rain.

In the rearview mirror, he saw Gabriel lean back with his arms crossed behind his head. "Hopefully this is a simple search mission. I don't like the idea of being outnumbered by a pack of vampires and werewolves."

Kain rolled his eyes. No one liked being outnumbered in any situation. In silence, he resumed his focus, listening to the conversations of the other lycans. He hadn't told them who he saw in the woods.

"Gabriel, the lycan at my cabin was Bard," Kain said. His tone lacked any form of emotion, hidden behind the reserve he held.

Gabriel leaned forward, his hands on the back of Damien's seat in the passenger's side and Kain's. His eyes wide in shock. "Kain, please tell me you didn't just say what I thought you said."

"Who's Bard?" Damien asked.

Kain told him, starting from the time in the Blood Wars. The recollection of Bard's treachery, the fight between him and Kain that resulted in his forearm being torn off, and the fire Kain and Gabriel thought he died in.

"What the hell?" Damien said in surprise. "How is this guy even alive? How'd he find you after all these years?"

Beside him, Kain shrugged. "I do not know. What I do know is there is something wrong with him. I sensed a malice, but it was not just his. Be careful, Damien. Bard is more than a match for an inexperienced lycan like you."

Gabriel cursed. Bard's treachery resulted in his brother, Azazel's death, as well as Pentacost's. His hatred of Kain was deep and common knowledge to anyone who knew about the fight.

The sight meeting the lycans' eyes as they drove up to the cabin brought about an array of shocked expressions.

The front windows had been shattered by Kain's lounge chair which lay on the front porch. A gaping hole where the front door once stood stared back at them.

Kain got out of the driver's side and approached the house slowly. He motioned his hand to Gabriel and Jill to go around the back. He ordered Scott to stay near the car to guard their flanks while he and Damien crept through the front door.

With brows creased in anger, Kain inhaled the scent of not only werewolves but a lycan as well. He glanced into the living room to find his sofa and throw pillows torn to shreds. Their contents were emptied all over the floor.

Placing a finger over his mouth while looking at Damien, Kain moved into the kitchen to find his dishes in pieces all over the floor. The cabinet doors hung on loose hinges. Some had been splintered and torn apart, thrown to the tile below.

Gabriel came through the back porch, his shoulders drawn up, fists balled at his sides. "There's nothing here."

Kain knelt to pick up a patch of black fur snagged on the edge of the island in the middle of the kitchen. He sniffed it, finding the scent old. "They did this weeks ago."

Damien kicked the remains of a cabinet door, cursing.

After dropping the fur on the ground, Kain put his hand on Damien's shoulder, asking him to follow Kain upstairs. The two lycans went up to the second floor while Jill and Gabriel stood guard.

In the master bedroom, Kain gasped, his heart saddened to see all he had left of his family's lineage destroyed. Bard and his pack of werewolves went out of their way to shred the journal Kain let Damien read. The black and white pictures of his mother lie in the remains of a black frame on the circular rug.

Kain picked up the photo from amongst the glass and splintered wood. The woman sat with a young man next to her in a faded and yellowing photo that looked like it was taken many years ago.

Damien stood over Kain's shoulder. He spoke in a sad and angry tone. "I'm sorry. Your home was beautiful. They'll pay for this, Kain. I swear."

Silence loomed for a while as Kain thought about what Anthony Cardoza wanted. The hair on the back of his neck stood when he looked at the closet, remembering the safe under the floorboards.

When Kain rose and marched across the room, Damien tilted his head in question. He uttered Kain's name but the older lycan didn't respond. Kain knelt in front of the now ajar door. He tore the floorboards from the nails holding them in place with a grunt.

Staring back at him, a steel safe. He entered the code and opened the door. The contents inside consisted of nothing more than a box wrapped in what looked like a blanket.

"This is it," Kain said.

Damien's eyes widened in realization. "Is that what I think it is?"

Kain nodded as he took a gym bag and placed the box inside, zipping it up in time to hear Gabriel call from downstairs.

The crashing of window glass followed by the stifling smell of smoke and fire made Kain push Damien out of the room into the hallway.

"It's a gods damned trap!" Gabriel screamed.

Kain came up beside him. "Take them through the front door! Use the parts as a shield!"

Gabriel did as he was told. He ran through the front door with Jill on his heels. When they were safely outside, Gabriel called out to Kain.

The house went up in a blaze faster than Kain expected. He shoved Damien out of the way before a beam could land on him.

Coughing, Kain strained to look through his burning eyes to find an alternative route to get them out.

Damien shook off the dirt thanking Kain for saving him. "Do not thank me yet, this is far from over."

Kain found a part in the wall where it'd begun to crack beneath the roaring flames. He grabbed Damien by the forearm and kicked the door with a cry of force. The wood gave way and Kain gripped Damien, jumping over the embankment and rolling.

On their way down, Kain winced at a sting in his ankle. Beside him, Damien lay unconscious. Kain could see blood matting the side of his head.

"He doesn't look so good," came a dark, mocking voice above the crackling flames and shattering of glass.

Kain looked up from Damien to find Bard staring back at him. Jared stood at his side, smoking. The two of them smirked.

Gabriel, Jill and Scott slid down the embankment to join Kain and Damien. Jill dropped to her mate's side. Gabriel growled.

"What's it going to be, dog?" Jared asked like he was annoyed even to be there.

"Shut up, Jared!" Bard snapped, interrupting. "Kain's mine."

In a low voice, Kain told Gabriel to get Damien to the pack's house and to call Kyle.

"No way in Sun's hell!" Gabriel said with a low snarl.

Kain glared at him. "Do as I say. Damien will not last if he is not taken care of."

Gabriel appeared to want to fight more but the soldier's glare silenced any further argument he might provide. He motioned to Scott and Jill to follow him. Jill shifted to allow Scott to put Damien on her back.

Once his fellow lycans were safe, Kain returned his attention to his opponents. Jared remained where he was, allowing Bard to step forward.

"The dark one sends his greetings, Alexander Kain." Bard grinned a fanged grin as he removed his jacket, revealing the arm hidden beneath it. His missing right arm had been replaced with a dark claw much like the one that struck Damien before the Circle of Stones. The encounter nearly killed both he and Kain.

Kain's breath hastened in his chest. The wicked claw emitted a malevolence Kain knew all too well. He could almost feel its hunger to tear into his flesh, the scars on his body igniting into searing pains. "Bard, what have you done?"

Bard cackled, pointing the claw at Kain. "Taken power you're too much of a coward to accept. It's amazing, Kain. You have no idea."

Kain had every idea. In the weeks Barghast tortured him, he offered a taste of what it would feel like to be free from the suffering of the bane. It exhilarated Kain to feel so strong, so unstoppable. The problem was that it threatened to tear his soul apart, to corrupt him into a monster he never wanted to be.

"I hope it was worth your soul," Kain replied in a low, threatening tone.

Bard's brows creased in a scowl as he lunged, swinging the claw at him. Kain dropped to the ground and swept his leg, taking Bard's out from underneath him. The lycan fell to the ground, quickly recovered and hurled a handful of dirt and ash at Kain's face.

The cheap shot hit Kain, briefly blinding him. He cleared his eyes just in time to get hit with the claw in the arm he barely had the chance to raise to guard himself.

He clenched his teeth at the burning cold.

The blood in his body felt like it'd been ripped from him, much like the red tendrils he encountered when he freed Damien's mind from Barghast's influence.

Kain stumbled back, his chest on fire as he tried to catch a breath. His ankle ached and protested at being used despite the injury.

Bard held his arms, bowing up his chest. "Damn, seeing you like this is intoxicating. Why the Shadowed One wants you is beyond me. You're pathetic, Kain. Nothing like the legends make you out to be."

Kain straightened, still dazed from the claw's effects. He didn't give the satisfaction of a reply. He took the stance of a martial artist, ready for another round. He relaxed his body despite the pain, anticipating and dodging each of Bard's attacks with little effort.

Something he trained Damien to do for his fight with Nathaniel.

Bard screamed with rage as each attempt to hit Kain again failed. Kain dodged or blocked Bard's hits with little effort, keeping his distance and avoiding contact with the claw.

A surprise attack by Jared pushed Kain to his knee on the ground. The vampire joined in the onslaught, making it hard for Kain to handle the grazes of the claw and Jared's elongated nails.

The malicious power of the claw took Kain's strength the longer he stayed near it. He knew he had to get away or be overwhelmed.

Kain howled in pain when he grabbed Bard's wrist that held the claw. Jared bit down on his shoulder, tearing into Kain's flesh.

A large gray body rammed into Jared, sending the vampire flying across the forest floor.

The new lycan's arrival gave Kain time to recover enough to shove the claw away, twist Bard's arm behind him and hold him. "You are a fool, Bard. In the end, I will be the one to kill you."

Kain shoved Bard away from him. Two other lycans came out of the brush behind Kain. One, a chestnut furred female snapped at Bard. The other, a large gray male Kain recognized as Lune.

From behind Bard, a lycan larger than Lune with deep red fur sauntered forward. His scar covered body identified him as Cade. The "Silent Soldier."

Bard hissed. "Fine. This isn't over. It's just begun. Something I promise you, Kain, is you'll be the one dead at the end of this."

Cade roared at Bard, sending him fleeing into the woods.

Drained from the claw's effects and the loss of blood where Jared tore into him, Kain collapsed.

CHAPTER EIGHT

T he cold drop of water on Kain's cheek woke him to find he was lying on the soft soil of the ground. Above him, the sun shone bright, its rays warming him.

The voice of a man called to Kain through the fog in his mind.

Try as he might, Kain couldn't get his weakened body to respond. He blinked his eyes, moaning. The voice called out again and again until he could no longer ignore it.

Kain opened his eyes to see the blurred figure of a man standing in front of him. He squeezed his eyes, opening them again to try and clear his vision. What he saw made him gasp in surprise.

Pentacost Kain knelt beside his son, smiling a loving smile.

"You cannot be. You fell." Kain tried not show any emotions despite not seeing his father after so long.

Pentacost shook his head, rising, and offering a hand to help his son to stand. "This is the border of life and death. You were injured, my son."

Once he was on his feet, Kain held his hand against his throbbing head. He let himself remember his bout with Bard and Jared. The feeling of Bard's claw as it sucked the life from him, Cade's arrival, then nothing.

"Your mind called upon me to help you, Alexander," Pentacost said. "You have faced Barghast's power on the physical plane and felt its effects."

Kain had to sit down on a nearby stone because of the lingering weakness. "What does he want with me, father? Is my torture not enough?"

Pentacost joined his son. "He will test you more than he ever has in the upcoming days. Bard's reappearance is only the first step. You must remain strong."

"What can I do?"

"Live your life. As strong as you are, you have forgotten what it means to be more than a soldier."

Kain looked at his father, confused yet admiring him. The scar covered lycan had his head tilted towards the woods around him. All his life, Pentacost raised him to fight and defend the royal line. Kain never had the chance to live the life of a normal lycan youth due to endless hours of training and recovery.

Pentacost lowered his eyes. "Forgive me. I failed you. I never let you have the life of the other young lycans. Tenebris wanted me to tell you that you have a chance to know a life outside of bloodshed."

Kain asked his father what he meant. Pentacost told his son why Luna told him to take Tala. The gods wanted Kain to have a life outside of the Blood Wars. To know what it was like to be free in what time remained to him.

Kain felt his chest tighten with a mix of regret and relief. He longed to get back to Tala. He wanted to court her.

"Go," Pentacost said, reassuring his son. "Be watchful but live. Love the woman you care for."

Kain embraced his father in a tight hug. "Father, I miss you."

"I know. I will see when your time comes. Go."

Kain groaned, covering his eyes against the light of the room. His head ached behind his left eye. Using his fists, he pushed himself to sit up, feeling like he had a hangover.

He looked at the hand he used to catch Bard's claw to find it wrapped. A sharp pain in his shoulder brought attention to the condition of the bite on his neck.

The arrival of Kyle helped Kain focus on the fact he'd returned from the dream encounter with his father.

"Oh, thank the gods." Kyle walked over to Kain. He put his stethoscope buds in his ears and placed its end to Kain's chest.

"How long have I been asleep?" Kain coughed as Kyle asked so the doctor could move to his back.

"A few days. You came to us incredibly weak." Kyle asked Kain to take in a deep breath and let it out.

"Damien?"

Kyle pulled the stethoscope off and placed it in his bag. "He's doing better. The injury wasn't deep and as you know he heals faster than one of us. He was only out for a day before the wound healed. You seem to be feeling better so let me go tell the others. They wanted me to let them know."

Damien came in shortly after. He closed the distance between the two of them, taking Kain in a hug and pleading with him to forgive him for leaving Kain behind.

Returning his hug, Kain reassured Damien that he was okay.

Damien took Kain's hand. "Don't tell me you're okay when you've had a chunk ripped out of your shoulder, asshole. Christ Kain, I reiterate, if I had a brother in a past life, it would be your stupid ass."

Kain laughed.

"I'm sorry. You got hurt again because of me." Damien proceeded to unwrap Kain's burned hand, discarding the old bandage and replacing it with a new one.

Kain watched, his eyes soft and appreciative. "It is my duty to protect you, Damien. I told you once before."

Damien didn't say anything until he finished re-wrapping Kain's hand, asking what happened.

Tala came in, her misty eyes growing wide in shock and relief to see Kain. She lifted her hands to her mouth.

"I will tell you soon. For now, I believe I want some time alone, if you don't mind," Kain said.

Nodding, Damien left the two of them alone, reminding Kain he'd need to tell the whole story later.

Kain took Tala in his arms. Her small body fitting in his, comforting him to find her safe and wanting to show her how much he cared for her. He took her mouth in a kiss, pulling her towards him until she came to sit on the bed's edge.

His hands gripped her butt, making her squeak in pain.

Inside, he wanted to remove her clothes to feel her skin against his as he had with Jill during their heated make-out sessions. He didn't want to push her into too much too fast but his desire to feel her skin almost drove him wild.

Tala pulled emotions out of him he'd only truly felt for one other woman in his life.

With a heavy breath, he broke their kiss. "Tala, I--"

Tala's fingers on his lips silenced Kain. With a coy smile Kain had never seen, Tala stepped back and began to undress. The action baffled Kain. She'd been shy and reserved for most of their time together. Recently, she began to act on her more lycan features like a lack of fear of being naked in front of him.

"Hunt with me." Tala purred.

Kain got up from the bed and removed his clothes. A teasing grin fell across his mouth when he saw how he affected the female lycan. The two of them shifted and jumped from the window and into the night.

Following their hunt, Kain and Tala found themselves sitting on a ledge known as the Lookout to the people of Big Timber.

In front of them lay a sea of trees, mountains in the distance. The top of the town hall stuck out just above the canopy bathed in the blues and silvers of the night.

Neither one of them cared about being naked together. To the lycans, the body was something beautiful, something they didn't need to hide when they were together.

"Tala, tell me about your family. What your life was like before all of this?"

Tala leaned against Kain's shoulder, savoring its firmness and comforting smell of wild pine and male musk. "We lived in Great Falls with my cousins. I attended school there and eventually went off to college to be an environmentalist. To pay my way, I waited tables at two different restaurants. My half-brother Tobias worked construction and our mother taught at the local middle school."

"And your father?"

Tala sniffled, "He didn't live long enough to see me past four. He gave his life so my mother could stay safe."

Kain kissed her hair, his eyes sad. "I'm sorry."

Tala took Kain's hand, squeezing it. "What about you?"

"My father raised me to be a soldier. I never knew what a real childhood felt like," Kain replied with a remorseful tone in his voice.

Hours seemed to pass as Kain asked more questions about Tala's childhood. In return she quizzed him on whether he remembered a time before the Wars and if he had any friends outside of the pack.

In the end, Tala decided to introduce Kain to a world away from war and fighting. She would introduce him to her favorite kinds of music, show him how to play and share her favorite types of places to go to relax. She wanted to show him a life among the humans of Big Timber.

"Will you go out with me, Alex? On a real date? Not just to hunt but to see the life of the city?"

Kain thought about it for a moment. He'd remembered those times when Damien went out with his friend Rob and came back to recount it with Jill. Even Gabriel mentioned how he went out at times with Scott and Nathaniel to watch football games at the local sports bars.

Despite his raising Clint and dealing with a rebellious teenage lycan, Kain never really socialized. He found the transition from soldier to civilian to be more difficult than he thought.

Hesitant, he agreed to go out with Tala. Shifting back into wolves, they ran back to Damien's house.

When they finally arrived at their destination, Kain jumped up into the window, followed by Tala. He proceeded to put his jeans back on, but Tala stopped him.

He glanced at her to see her eyes taking in his body.

She took his hand and proceeded to trace the scars of his forearm, her eyes sullen. "I know you don't want to tell me, but I can't help worrying about you." She placed a soft kiss on one of the scars. "Do they hurt?"

"At times but they look worse than they feel. In truth, I've grown used to them," Kain replied bluntly, his voice gentle. He didn't share the details of the bane with many, not even Jill knew the full extent of his story.

Tala kissed one of the scars on Kain's bicep before leading Kain to the bed. She laid down without putting on any clothing, her heart racing and hoping he'd join her.

A wide grin crossed over Kain's mouth at the open invitation. He crossed the distance and lay down next to Tala, propping up on his elbow and using his arm across her waist to draw her into his body. His fingertips brushed over her arm, down her side to her thigh. The tender skin felt warm beneath them.

"Will you stay with me tonight?" Tala asked, a bit embarrassed at such a frontal request.

Kain took in a deep breath full of her scent. "It would be my pleasure. Thank you for showing me a life outside of battle. For showing me I can love another without fear."

Tala turned her head, confused.

Kain blew a breath out of his nose, half-giggling through closed lips. "It's nothing." He kissed her hair and settled in behind her. "Good night."

Tala wasn't satisfied with Kain's answer. She knew he was hiding something from her and tended to dodge her when she approached the subject of his scars. It made her sad and a bit upset since she shared the vampire side of her.

Due to the heat of Kain's body, she fell asleep, pushing the thoughts away and enjoying the muted sounds of him breathing.

The following morning, Tala woke up startled after a nightmare. Her eyes met the sight of Kain's handsome face still asleep with his head resting on his forearm, using it as a pillow.

Tala's cheeks heated at how perfect he was. She wanted to reach out and pet his hair but didn't want to wake him. Instead, she snuck out of bed, got a quick shower and dressed to head downstairs.

Jill was still in her pajamas in the kitchen making coffee. When she noticed Tala, she smiled and greeted her.

Tala nodded and offered a greeting. "Jill, do you happen to have some time today to spend a little girl time with me?"

The older female pushed her loose ponytail to her opposite shoulder. Her raven hair refusing to be tamed, defied her. "I can. Let me ask Ivy if she'll watch the pups. Any particular reason why?"

Tala's cheeks heated, earning a laugh from Jill. "I want to take Alex out, but I don't know where he likes to go. I thought you might show me some of his favorite spots or a good place to –

"Make-out?" Jill replied, a teasing smirk on her face.

Tala nodded.

Jill repeated what she said about Ivy and left the kitchen.

Tala loved Jill. She saw the older female as a sister and role model. The relationship between Jill and Damien made Tala envious. She wanted to build a bond with Kain in the same way.

It hurt her that they still hadn't shared blood. Tala wanted nothing more to know what such a bond felt like. She'd heard stories from her mother and some of the other females of her pack. It often made Tala feel like a princess waiting on her Prince Charming in one of those fairytales.

It made her laugh at the irony since Kain's bloodline was indeed a line of knights.

Kain woke to find Tala already gone. Her scent lingered in the room showing him she hadn't been gone long.

He lowered his eyes, disappointed. The night before he wanted to make love to her, to seal their bond and make her his. His body burned with a desire to show her a side of him only Jillian truly knew.

A resigned sigh escaped his throat as he sat up to check his phone to see a text from Gabriel telling him he needed to speak with Kain. With a quick reply, Kain got up to go downstairs, not bothering to put a shirt on.

Damien met him in the kitchen while Kain poured a cup of coffee. When he saw the younger lycan, Kain offered to pour Damien a cup as well.

Curious as to where Tala might be, Kain asked, "Have you seen Tala this morning?"

Damien took a quick drink of his coffee. "She went out with Jill earlier. They should be back in a couple of hours. How're you doing, Kain? Your ankle alright?"

Kain joined Damien at the small table. "It's healed up for the most part. My shoulder as well," Kain looked up to find Damien staring intently at him. From their time together, Kain knew Damien acted like this when he had a vision. "What have you seen?"

Damien jerked his eyes away. "Nothing. Just a rough last few nights. We'll be taking Maggie to her First Moon event in a couple of days. I'd like it if you went."

Kain glared at Damien. Instead of pressing the issue for the moment, Kain agreed to go with Damien and Jill to the First Moon. He hadn't been to one since his time as an alpha. It always made him happy to see the pups accepted as members of their packs.

"Did you speak to Cade?" Kain asked.

"Yeah. He's on board. All we have to do is send out a howling call."

"Good. I have a feeling when the time comes, we will need all the help we can get. We still don't know what Anthony's plans are. He's been quiet, at least here."

Kain thought about the encounter with Bard, deciding to tell Damien about the cause of the burns on his hand. "Damien, Bard's accepted an evil gift from the dark god. His missing forearm has been replaced with a claw like the one that attacked you in the snow a year ago."

Damien's brow creased. "How's this possible? Before, all Barghast did was attack us in the celestial realm. How is he able to manifest like this, now?"

Kain shook his head. "That I do not know. When I got close to Bard's arm, I felt like my blood, my life, was being ripped from me. Much like those red fibers we encountered. It is the reason I was so weak."

"What can we do?"

"Nothing yet. Just be on your guard and keep your thoughts open to me. I will do the same. Whatever is going on, it is worse than the Circle of Stones. Barghast was paid a great insult there. He will not be so quick to forget."

Damien clenched his teeth, growling through them. The heel of his hand landed against the edge of the table, jarring it. Once again, Kain got the feeling that Damien hid something from him. A portion of the young alpha's mind remained in shadow, hidden from Kain's bond with him.

It impressed Kain to see how strong Damien had gotten. Not just anyone could block Kain from their thoughts or feelings, yet Damien managed to do it.

CHAPTER NINE

T ala and Jill returned two hours following Kain and Damien's talk in the kitchen. The women carried a few bags, dropping them in the foyer. Jill called to Damien to help her carry her bags upstairs following a heated kiss and some sensual touching.

Tala's cheeks heated at the sight. Her eyes met Kain's as he came out of the living room into the foyer, stepping around the embracing lycans. She almost said hello but Kain stopped her by wrapping his arms around her, his hands gripping her hips as he kissed her.

The passion she could feel in the firmness of his embrace excited her. Warm, hard muscles met her hands as she reached to caress his bare chest and stomach. His hands on her hips made her breath hasten. Her mind filled with images of them tangled together under the sheets of his bed, the scent of him drove her carnal senses mad with need.

When he pulled away, their eyes met briefly. Kain offered to help her take her bags up the stairs. It confused her when he took them to his room instead of hers.

After setting the bags down, Kain took a small portion of Tala's hair between his hand and thumb, caressing the velvet strands and kissing them. "I will explain later. For now, welcome home."

Tala's belly filled with butterflies at the sensual tone in Kain's voice. Her thighs drew together at the growing wetness between her legs. She imagined what it would be like to have sex with Kain if hearing his voice drove her this crazy with desire.

"How did your time with Jillian go?" Kain asked, intrigued by the effect he had on Tala.

"It was fun. Nice to have some girl time." She playfully shoved his chest. "Are you still wanting to go on our date?"

Kain nodded, excusing himself to go get cleaned up and dressed.

While he was gone, Tala hung up the new clothes Jill got her in Kain's closet. She took the books she got and put them on the nightstand. One of them, she got for Kain as a gift since Jill told her he liked to read.

She set it on his bedside, wondering when he would notice it.

Kain returned freshly dressed, sat on the bed and proceeded to put his boots and jacket on. He took his keys from the nightstand, chuckling when he noticed the new book.

That didn't take long, Tala thought, catching a teasing glance from Kain.

The two of them left the room to Kain's waiting car in the driveway. Tala neglected to tell him where they were going so he waited on her cue.

"There."

Tala pointed to a coffee shop Kain was all too familiar with. It was the place where Damien often stopped to get his favorite tea and talk with his friend Rob or his dad, Charlie.

Kain pulled the car into a parking spot and turned off the engine prior to getting out and opening Tala's door for her.

Tala thanked him, giggling. When he offered his arm, Tala bypassed it and took his hand, tangling her fingers with his. It made Kain happy to see she accepted his advances. She pulled him through the door and up to the cash register.

Betsy McClaine, a fellow lycan froze, her wrinkled eyes widening when they fell on Kain. Her hands drew up to her mouth, hiding yellowed fangs.

"Here I swore I saw the last of them," she said, her eyes misting. "I heard the rumors there was a Kain at the battle with Lilith. I didn't believe them until now."

Betsy kept the conversation within an ear shot of her daughter Rayna. The two lycans stared at Kain until Betsy handed him the drink he ordered.

Kain could feel their eyes on him as they left the shop. The look in Betsy's eyes lingered in his mind. Her daughter wiped away a single tear from her eye, probably thinking she'd hidden it.

"I didn't realize how important your family was until I came here," Tala said, sitting down after Kain opened her door for her.

Kain sat down in the driver's side, turning the key. The engine purred to life. "Reactions like that are not uncommon. Since I came to the States, I've been visited by many lycans. Most of them shocked to find a Kain still lived. Others needing guidance on what to do after discovering vampires lived here as well."

The car pulled out of the lot onto the road. Tala directed Kain to a spot in the woods where he parked his car and the two got out to walk.

Tala asked multiple questions about the importance of Kain's family and why so many lycans almost seemed to revere them. Kain told her the story of his father's legacy. How he did more than just defend the royal line. He defended families who were trying to live during the Blood Wars, often leaving his charge to answer howling calls of help and desperation.

Pentacost's sacrifice earned him the respect of the lycan race. A legacy Kain did his best to keep alive the best he could.

Tala took Kain to an old wooden bridge overlooking a bubbling creek overflowing from the abundance of rain. She sat on a wooden bench overlooking the scenery.

"I thought you'd like this place. It's calm and quiet. A great place to talk or--" Tala paused, her cheeks hot.

Kain sat next to her, grinning at the not so subtle invitation. He lay his arm around Tala who snuggled into his chest with a satisfied sigh.

The two sat in silence, enjoying the fading light of the evening, stealing a kiss every now and then.

A foreign scent followed by the rustling of the leaves grabbed Kain's attention.

Tala's ears perked at the sound.

Kain stood up slowly, his eyes locked on a bush on the other side of the bridge.

"Tala, go towards the car." Kain kept his voice low. He stalked towards the rustling brush, his nose focused on the scent. It didn't smell like a werewolf or a vampire. However, he couldn't make out the scent of a lycan either through the heavy scent of blood.

When he was sure Tala was a safe distance away, Kain quickened his pace, eventually leaping through the brush and landing on a large wolf, dragging it out of the brush.

The wolf whimpered against the wounds covering its body. Kain pinned it by the throat beneath his boot.

"Tobias!" Tala screamed. "Alex, stop! Please!"

Kain looked back to see Tala running towards them, annoyed she hadn't listened but relieved to find she knew the wolf beneath his boot. He let the wolf up.

It shifted into the form of a young man covered in bruises and cuts. His breath heaved.

"Who is this?" Kain asked.

"He's my brother." Tala rolled Tobias onto her lap. "Tobias, by the gods, what happened?"

Tobias struggled to speak but was unable to.

Tala's eyes filled with tears at the terrible state her brother was in. "We need to take him to the hospital. Please, Alex."

Kain couldn't help but feel a bit uneasy. The wounds covering the young lycan's body were interrogation wounds.

Much like the ones he'd inflicted to get information in the Blood Wars. Despite his instinct, Kain helped Tala get Tobias in his car.

Kyle met Kain in the waiting room after receiving a phone call from him concerning an injured lycan. The look on the soldier's face told the doctor their visit needed to be as private as possible. Kyle obliged, taking them to the examination room he kept empty in case he got any lycan patients in the ER.

The two lycans lifted Tobias onto the bed where Kyle proceeded to check on his wounds. "What in Tenebris's name happened?"

Kain told him about the events on the bridge and the circumstances surrounding Tobias' appearance. "Something is not right, Kyle. I recognize the types of wounds on his body."

"What're you thinking, old friend?" Kyle asked, concerned.

"I am not yet sure. He is Tala's brother. I am conflicted on how suspicious I should be," Kain replied.

"That's not like you."

Kain gritted his teeth. "I know. It is frustrating."

Damien tugging at Kain's mind forced him to end the conversation with a request to be kept up to date regarding Tobias's condition.

After Kyle stabilized her brother, Tala sat next to his bedside, his hand in hers. Tears fell down her face.

Kain entered the room and sat next to her.

"I thought I was the only one who survived," She said. "What happened to him?"

Kain didn't answer. He stared at the bruises on Tobias' face. Whoever inflicted them let him go, that much Kain knew. It was a tactic lycan generals employed to lower their opponent's suspicions and it was effective.

"We should go back to the house." Kain stood from the chair. He placed a hand on Tala's shoulder. "I promise I will bring you back to see him."

Hesitant, Tala stood from her chair and followed Kain out to his car, leaving her cell phone number with Kyle in case her brother woke up.

On the drive home, Kain and Damien spoke in their minds.

Damien informed Kain about a message Gabriel got from Ramona involving an emissary the vampire's mother planned on sending to the pack's house later that evening.

Tired and frustrated by the night's events the last thing Kain wanted was to see a vampire. When asked where he and Tala had been, Kain responded by recounting the evening's events. He told Damien about Tala's brother, leaving out the suspicion he had regarding the lycan's appearance.

Beside him, Tala stared outside, watching the trees rush by. Kain admired how the leather pants she wore hugged her hips closely, showing off her curves. Her deep red hair lit up with strands of amber in the passing lamps. How he longed to hold her as he made hot love with her.

"I am sure your brother will be fine. Kyle is one Sun's hell of a doctor," Kain said to reassure her.

Tala offered a weak smile in reply.

Kain let the subject drop upon seeing she didn't want to talk.

"I'm sorry our night was ended like that." Tala turned her body towards Kain, leaning against his arm on the rest between them.

"There is no need to apologize. Family is important. I'm glad your brother is alive and well. You know you are no longer alone," Kain replied.

"Did you have any siblings? I don't think you've told me, yet."

Kain exhaled through his nose. His heart hurt at the memories of so many of his adopted family. "I do not know if I had any biological brothers or sisters. My adopted mother had pups of her own when my father married her, but he never told me if he had any."

Tala lay against Kain's arm. She asked Kain about who his real mother was. "I do not know. My father rarely spoke of her. When he did, he always looked so saddened, but I could tell she was the only one he ever truly loved."

A pregnant silence resumed until Tala turned on the radio and proceeded to sing along with REO Speedwagon's "Can't Fight This Feeling."

The jovial mood she exhibited made Kain curious. He asked Tala about the types of music she liked, what her favorite food was and what types of books she liked to read.

As they exchanged favorites, Kain felt his heart lighten despite his leeriness. It delighted him to learn so much more about the woman he'd come to love. She made him happier than anyone in many years.

His desire to do so much more than make-out with blossomed inside of him. No longer did he want to court her, his mind was made up. He wanted Tala as his mate, remembering the goddess' word to protect him from Barghast's wrath.

Kain parked his car to see Damien standing with his back to them. Gabriel, Scott, and Clint all stood with him. They appeared to be talking about something.

"Go inside, sweetheart," Kain said to Tala. "I will meet you as soon as I know what this is about."

Tala kissed Kain's cheek before running into the house, greeting Damien on her way past him. Damien returned the greeting with one of his own.

Kain joined the other lycans, his face emotionless. "My apologies for my lateness. I had something to deal with."

Kain's eyes met Damien's, the only lycan he told about Tala's brother.

"No problem," Gabriel said. He cocked his head, shrugging his shoulders. "The emissary isn't here yet. Being a vampire, he has to wait until moonrise anyway."

"Do we know what this meeting is about?" Kain inquired.

Damien straightened up from his leaning position. "We don't know yet. Personally, I'm not keen on having another vampire in our territory."

"Calm yourself, Damien. Meetings like this occurred many times in the Blood Wars. Let us hear what he has to say." Kain patted Damien's shoulder to comfort him.

The trembling beneath his hand made him aware of Damien's unease.

Gabriel straightened from the position on the wall. "In any case, if I had to guess, Desdemona wants to end things as quickly as we do. The matriarch can't risk showing a lack of control in light of Darius' death."

After a couple of hours, the waxing crescent of Luna's face could be seen above the tree-line.

Kain stood with his arms crossed, his back to the house, eyes closed to allow his acute sense of hearing to tune into the engine of a car. He opened his eyes to see two specks of light coming up the driveway. The Cardoza crest didn't appear to be on the hood.

The missing emblem seemed strange since the emissary supposedly followed Desdemona's orders. It surprised Kain to see the car wasn't a limo or the BMW so popular among the vampires of Big Timber.

Instead, a deep blue Firebird with a racing stripe painted down its body pulled up into the driveway next to Kain's car. A modern make for a family as old as the Cardozas.

Interesting, Kain thought as the vampire departed the vehicle.

CHAPTER TEN

K ain observed the vampire staring back at him from the Firebird. From what Kain could tell, he appeared to be a young man no older than his early thirties. His short hair a silver so radiant, the moon's faint light bounced off it in waves.

Instead of the typical ruby red eyes of the vampire, the young man sported two burning eyes the color of amber with flecks of what appeared to be gold. He wore a plain black shirt and blue jeans.

On his wrists he wore what looked like leather bands. The Semper Fi tattoo of a US Marine lay on his right wrist.

The longer Kain stared at him, the more intrigued he became. This young man didn't resemble a typical vampire.

The vampire walked up the cobble walkway, stopping short of the porch. "My name is Zane. I've come on behalf of Desdemona Cardoza."

Kain watched Damien greet the vampire. His confidence shining through made Kain proud at how much he'd grown in such a short time.

"What do you want?" Damien asked in a direct, authoritative voice.

"I'm here to deliver an invitation to dinner at the coven here in Big Timber," Zane said. His accent betraying his southern roots.

Kain saw Damien shudder. Despite wanting to intervene, he remained where he was.

Gabriel joined Damien in addressing Zane. "Why in Sun's hell should we accept?"

Zane's eye seemed to flash. "Above all, Gabriel, I can imagine Ramona wouldn't mind seeing you again."

The mention of Ramona's name made Kain cover a snicker at Gabriel's apparent blush.

One question lingered in the air. Kain advised Damien in his mind to ask.

"Why does Desdemona want to meet?" Damien asked, glancing at Kain, earning a nod from the older lycan.

Zane adjusted his weight, his hand in his pocket. The other hanging at his side. "She wants to talk about a common problem we're all facing. Anthony and his pursuit of the lycan packs. She wants to extend proof she doesn't wish this bloodshed any more than you do."

Kain glared at Zane. However, it was Gabriel who requested to know why Desdemona hadn't done anything to stop her son's rampage.

"She can't," Zane replied, sighing. "She can tell you more. What's your answer?"

Kain raised his brow at the vampire's abrupt openness. It reminded him of himself. Damien tugged at his beta's mind, asking him what he should do.

Accept the invitation. I sense no deception in Zane's words. He is a soldier, much like me. He would not risk disobeying his mistress' orders, Kain answered Damien's thoughts.

With an uneasy glance, Damien informed Zane they'd meet Desdemona on one condition. Damien would bring at least three lycans with him due to his lack of trust in vampires.

Zane nodded. "We're aware of your experiences with Lilith, Damien. Bring who you want. Desdemona will have me contact you with the time of the meeting."

Damien agreed despite the fear Kain could feel inside of him.

The vampire got back in the car, did a three-point reversal, and pulled back out onto the driveway towards the main road.

Gabriel kept his voice low as he spoke to Kain. "Well, what do you think?"

"I think we should do what we did in the past. Listen to what she has to say. You did well, Gabriel." Kain grinned, impressed with Damien and Gabriel's handling of Zane's visit.

Gabriel replied with his own grin, going back into the house.

Damien remained outside, his head lowered. From where he stood, Kain saw the trembling in his friend's hands as they gripped the wood railing.

"I don't want to go back there, Kain," Damien said, his voice shaking. "I remember what happened in that place."

Kain put his hand on Damien's back. "You will be fine. As Alpha you must do things you might not want to. I will be there. Who else are you taking?"

Damien pondered for a moment. "I was thinking Gabriel and maybe Scott or Jill."

"Take Jillian. She is immortal and will likely ignore your orders to stay anyway," Kain replied, chuckling.

Damien burst out laughing. "Yeah, you're right. She wouldn't want me to go back there without her. Thanks, Kain."

Kain smiled, nodding.

Tala waited for Kain in their bedroom like he asked her to. Her thoughts turned to her brother lying in bed at the hospital. The memory of him howling to her telling her about their mother came forward in her mind. She wanted to know how long he'd been alive and who hurt him so bad.

Anger niggled at the back of her mind. She was so distracted, she didn't hear Kain come into the room. His sudden arrival made her jump.

"I apologize for scaring you. What were you thinking about?" Kain asked, sitting on the bed beside her.

Tala adjusted her sitting position on the bed so she could face Kain. "About my brother. For weeks I thought I was the only one who survived."

Kain didn't respond. After their date, he'd returned to the hospital late in the night to find Tobias awake and asking for his sister. Kain told him he could see her after the young lycan answered some of his questions. Conveniently, Tobias claimed he didn't remember too much about what happened after the pack was attacked.

"How did the meeting with the vampire go?" Tala asked.

Kain put the thoughts of his visit with Tobias aside. "It went well. Desdemona wishes to have a meeting here at the coven in Big Timber."

"Why?"

"She wants to assure us she has no hand in Anthony's actions. My guess is she'll offer to help us in any way she can without alerting Anthony to what she is up to," Kain replied.

Tala sighed a worried sigh. "I'm guessing you're going to go."

Kain nodded.

Tala stared at Kain, once again taking in the beauty of the man in front of her. She wanted to reach out and touch him, to kiss him as they had so many times. Their date had been interrupted which forced her to change her plans to ask Kain to make out with her.

She almost asked Kain if he'd be willing to continue what they started. Kain's mouth against hers silenced any words she might've spoken.

The force of his kiss exhibited the same deep need Tala had seen in Kain before. A need she'd felt almost ever since she first saw him. They'd been avoiding acting on their lust for each other for too long.

Kain rose from the bed, bending at his waist to lift Tala from the bed and onto his hips. He settled her against the wall, his mouth holding hers, teasing her lips to let him in.

Surprised at the sudden intensity, Tala opened her mouth, letting him invade her as far as he wanted. The words Jill said about Kain being one Sun's hell of a lover came into the forefront of Tala's mind. He'd only just started but already Tala could feel a glimmer of what Jill meant.

Kain held Tala's thighs firmly as he kissed her, his breath hastening. Every need, every hunger flooded into him. He pressed his body close to Tala, inhaling her scent.

Guided by Kain's hand, Tala tilted her head to allow him access to her jaw kissing along its length.

The brush of his fangs made Tala wince in anticipation. She said nothing but his name between pants. She wanted him to do so much more, to go as far as he wanted.

Desire flooded between her legs, making her use the muscles in her thighs and calves to pull him closer.

Her hands ran over the firm muscles of his shoulder blades up to his hair where her fingers tangled in the strands of dirty blonde.

Kain withdrew, his head lowered, breathing heavily. He lowered Tala to the ground, his hands moving from her butt up her back. He wanted to remove her shirt, take her breasts with his mouth and make love to her.

When he opened his mouth to speak, Tala brushed his lips with her finger tips, whispering to him not to talk. Her hands on Kain's hips made him shiver with eagerness. Moving slowly, she began pushing his shirt up; the nails of her thumbs tickling the scars on his side and pecs. He let her remove it, hissing through his teeth when she nipped his right pectoral muscle.

Tala pushed Kain back until the backs of his knees met the edge of the bed. Making sure she kept his gaze, Tala began rubbing Kain's length behind his jeans. For this moment, she didn't care to be shy. She knew what she wanted and grew tired of waiting. She let her tongue taste the heat of Kain's copper skin while she explored him.

When she got to the spot on his hip where the crest of a wolf baring a medieval shield lay, she bit firmly down. Her hand held his thigh in a tight grip. The act brought about another hiss through Kain's teeth which made Tala eager. She rose to kiss Kain's collar bone, desiring to share blood with him so she could understand a fraction of what Jill experienced with Damien.

The sacred sharing of blood between mates was supposed to be a bond stronger than even sex. From what Tala was told by her mother, mates could feel one another's emotions, see each other's memories and talk while they were miles away from one another.

Many times Tala spoke to Jill about it, her desire to experience it with Kain grew stronger.

The hard length under her hand made a coy grin curl across Tala's lips. She started unzipping Kain's jeans, licking her lips and fangs, eyes half-open.

Despite what his body told him, Kain caught Tala's wrist, careful not to hurt her. "Are you sure? I'm not sure I could stop."

Tala ran her thumb over Kain's lips, silencing him. "I want you. All of you."

She finished unzipping his jeans and opened them, following them down his legs, thrilled to find he wore no underwear.

She'd seen him naked before when they hunted together but now she saw him as something more. Someone she wanted to give her body to and eventually bare pups for.

Kain let Tala push him to lie on his back while she mounted him. It'd been too many moons since he last had any sexual encounters with a woman.

Tala's smoldering eyes met his as she positioned herself over his erection. She leaned into his face, rubbing his tip with her wet opening. "Alex, I want to share blood with you. To bind myself to you in the most powerful way our kind can."

Thoughts blurred as Kain's lust grew. He managed to focus enough to speak between breaths. "My memories are not easy to bear."

Tala shook her head, telling him she didn't care. Her pleading eyes bore into Kain's, pulling surrender so easily out of him, it surprised him. Tala smiled, satisfied as she lowered herself onto him. Tiny whimpers escaped Tala as her small, virgin opening tore to make room for the man she loved.

Gods, how she wanted this.

Kain felt so good, her heart leapt into her chest from pounding so hard. Finally, he was hers. The game they'd been playing had ended and she'd been able to push away her shyness to take him.

To have such a powerful, strong soldier beneath her gave Tala a sense of confidence she hadn't experienced before. He'd allowed her to take control. Something she never thought she'd be able to do with a male. It elated her so much to see he trusted her.

A dazing rush sent the blood from Kain's brain from the pure pleasure.

Despite his usual preference for being on top, he found himself holding onto her hips moving in time with her rhythm.

Tala's nails dug into the flesh of Kain's chest, her head lulled back the higher her pleasure soared. He felt right to be with.

Something inside of him reminded Tala of herself though she didn't know what. The movement of his hips drove him deep into her warmth.

Before Tala knew it, she started screaming as the orgasm rocketed through her entire body, her muscles convulsing around his length. Her nails dug so deep into Kain's chest, they left red marks. A few minutes after Tala experienced her orgasm, she felt her womb filled, her belly tingling at the sensation. Her hands rested on his chest in an attempt to hold herself up, her body trembling from the remnants of the intense pleasure.

Kain's chest heaved, his mind stunned at how good Tala felt. He'd almost forgotten how nice it felt to be so intimate with another of his kind. The sting of the scratches her nails left on his chest delighted him. For once, the pain was welcome.

The trembling in Tala's legs against his hips had Kain helping her off of him to lie beside him on the bed. He propped his head up in his hand, the other ran down her side to her thigh.

Despite her fatigue, Tala forced herself to sit up, her eyes meeting Kain's, reminding him of his promise to let her share blood with him.

Kain sighed in exhaustion and concern. His memories weren't the type one shared with their mates. They were full of pain, betrayal and an evil, vindictive god. If he shared blood with Tala, she'd experience every emotion Kain ever experienced. However, he gave his word and understood why she'd want to form the powerful bond mates had with one another.

"Tala, before I do this, I need you to know what you might see. It can get overwhelming and some of it, you might not be able to understand."

Tala scooted over to Kain, bending to kiss the base of his throat. "I don't care. I want to be with you. I want to help you deal with whatever it is you're going through. You've helped me find a confidence I never knew I could. I don't feel so helpless or shy when I'm with you anymore."

Kain closed his eyes in preparation for Tala to take his blood. The bite of her nail against his skin did nothing to him as a thin line of crimson began to drip from his collarbone. Her warm, soft tongue relaxed Kain as it traced down the small wound. He couldn't keep from feeling a bit nervous.

The only other lycan who knew Kain's secrets so well was Damien.

The moment Kain's blood met her tongue, Tala saw flashing images of his childhood. At first it seemed normal until the images shifted to his teen and older years. He spent so many hours alone except when he was with his father training.

Tears began to fall down Tala's cheeks at the overwhelming loneliness, the sadness and isolation. She could feel the love Pentacost had for his son but at times, the images of Kain's father looked as sad as Kain did.

As the images ran through Kain's life, Tala stared into the burning eyes of something so evil it made her scream and jump only to be caught by Kain.

Kain held Tala against his chest as their bond formed. She thrashed against him, crying out at times. It tore his heart out to know what she might be seeing. He uttered a silent prayer to Tenebris, begging him to protect Tala and to forgive Kain for what he'd exposed her to.

It seemed like hours before Tala eventually settled down, panting and covered with sweat; her body limp.

"I am so sorry, sweetheart," Kain whispered into Tala's ear, rocking her in his arms. He could only imagine how she felt since he hadn't taken her blood.

Tala whimpered, reaching for Kain's face, her tear-stained eyes meeting his. She said nothing but took his mouth in a passionate kiss full of understanding of the pain Kain went through.

She could feel every emotion he was feeling, hear his heartbeat and see the blood running through him like the image of a CAT scan.

Kain could taste the salt of her tears in their kiss. He held her close, thankful she hadn't fled from him. There was one thing he suspected would scare her away from him. The vampiric side of her probably served as protection against the dark god. He still didn't understand how being a hybrid worked. They were so rare, he'd never met one.

Tala pulled away, her hand on Kain's face. "I want you to see my past, Alex. I think we have more in common than you think." Tala ran her thumb over Kain's lips, pushing down his lower lip to reveal his fangs to her.

Kain closed his eyes, relaxing into the caress of her thumb over his fang. The subtle taste of copper teased his tongue. In an instant, he saw Tala's memories in his mind.

The images of her as a pup, dejected by her pack save for her mother. Confusion when she asked her mother why everyone treated her differently or refused to look at her. Then came the image of a vampire with hair the same shade as Tala's.

From what Kain could tell, this must be her father. Tala couldn't have been older than five or six. She was crying, holding a teddy bear and asking her dad why her pack seemed to hate her.

Her father smiled and lifted her into his arms, promising her it was because they didn't understand how special she was. They couldn't see that she would one day become something great.

Kain's heart stalled. It'd been the same thing his father told him when his adopted brothers and sisters refused to play with him.

He blinked, gasping as he focused back into the bedroom. Tala was above him, her eyes full of concern.

"Now I know," Kain gasped. "I know why the gods gave you to me."

Tala waited for him to go on.

Kain sat up to pet her face. "We understand each other's pain regarding our families. I have never found someone to relate to where my father was concerned. I think you do. I saw your father. Christian, I believe his name was."

Tala nodded. "I related to him more than my mother for obvious reasons."

"I take it Tobias is not your father's son."

Tala shook her head. "I hated my step-father. Not because he was bad but because I couldn't make him understand."

Kain pulled Tala to lie back down beside him. She conformed her body into his, her butt meeting his groin. "I love you, Alex."

"And I you," Kain whispered into Tala's hair. "Tomorrow, I want you to move into my den. I want you beside me."

Tala's heart raced. She smiled a wide smile at the thought of being with the man she loved for the rest of their lives.

Kain woke the following morning to Damien calling to him in his mind. The younger lycan told him that Gabriel heard back from Ramona about the dinner. According to Damien, it would be held in two days.

Gives us time to celebrate the First Moon, Damien said.

Indeed. Have we given thought to dispatching a messenger to Galek to ask for his help? Kain replied.

Damien told him that Nathaniel and Vincent had been dispatched by Gabriel the day before. They were still waiting to hear back from them.

Good. Well done, Damien. I will meet you downstairs. Kain got up from the bed, careful not to wake Tala. She'd woken up a few times in the night because of nightmares and Kain didn't want her to be tired.

Especially since he planned on asking her to attend the First Moon event with him that night.

Kain got up to catch a shower to wash off from their love making and relax his aching muscles. He let the hot water turn his skin a shade of red. The scratches on his shoulder blades and chest complained beneath the temperature but Kain didn't care.

Thoughts of his own nightmare came to the forefront of his mind. He'd fallen into Barghast's plane but the god wasn't there.

The idea unnerved Kain. Barghast never gave up a chance to torture him.

Where are you? Kain thought, disturbed he even wanted to know. At least if the dark god was torturing Kain, he wasn't hurting anyone else.

The sudden arrival of Tala's hands on his back relaxed Kain.

"Good morning," Tala said, her voice tired.

"Good morning. Did I wake you?"

Tala rubbed Kain's back before wrapping her arms around his waist. "You could say that. Your body is like a furnace. Things got a bit drafty once you left."

Kain chuckled. He turned and took his mate into his arms. "I have something I want to ask you."

Tala's brow raised.

"Have you ever been to a First Moon event?"

The confused look in her eyes answered his question.

He laughed, inviting her to go with him and explaining the intricacies of how it worked. Something he probably had to teach Damien since the young alpha likely hadn't done one yet.

Intrigued, Tala agreed.

When he started to wash his hair, Tala took the shampoo bottle from him and began washing it for him. "Are you still going to the dinner?"

"We are," Kain replied.

Tala bit her lower lip. The idea of Kain going to the vampire coven made her nervous despite how strong he was. "Alex, I know about your scars. I know what they mean and how you got them."

Kain proceeded to rinse his hair. He didn't respond but fought the frustration building inside of him.

Tala didn't continue her thought. She knew the subject of his scars made Kain agitated.

"I have to meet Damien," Kain said, petting Tala's face to show he wasn't mad at her. "I want you to get some more sleep if you can. You will need it for tonight." He placed a soft kiss on Tala's lips then got out of the shower.

Kain went downstairs to find Damien pacing the floor and muttering to himself. The alpha appeared frustrated, confused and pissed off all at once.

"Damien, what in Tenebris' name has you so wound up?" Kain leaned against the door, trying not to laugh.

Damien didn't stop pacing. "I've never done a First Moon event, Kain! Not sure if you've noticed but my pack's grown. They're all expecting me to welcome their pups like an alpha should. You never trained me on those customs."

"The first step is to calm down. All you need to do is change into your wolf skin and greet and welcome the shifting pups into your pack. It's not hard and you have seen it before."

Kain's words didn't seem to help Damien calm down. He actually looked more wound up. "Come spar with me, Damien. It has been a while and you seem to need to vent some energy."

The pacing stopped. Damien's eyes almost appeared to light up at the idea of sparring with his old mentor. "Just make sure I don't kick your ass, old man. I've been practicing since you've been gone."

Kain grinned a coy, mischievous grin. If he remembered correctly, every time Damien said those words, he wound up on his back. He offered his friend to go outside first and followed him onto the front lawn.

CHAPTER ELEVEN

L ater that afternoon, Jill arrived with Tala to find Damien holding an ice pack over his eye while Kain leaned against the marble counter enjoying a cup of coffee.

Tala glanced at Kain. In her mind, she heard him explain what happened.

"Damien, tell me you didn't. Not the old man comments again," Jill sighed, examining Damien's eye.

Damien huffed, changing the subject. "How's your hand, Kain? Didn't get the chance to ask between landing on my ass and getting up."

"The burns have healed for the most part. The damage has left me with limited use, but I can still throw a decent punch." Kain smirked at Damien's sarcastic eye roll.

Tala took Kain's hand, her fingers tracing the distorted scar, wondering why she hadn't seen it when they made love. She looked up at Kain concerned.

Kain responded with a gentle, reassuring smile and whispered he was alright.

The smell of blood took Kain's attention from the conversation. He glanced at Damien. "Do you smell that?"

Damien nodded. "Yeah. We better go see what's going on."

Kain told Tala to stay in the house while he, Jill and Damien went out to the front lawn. Vincent limped up the gravel walkway, his body dripping with blood and reeking of silver. His tongue hung loosely from his mouth. One of his eyes had been gouged from his skull.

The stinging in Kain's scars and hand revealed to him who the culprit was. He ran forward, catching Vincent just as he shifted and started to fall.

Vincent coughed up blood, choking as he tried to speak.

"No, do not try to speak, my friend," Kain said, taking off his jacket and covering Vincent's shivering form.

It took everything he had to keep from dropping the injured lycan due to the burn of the silver in his wounds.

Kain lay Vincent down in the soft grass. His eyes were a mix of sadness and great anger at how badly a condition Vincent was in.

"Gone ..." Vincent gagged from the one word.

Damien knelt next to Vincent and asked what happened.

Kain could tell Damien was trying not to sound angry to keep Vincent comfortable.

"He need not speak, Damien," Kain replied.

Vincent coughed again. "Need to know ... Galek ... Channon ... Dead ..."

Gasps erupted from Jill, Damien and Kain.

"Galeck is ... dead?" Damien's fists clenched on his thighs. He dropped his head, drawing up his shoulders.

"Vampires ... werewolves ... too many ..." Vincent choked. "Nathaniel ... captured." Vincent's breath grew shallow. A single tear mixed with the blood on Vincent's face as it met Kain's.

"Forgive me ..." Vincent's body stilled, his breath ceasing.

Kain pushed Vincent's blood-soaked hair away from his face, closing his friend's eye and raising the jacket over his head. He uttered a peaceful prayer to the gods to take the soul of another fallen brother before rising to his feet.

"Dammit!" Damien got to his feet and threw a fist into the nearest tree.

"Kain," Jill said, her voice void of emotion.

"They are trying to cut us off. Stoker must have mentioned who our allies were in the battle against Lilith. It would be difficult for Anthony to fight so many." Kain's brow creased, his fangs clenched against what he saw as cowardice. He held onto the calm reserve despite his anger.

"We need to pull our remaining allies closer. We can't risk Yuna or Gabriel falling prey to the same thing," Jill commented.

Damien picked up Vincent's body and carried him around the house. Kain and Jill joined him.

Tala came out of the back door and covered her mouth. She ran to Kain's side, wondering what happened.

Kain stared at her with sadness in his eyes then back at Damien who proceeded to shift and dig a hole.

Once Damien finished, the four of them shifted and let out a mournful howl which echoed across the mountainsides. All along the ridges, howls joined theirs in a song sending off another soul to the arms of the gods.

Following Vincent's burial, Kain contacted Gabriel over the phone to let him know the tragedy that had occurred. Gabriel responded with a line of cursing and after some calming words from Kain, gave his word he'd be at the First Moon event later that night.

Kain hung up his phone and set it down on the bedside table. He'd been spending the greater part of the afternoon helping Tala move into his room. He stared out of the paned window down at the fresh mound of earth covering Vincent's body.

Tala's arms around his waist helped ease the tension. She didn't say anything but snuggled into his chest, wrapping his arm around her.

They stayed that way until the late afternoon hours faded into the gentler colors of the twilight hours.

The First Moon event would start at moonrise.

Kain instructed Tala to get dressed in something warm and to put a change of clothes in the backpack he set on their bed.

Tala kissed Kain then went to do as he asked of her. She'd never been to a First Moon but was always curious about them. She'd only heard about them from the older lycans in her pack. Her pack lacked leadership like alphas and betas, so it all felt new to her.

After she finished packing, Kain took the backpack and the two of them went downstairs to find Damien and Jill waiting with their pups. Maggie stood next to her mother, smiling wide upon seeing Tala and Kain. She ran to Tala and begged her to pick her up.

Tala obliged, earning a hug around the neck. Such a sight brought a hint of warmth to Kain's heart despite the day's earlier events. He wondered if he would live long enough to see his pups reach Maggie's age.

"We'll be taking Jill's car, Kain. It has the girls' seats in it. Meet you at the Woods Edge." The moment that should be something to be proud of did little to lighten Damien's mood.

After agreeing to meet there, Kain took Damien aside. "I know your heart is troubled, brother, but let this moment be one of great pride. Maggie is advancing fast. Do not let her see her father so broken. There will be time to grieve."

Damien let out a deep breath. "You're right. Thanks, Kain."

Kain smiled and let his friend go out with his family. Tala put Maggie down and went with her mate to his car.

During the drive to the Woods Edge, Kain's thoughts circulated through all that happened starting with his cabin. The way Anthony went about his strategy baffled the lycan soldier in some ways but made sense and impressed Kain in others.

If Desdemona wanted to extend aid, then she had to have known about the storm on the way. The question remained as to why she wouldn't openly help against Anthony. It had to have something to do with her being a pacifist. She'd refused to get involved with Lilith as well and appeared to make sure the damage to the coven was minimal and could be repaired.

Kain's thoughts went to Zane. Something about him seemed familiar, but Kain couldn't put his finger on it. The vampire was clearly younger than even Jared but the way he carried himself and the color of his hair and eyes were different than any of the vampires Kain knew.

"Pheasant for your thoughts?" Tala asked in a jovial tone.

Kain snickered. "That actually sounds wonderful. I was thinking about everything going on. Your father, Christian was killed by Anthony. Why is that?"

Tala scowled. "He worked for Anthony as a hit man. During one of his jobs, he met my mother who was nothing more than a pleasure slave for his mark. After he killed the vampire Anthony wanted killed, my father took my mother away and nurtured a love affair with her. He managed to keep it a secret until I was old enough to know who he was and then--"

Kain took Tala's hand with his. "It's alright. Your father risked a lot to be with your family, Tala."

"I hate Anthony so much! I don't understand why he suddenly decided to go insane."

Kain understood what caused the problem. Bard's arrival, the interest in the talon. Barghast orchestrated it all. The thought unnerved Kain.

Once they arrived at the Wood's Edge, Kain parked his car next to Damien's and got out.

The stillness of the woods perturbed Kain. A familiar smell lingered in the air. Its rotten, putrid scent brought back memories of Kain's encounter with Bard.

Oh no. "Damien! Hurry!" Kain shouted, shifting into his lycan form and sprinting into the woods.

The sounds of gnashing teeth and growls echoed in the clearing. Kain slid to a halt in the sacred space overlooked by three huge boulders used by the alphas during the First Moon events. Gabriel, Lune, Cade and a few others Kain didn't recognize battled werewolves while trying not to trample the frightened pups whose mothers either lost them or died.

The scene reminded Kain of times he'd arrived too late to save anyone when the Blood Wars raged at their worst. Snarling, he grabbed the nearest werewolf and threw it yowling across the sky. It landed on one of the boulders the alphas stood upon when greeting pups.

Gabriel grinned a fanged grin and sank his teeth into the throat of another werewolf, lashing his head from side to side. Kain heard Gabriel reach out to him telepathically to tell him what went on before he arrived.

The werewolves arrived not long before the lycans and began killing whoever they found. Thankfully, not many had gotten there yet so the carnage wasn't as bad as it could've been.

A howl like the call of a loon rang out in the clearing. The werewolves froze when Damien leapt through the trees, landing on two muscular legs. Runes glowed a bright blue on his white fur.

"Finally." A voice rumbled from beyond the platform of boulders. Bard stepped up in his full lycan form, his fangs drawn back over his lips in a wicked grin.

The presence of the dark god's power made the scars on Kain's body burn. It threatened to force him to his knees, but he stood fast, ready to protect his fellow lycans.

"I was wondering when you'd arrive, Kain. Have you decided to surrender what we want yet?" Bard spat.

Kain stepped forward, growling. *"I do not barter with cowards. Leave now or I will kill you, Bard. What you have done is beyond my contempt."*

Bard leapt from the rock, landing mere feet from where Damien stood, his fangs snapped in obvious frustration. His eyes radiated a deep hate as he drew closer to Kain only to be intercepted by Damien.

"Back off. I don't know who you are personally, but I'm beyond pissed," Damien snarled.

Bard glared at him, smirking.

Seeing what was about to happen. Kain pushed Damien aside, receiving a hit by Bard's foot. The proximity to the claw dazed Kain as he pushed Bard's kick away. *"Damien, you are not ready. Stand down!"*

Bard threw another punch which Kain met with his own. The sound of the collision emulated a crash of thunder when bone met bone.

The demented lycan's eyes met Damien's. *"Listen to your boyfriend, kid. Who do you think trained me?"*

Damien's eyes widened. He watched as the two fought. The way they moved matched perfectly except for the fact Kain seemed to be taking more hits.

Kain felt sick to his stomach. The claw's darkness threatened to sap every last drop of strength from him, but he was determined to keep Bard from attacking Damien or Gabriel.

A stray hit from Bard forced Kain to his knee. All around the fighting between the werewolves and the lycans continued. The whimpering of pups and the cries of desperate mothers filled Kain's ears.

The only difference was the intense light out of his peripheral vision. Damien lunged at Bard, his body so bright, Kain had to avert his eyes. He'd seen this before during the fight with Lilith, only it radiated the same crushing power Kain felt from the woman he met in the celestial plane.

When he could focus, Kain saw Damien gripping the demented claw, its flesh writhing and screaming beneath his silver nails. Bard yowled in pain, struggling to get free.

With his free hand, Bard slashed at Damien's face, his claws raking across the white lycan's flesh, leaving no marks.

*"What the hell?!"*Bard screamed.

*"I said back the fuck off. I won't let you hurt Kain or any of my people anymore. If I see you again, I'll kick your blood loving ass."*Damien shoved Bard away.

The black lycan stepped away, holding his injured claw. Gabriel, Lune and Cade all formed up behind Damien. Kain rose to his feet, careful to keep his face hidden but still ready to back his fellow lycans.

Bard snarled, ordering what remained of his werewolves to back down. His eyes met Kain before laughing and fleeing into the woods.

Kain watched Damien turn to face him. The light around him faded to a manageable level so Kain could stare at him.

Damien shifted back, his eyes locked on the fresh wounds on Kain's face.

The look in the lycan alpha's eyes was unmistakable. Damien wanted to talk.

Due to the night's events, the First Moon event had to be canceled. The lycans spent hours taking care of the remaining visitors from neighboring packs. Not many had been killed or injured in the scuffle.

"Damien, that was incredible," Gabriel said, while the lycans walked back to the Woods Edge.

Damien didn't reply. His fists at his side told Kain he was clearly upset.

Tala ran up to Kain and reached up to touch his face.

He stopped her, shaking his head and asked for a gauze pad from the first aid kit in his car.

Damien met Jill and hugged his pups. He motioned to Kain to follow him.

Kain took the gauze Tala handed him and followed his friend until they were out of listening distance.

"Talk," Damien demanded.

Kain sighed, leaning against a nearby tree, holding the gauze to his face. "It is true. I trained Bard, but it was many moons ago."

"And you think this wasn't important enough to tell me sooner?"

"There are many things about my past I have yet to share. As I am sure there are some things you have yet to tell me. Damien, this is not the time. Bard is injured. We need to focus on finding a way to stop this."

Damien whipped around. His lips drew up around his fangs. "What about your face, then? What did you do, Kain?"

Kain explained the deal he made with Tenebris. How he believed protecting Damien was more important than his previous chosen. However, Kain refrained from mentioning the encounter with the goddess. "Damien, all I have ever asked is for you to trust me. It is all I ask now, brother. Please."

Damien's eyes softened. "I know, Kain. I know I need to trust you and I know I shouldn't demand for you to tell me about your past. I just wish you would trust me with more of it. Promise me you won't do anything reckless. That you'll come to me."

Kain took Damien's hand in a firm shake. "I promise."

Damien embraced Kain. The gesture saying more than any words. Worry, concern, fear and love flowed into Kain the longer Damien held him. It was something not even Kain's siblings gave him when he was younger.

Damien meant more to Kain than many of the lycans he knew. No matter what it took, Kain would keep him and his mate safe, even if it cost Kain his life.

CHAPTER TWELVE

The morning following the disaster at the Wood's Edge, Kain received a rather unwelcome visit in his dreams. Kain wondered if the injury Damien had inflicted upon Bard had something to do with it.

"I am in no mood to entertain your company." Kain felt the heavy claws on his shoulders squeezing his flesh.

"*To my greatest regret, my soldier, you never are.*" The god folded his leathery wings around Kain's upper body. The gesture took on an air of protection. *"Why continue this fight? Be mine, Alexander. Serve me."*

It appeared as if Barghast was pleading. Something Kain had never seen or expected of the god during their time together. Kain shoved the god's claws off.

"Enough. I am not your soldier. I will never serve you nor accept any gift you may want to give."

The dark god's chuckle held a sense of malice and surprisingly, sadness. His burning red eyes closed to tiny slits. *"You will be mine, Alexander. The precious Purifier you seem to care for cannot save you. Make whatever deal with whatever goddess you wish but your soul is mine."*

A feeling of terror flooded over Kain. He didn't know how the dark god knew of his encounter with the goddess, but the pledge Barghast made caused Kain's stomach to churn. He had thought to ask why Barghast wanted him so desperately and why he'd become so hellbent on Kain serving him.

Before Kain ventured to ask, he found himself alone in the black plane.

Kain opened his eyes to find he was still in bed. He was so upset after the Wood's Edge that he and Tala went on a hunt during the wee hours of the morning.

Tala lay asleep next to him. The gentle breath coming from her helped Kain calm down after his encounter with Barghast. He smiled, caressing the exposed skin of her side down to her thigh where the bedsheet fell to her knee.

She smiled in her sleep, purring and nuzzling deeper into the soft sheets.

To avoid waking her, Kain slipped out of the bed, put on his jeans and left the bedroom to go downstairs.

A gentle rain began pattering over the landscape, echoing in the vivid green made more prominent by the light of the sky. A fresh scent greeted Kain as he stepped out onto the front porch. Its cooling touch upon his senses eased the flames of the dark god's glare.

"Morning, Kain," Damien said and took a drink of his coffee. His eyes were locked on the landscape with his brow furrowed in agitation.

The intense focus Damien had in his eyes and the nervous tapping of his foot gave Kain the idea the young lycan had something on his mind.

"Morning, Damien," he responded. "Mind telling me what it is you're thinking about?"

After placing his empty coffee mug on the table, Damien sat down on the top stair of the porch, motioning for Kain to join him. "I've been thinking about some things."

Kain tilted his head in curiosity, waiting for his friend to continue. The last time Damien wanted to discuss such things, the young lycan came up with a plan which led to the lycans' victory at the Circle of Stones. Here recently, Kain saw his friend becoming more distressed - his emotions a scrambled mess of fatigue and confusion.

"Damien, whatever it is that's bothering you, you know you can tell me. I can see how stressed and upset you are. Tell me." Kain encouraged Damien, taking on the air of the mentor Damien came to trust and believe in.

Damien glanced at his mentor in his peripheral. "It's how Anthony seems to be going about things. He's not flaunting his vampiric god-complex like Lilith did."

"Interesting. What do you mean?" Kain listened intently as Damien described Anthony's actions to be more like those of a modern-day mob boss.

Despite using Bard and his werewolves as an attempt to capture Kain's attention, Anthony seemed to be methodical. He was avoiding the typical vampire tactics of outright attacking people or hunting mortals to frame the lycans, unlike Lillith who'd attack anyone without restraint.

"It seems like he's using his influence in the human world to get to us, namely you," Damien said putting his hand through his hair. "What does he want with you, Kain? All of this can't be over the talon or he would've stolen it already."

Theories swam in Kain's mind. The way Barghast remained absent or did what he could to win Kain to his side gave a deeper meaning than just the talon. Why Anthony wanted Kain remained a mystery because Kain didn't encounter the young vampire save for a few meetings.

"I do not know why Anthony wants my attention, Damien. If I did, I would tell you. You do have a point about his methods. The Cardozas are a powerful family with many followers and those loyal to them. Perhaps he has no need to use his darker influence."

Damien lowered his head. "I spoke with my dad. He's going to make arrangements for Gabriel, Cade, and Lune's packs to stay in the motels. It's hunting season and a mass influx of people won't seem suspicious. Jill is sending the girls to stay with him and Sarah along with Ivy and Astrid."

Kain took a moment to realize something. "Wasn't Sarah your adopted mother's name?"

Damien's eyes creased into an uneasy gaze. "Yeah, I caught that too. I just hadn't said anything to avoid hurting my old man. I doubt it's registered or if it has, he's not saying anything."

Letting the uncomfortable matter drop, Kain continued, "When do you expect the other packs to arrive?"

"Gabriel sent me a text telling me they were on their way. Cade sent a howl last night and Lune was spotted moving down the river side with his pack. They should be here by tomorrow or the next day at the latest."

The two men stood in silence until Damien broke it. "I've been thinking about pulling some modern tactics of my own. You've taught me to look for signs and to anticipate your enemy."

Kain grinned a proud grin.

"I think we should try to get a hold of one of Anthony's men. Someone we can beat the Sun's hell out of to get information. If Anthony wants to play the mob card, then let's play it."

"Who do you have in mind?" Kain asked.

Damien picked up a nearby rock from one of the flowerbeds. He twirled it in his hand for a moment before crushing it into dust. "I want that bastard, Stoker Cromwell. I know he's still alive. How else would Cardoza know where all our sacred sites are? I'm not done with making him pay for all the shit he put me through."

Kain recalled the incident with Damien's friend Chelsea. The young woman had been so overwhelmed with grief, she'd been lured into a trap and changed into a vampire. The result ended in tragedy.

In other encounters, Stoker nearly killed Damien, and had Jill not turned him, they wouldn't be speaking.

"How do you propose getting to him?" Kain questioned, both curious and feeling the same way Damien was. "Odds are he has remained close to Anthony to avoid you."

"Zane. The vampire who works for Desdemona. I don't know what it is about him, but I feel like we can trust him. At the dinner, I want to ask Desdemona to have Zane get a hold of Cromwell. We'll wait until he does and then he can have some time with me and you." Damien picked up another rock and fiddled with it.

Silence resumed while Kain mulled over Damien's plan to get a hold of Stoker. As far as guerrilla tactics, it was masterful. Interrogation was one of Kain's specialties in the Blood Wars. It both excited him and made him angry looking forward to it.

A question lingered in Kain's mind since Damien acted strangely to him not a few days ago. He could tell Damien hadn't told him something. "Damien, since the fight with Bard, have you sensed anything in regards to the dark god?"

The fiddling stopped. While Damien gritted his teeth, Kain watched his eyes intently. It was as though the young lycan's thoughts wandered to a corner of his mind he didn't want Kain to go. A dark part Damien kept hidden.

A short moment passed then Damien looked up at Kain. "I hadn't really seen anything. During the fight with Bard, when I gripped the claw, my mind was suddenly filled with what I thought were screams of agony. The damn thing moved under my claws like a worm on a hook. It disgusted me, honestly."

"What did it feel like?"

Looking at his hand, Damien appeared to ponder how he might say what he wanted. "It felt like I was touching Barghast himself. Cold and dark with a slimy, leathery texture. I can't think of any way to describe it."

The disgusted look on Damien's face while he spoke made Kain curious. Great details like the texture of the dark god's skin were things Kain never shared. It made him think Damien had experiences of his own while his mentor lived in isolation.

"What about you, Kain?"

Kain thought back to the emptiness of Barghast's plane until after the battle with Bard. The god's behavior seemed angry though he didn't show it like he usually did.

Damien listened while Kain told him of the dark god's absence from his plane. How he hadn't gone out of his way to torture Kain in the usual manner and when he did appear, he seemed almost sad to do what he'd done for centuries.

"Do you have a theory as to why he's acting so strange?" Damien asked.

Kain shook his head. "No, and in truth, it is more than a little unnerving."

The following morning Gabriel and his beta, Dolph arrived at Damien's pack house. He greeted Kain with a sullen look in his eyes, his head hung low. Dolph looked angry enough to start a fighting match with Scott who sat in the living room with Clint.

"It is good to see you, Gabriel. I know you have been traveling a lot lately." Kain took his friend in a hug.

Gabriel held Kain close. The gesture held an air of concern and overall sadness. "It's good to see you as well, Kain. How's your hand?"

Kain showed Gabriel his hand. He'd been wrapping it in fighter's tape to hide the horrible, wax-like scars. "I still have little use. Kyle says the burns may have removed my ability to recover from it completely. It still serves a purpose though."

Gabriel smiled a weak smile. "And, Vincent's death?"

Kain offered Gabriel to join him in the living room. Damien sat in his usual spot against the big black wolf sleeping on the floor. Between the two of them, Jill and Tala took turns watching over the pups.

It'd been hard since Damien made the choice to send his girls to stay with his father, Ivy, Astrid and Sarah. His reasoning was to protect them and keep them as far away from the fight as possible.

The choice devastated Jill who hadn't shifted back since her children left. She said nothing save for a few whimpers, her cheeks moistened by tears.

Damien stroked the black fur, murmuring to his mate when Gabriel came into the room with Kain.

Gabriel sat on the floor across from Jill. "So, you really sent them away?"

Damien nodded. His eyes sad.

"Sun's hell. Will the gods not find it in themselves to give us true peace?" Gabriel dropped his eyes. Kain could hear the grinding of the alpha's fangs, a low growl rumbling in his chest.

Lune and Cade arrived with their betas hours after Gabriel's arrival, informing Damien and Kain that they'd gotten their packs set up in the motels Charlie made available to them.

Once the leaders were all assembled, Damien brought everyone up to speed about Vincent's death and the message he gave before joining the gods. He went into his thoughts regarding Anthony's choice of guerrilla or mob-like tactics and what Damien came up with to counter the Don's actions.

Lune glared at the floor in front of him. His beta, Justin, sat beside his alpha. Cade's beta, Adam, mirrored his alpha's leaning stance against the wall. Kain could tell Cade had chosen a lycan much like himself, a hardened soldier, to be his beta.

Kain stood behind Damien, his arms crossed over his chest.

"What you're saying is, this vampire isn't fighting like a vampire? He's relying on human world tactics? Why choose to go that route?" Gabriel questioned.

"It's the modern day, Gabriel. The Cardoza family is as big as the Italian mob. Why not use that influence? It means he can reach us no matter where we try to hide and can hire human hitmen who aren't affected by the sun," Damien replied.

Lune moved his glare to meet Damien's eyes. "This madness you plan on going through to obtain Cromwell. This isn't only for vengeance is it? If it is, you better put your petty fit behind you."

Cade echoed Lune's sentiment. "I for one don't like you leading this, Damien. Nothing personal but everyone in this room has more experience with vampires."

"Enough, Cade," Kain snapped. "Have you forgotten who it was who developed the plan at the Circle of Stones? Seems to me it is you who needs to put your petty differences behind you."

Cade snarled at Kain. The rivalry between the two soldiers became legendary in the world of the lycans. Despite Cade's size and his military training, Kain always came out on top in the ring.

"I remember. My alpha was murdered in that battle. Bite your tongue, Kain. I only meant a trained strategist should be leading, that's all." The Silent Soldier averted his eyes when Kain's almost seemed to burn with challenge.

Damien didn't respond to Cade's biting. It was no secret to anyone in the room how much Cade didn't like Damien. Kain stood in the same room when Cade said the packs should leave Damien to his own defense against the vampires.

Gabriel rose from the floor. His size brought him equal to Cade's. If the two fought, one of them would have to die before either of them backed down. "I've had enough of you Cade. Holt died honorably getting rid of Rayes. Let him rest in peace for the gods' sake. We could always leave your worthless ass in the hands of the werewolves and see how you do."

"Stop!" Damien shouted. He'd gotten between Cade and Kain who stood on opposite sides of the room. "I've had it with the bickering! We're up to our asses in problems. Cade, if you won't trust me, get the hell out of my territory! I don't need you. Lune, you're out of line! No one hates Stoker Cromwell more than I do but fuck my reasons! This is for our packs, not for me."

Every eye in the room, including Kain's were wide as dinner plates. This new part of Damien impressed Kain and filled him with pride.

No one said anything else as Damien resumed his spot on the floor. Kain could swear he heard Jill snickering below him. It made his heart smile.

Damien rubbed the bridge of his nose with his thumb and fingers. "Now, can we please focus? Tonight's the dinner at the coven here in Big Timber.

We need to come up with a plan in case it's a trap. Gabriel, I want you, Kain and Jill to come with me. The rest of you can stay here. Make sure the packs are settled in and inform us if anything happens. Remember, think like a human or a hunter. Anthony isn't targeting lycans, he's targeting humans."

CHAPTER THIRTEEN

Tala met Kain in the kitchen after the talk in the living room. She could tell by how high his shoulders were drawn and how tight he gripped the marble counter that he was stressed.

She sashayed over to him and lay her head against his shoulder and running her nails over the scars on his forearm. In his injured hand, he gripped the keys to his car, the other held his cell phone.

"You're really going?" she asked, concerned.

Kain said nothing. He didn't need to.

"I don't like this and think it's beyond insane, but if you believe it's the right thing, I'll support you and wait for you." Tala stood on her tip toes and kissed the bottom of her lover's jaw. "I want to be with you when you get home. Can we go hunting together again?"

The suddenness of Kain's embrace made her jump, bringing about a shocked squeak. His arms held her tight to his body, the smell of him captivating. Their lips met in a brief kiss.

"Nothing would please me more," Kain purred while running his hand through his mate's silken hair. "Keep our bed warm. I will be home soon."

Tala walked with Kain out to the front lawn where Gabriel, Damien, and Jill waited beside his car.

Tala kissed Kain one last time before watching him walk down to the car. Their eyes met for a short time before he got in the driver's side and pulled off.

When the lycans arrived at the metal gate surrounding the coven's mansion in the high mountains outside of Big Timber, Kain felt Damien tugging his mind. The feelings and memories of the night they had to save Damien from Lilith ran through Kain's thoughts as if they were his own.

Kain reassured Damien that this visit wouldn't be like his last one. To distract the young lycan, he told Damien a story between the two of them about how Kain attended many of these meetings with his father. They were often used to either promote peace or to try and come to terms before a major battle.

As Kain thought, Damien quizzed him about how the meetings often went. Despite the number of questions, Kain was glad he'd managed to distract his friend long enough for them to go through the automatic gate.

Zane stood at the base of the concrete steps leading up to the large double doors of the house. Damien stopped beside Kain, his eyes glancing toward the second-floor window to the right of the door. He squeezed his eyes closed.

Kain placed his hand on Damien's shoulder, once again reassuring him Kain wouldn't let anything harm him. Kain focused on Zane and reminded Damien of the feelings the alpha had about trusting the vampire. Inside, Kain couldn't explain it but he too felt he could trust Zane. Something about the vampire reminded him of his early days in the Blood Wars.

Damien shocked Jill and Gabriel by walking up to Zane and taking the vampire's hand in a firm shake.

"Uh, Kain, explain please?" Gabriel asked.

Kain didn't explain. He only shrugged and followed his alpha's lead, leaving Gabriel baffled.

They walked into the halls to find them lavishly decorated much like the many mansions Kain attended the most luxurious parties in. Through his boots, he could feel the plush carpets. Along the walls, paintings of the coven's monarchs lined the crimson red wallpaper.

Zane stood close to Kain, his eyes glancing at him occasionally. Kain nearly said something before the vampire spoke. "Damien is impressive. He held no fear when he approached me."

"The Purifiers feared neither race according to legend. Damien has had his fair share of problems with your kind but still he chooses to try and bring peace." Kain's reply came without emotion.

Zane half-chuckled. "You should be pleased. He trusts you, seems to care for you. A good trait to have in a leader with so much on his shoulders."

The vampire's words made Kain both curious and uneasy. He didn't say anything else but didn't let the lingering discomfort go considering the vampire's interest in him and Damien.

They arrived in a grand hall with a table so long it looked like it could seat at least thirty people. At the far end, Desdemona sat with her fingers laced together. Her daughter Ramona sat to her mother's right. Both of them so astonishingly beautiful, Kain had to remind himself of the vampire's secret weapon he'd fallen for once in his life. He still dealt with the consequences.

Desdemona rose from her chair once Zane returned to her side, greeting her subordinate and accepting a kiss to her hand before he stood behind her. His hands behind his back like a soldier at attention. Ramona smiled briefly at Gabriel before returning to her reserved posture.

The lycans sat close together near the vampires.

"Welcome, my esteemed guests," Desdemona said in greeting. Her voice a sensual purr echoing in the room. Its tone betrayed a subtle Transylvanian accent. "I trust your journey here was a pleasant one."

"We appreciate your invitation, Ms. Cardoza. If our hostess would forgive us, we wish to cut the pleasantries and get to the reason she chooses to call," Kain answered, his voice holding the formality befitting a noble as old as Desdemona.

A smile of pleasure at Kain's greeting fell across Desdemona's face. "It is good to see one who remembers the old customs. Alexander Kain, I have not seen you since my late husband's unfortunate demise. The reason I invited you here is twofold. One, I wish to persuade you to know neither me nor my family condone the rash behavior of the Don of Great Falls. Two, I wish to offer a gesture of goodwill. Anything you may ask of me as long as it does not cause conflict between Anthony and myself, you are free to ask."

The mention of the latter perked Damien's ears. "Let's skip the persuasion. I don't give a damn what you say. You're letting this psychopath murder our people and doing nothing. Prove you want to help us."

Kain covered a smirk at Damien's boldness. It was just like him to give customs the middle finger and get to the point.

Instead of reacting the way Kain expected a vampire who was just insulted, Desdemona laughed. "Ah yes, the young Purifier. It makes sense you would not know our ways. Forgive me, I am still getting used to such modern ways of speaking. What is it I can do to prove what I say is true?"

"Lend us someone who can get a hold of Stoker Cromwell. He's been hiding behind Anthony and feeding him information. I want the bastard brought to us." Damien's hands landed hard on the wood of the table.

Desdemona motioned for Zane to lean down to whisper in his ear. Kain watched and listened as best he could but Desdemona kept her voice low enough not even a lycan could hear.

Following the short exchange, Zane nodded and returned to attention.

Desdemona sighed. "You will have Zane's full cooperation. He is former American military and more than capable of obtaining the vampire you want. I am familiar with this Cromwell. We do not much like him either. Is there anything else, Mr. Pierce?"

Damien continued, "I want Anthony cut off from Big Timber. This is too close to your territory. I doubt you want your son's actions drawing unwanted attention to your coven. If he wants to talk in neutral territory, fine."

Desdemona appeared to think for a moment. Taking such actions could make it seem like she acted openly against her son which could result in conflict. "Zane, do you have such influence in Anthony's organization?"

"I can arrange whatever you want. There are many in Anthony's employ who are loyal to me or who would betray him at their earliest convenience. Magnus, Dante and Steele are among the most loyal. Of course, you know the others," Zane replied.

Kain could see him stifling a grimace at the latter part of his sentence. He had a feeling he knew who Zane spoke of.

"Very well. It will take some time to give you what you requested, young Purifier, but we will assure it gets done." Desdemona raised her hand.

As if out of nowhere, servants carrying trays of various types of food arrived and began setting them down in the middle of the table.

Succulent filet mignon sat dripping in its own juices next to a platter where the most delicious pheasant hung on a spit. Scents of dinner rolls and fresh salad mingled with the meat, filling the room.

Desdemona gestured her hand towards the dishes. "We were not sure what you would want so we relied on our information regarding previous visits from lycan nobles."

Each dish looked delicious but Kain hesitated to eat any. He didn't trust Desdemona not to try poisoning or drugging the lycans in a strategic attempt to get rid of them. He'd seen them try such things at dinners meant to promote ceasefires in celebrations of holidays or to end battles.

Beside him, Damien sat with his arms crossed over his chest, refusing to eat anything as well.

"Is there something wrong?" Ramona finally spoke after remaining silent since the lycans arrived.

Her soft, ruby eyes were nothing new to Kain. His history with Ramona showed in the awkward glances the two shared throughout the dinner. However, she showed no such awkwardness to Gabriel who didn't stop himself from flirting back.

Kain rolled his eyes at his friend's behavior.

"You'll have to forgive me if I'm not openly trusting. It's not like I wasn't almost raped, turned and had my head bashed in by this place's former mistress." The tone in Damien's voice held a sharp sarcasm and blatant disdain for the coven.

"Damien, I was there the night Lilith held you prisoner. I did my best to get her to see reason and release you, but she refused to listen. My daughter and I hold a manner of pacifism regarding the war. We too have lost many. I ask you not judge us the same as you have the Stones," Desdemona responded with her own level of severity. The insult and hate for the Stones evident on her face.

Damien scoffed, averting his eyes.

Desdemona's gaze met Kain's with an interest capable of bringing about a sense of agitation in him. He'd seen the look a couple of times in the grand hall. "Alexander Kain, may I request your presence in my private study following our meeting here? You and your kin are welcome to stay for the evening. We have a guest room prepared for you."

Kain's first instinct was to stay next to Damien and close to his pack in case they fell under surprise attack. However, a nagging feeling in his gut told him he should accept the invitation. He nodded to Desdemona in agreement.

Kain made sure Damien, Jill and Gabriel were safe in the guest room before being led by Zane to Desdemona's study. He opened two large double doors and let Kain in, closing them without a word.

Desdemona stood next to the window. Her slender body outlined in the light of moon. Her pale complexion and the way she held herself gave Kain a glimpse back into ancient times when the Wars were at their worst. The beauty of her kind radiated an agelessness and a sense of danger, warning any potential lover to stay away from her.

Her saddened eyes never left their vigil from the cobblestone circular driveway. "Thank you for agreeing to see me. It has been many moons since I have had the company of the legendary Kain line. I, like many, believed you all deceased."

Kain stayed close to the door, leaning his back against the wall. "Why am I here, vampire?"

"How is your hand? I was informed it had been damaged."

The casual question shocked Kain. He'd expected her to attempt to pick his brain regarding recent events, not to ask him how he was personally.

"My hand is none of your concern. I ask again, why am I here?" Kain clenched his injured hand into a fist. It tingled from the nerve damage and still offered little use despite the effort his healing ability doing all it could to repair it.

Desdemona ignored the blunt question. She moved to her desk with a serpentine grace and reached into a drawer to pull out a black cell phone. Cautious, she walked to Kain and reached it out to him. "Take this. It will connect you directly to Zane. Call him anytime you need."

Kain took the phone and unlocked the screen. Only a single number with no name stared back at him from the contacts. "Why give this to me? Should it not go to Damien?"

The smile across Desdemona's lips looked melancholy. "I want it to be yours. Damien is young, and I fear he has much to learn regarding our worlds."

Kain put the phone in the back pocket of his jeans. He hoped Damien could see and hear his thoughts since Kain kept a channel open once he'd entered Desdemona's study. "Is that all?"

Desdemona returned to her spot next to the window. "You remind me so much of your father. He was always so distrustful of everyone outside of his pack. A wise trait for a time ravaged by war and death but not so much now."

"It does not surprise me you know of Pentacost. He once met your husband and nearly killed him in the middle of the courtroom." Kain responded, annoyed at the open mention of his father's name by a vampire. "If that is all you have to say, I will be taking my leave."

"I know where he is buried." Desdemona admitted.

Kain halted, his eyes wide. To his knowledge, his father's body had been left on the cold shores where he died. It never occurred to him that Pentacost might have been brought to the States and laid to rest.

Desdemona sat on the nook in the windowsill, offering for Kain to sit in the chair next to her desk. "When this is over, I would be honored to escort you to his resting place. For now, there is much you need to know."

Questions raced in his mind regarding Desdemona's statement. He kept his eyes emotionless to keep from giving his feelings away in the face of an enemy.

When he said nothing, Desdemona began. "My family line originated in Spain. The Cardozas held high ranking standing in both the human and vampire worlds. My father had the pleasure of meeting Lucius Wolf and offered to help the Purifier in any way to end the Wars. We did not become militant until I took over the family name.

"No one at the time believed a woman could hold as much influence as a man so I was set to be married to Darius. We let him be the face while I ran things. Unfortunately, in a meeting meant to be one of peace, Darius insulted your father and the king at the time. He threatened to kill Pentacost to prove we could never live in peace."

Kain listened to every word intently. He'd been young at the time but recalled the incident in detail.

It was one of the only times he remembered seeing his father so angry.

Desdemona took a moment to pour a glass of red wine. She offered Kain some, but he politely turned it down. "Darius did not know I met your father prior to our getting married. He blatantly ignored everything my family stood for. His many trysts resulted in illegitimate children and tarnished our reputation to be nothing more than that of a mob."

Kain inquired about the legitimacy of Ramona and Anthony. Desdemona shook her head. "Neither are mine. Ramona renounced her father's ways and remained loyal to the ideals of my father. Anthony was not so inclined. He wanted to earn Darius' love and as such became ruthless. As you can see, it did not stop once he came to the new world."

"What does he want with me?" Kain asked.

Desdemona took a drink of the wine. "He blames you for his father's murder. He believes destroying the son of his father's murderer will bring him a manner of power in our world. I fear he has begun falling into madness and tasted the hate of the dark god."

Kain's heart quickened. The god's absence and Anthony's sudden interest in the talon and the knowledge Kain had it became clearer.

"Despite popular belief to the contrary, many vampires do not worship Barghast. He showed long ago he had no interest in those he made. Many of us despise him. Those who do not act out of blind devotion. Anthony's madness is living proof the god does not care."

Kain remained silent. Desdemona said nothing more, leaving a looming sense of dread. If Anthony acted in Barghast's stead, blindly following the god's will, things would only get worse.

Tala sat in the nook of the windowsill staring out at Luna's face. She'd worried about her lover, Damien, Jill and Gabriel at the coven. Images of them being hurt in an ambush or poisoned ran through her mind. She did what she could to push them down.

A mix of emotions spun in her mind, her bond allowing her to feel what Kain felt. She'd never felt such confusion or sense of dread. She wondered what could be causing him to feel those things. She opened the window to let in some fresh air to help cool her head.

The crunching of a twig in the nearby brush caught her attention. She stared at the bush behind the pack's house to try to get a glimpse of what could be there. Her senses tuning into a familiar scent.

Gasping, she jumped from the window onto the nearby tree and slid down to the ground. Out of the brush, a wolf with ash grey fur sauntered out of the shadows.

"Tobias!" Tala ran to her brother, embracing him around his neck just as he shifted to human form.

"Hey, sis." The lycan's voice sounded weak. "I need your help."

CHAPTER FOURTEEN

T ala slapped her brother across the face, her eyes full of fury. "Why did
you run from the hospital, you idiot?"

Tobias rubbed his cheek, looked at his hand and then back at his sister.
"Kain came and interrogated me shortly after you left. The man's terrifying.
Tala, what was I supposed to do? I'm in trouble and technically on the run
from the Don. Was I supposed to wait for one of his hitmen to come and put
a bullet in my brain or poison me?"

"You could've come here and asked for help! Where've you been?!" Tears
streamed down Tala's face.

Tobias recounted the events that happened while he'd been held
prisoner by Anthony. The Don of Great Falls promised to spare he and Tala's
life if Tobias would do but two things for him - steal the talon from Kain
and set him up to be taken prisoner.

Tala's heart pounded. "Tobias, you need to go to Damien. Tell him
exactly what you just told me."

Tobias rolled his eyes, scoffing. "Right. What's he going to do? You can't
win this, Tala. Anthony has connections. He can get to whomever he wants.
Kain. Damien. It doesn't matter. I came here to see if you wanted to come
with me. I don't want my big sister involved in this. It's dark shit. Darker
than anything I've ever seen."

With fists clenched at her side, Tala grew angrier at the thought of her
brother's offer to abandon the pack just because things looked dangerous.

She'd come to love them in the short time she'd been there and wanted to do whatever she could to help.

Kain was her mate. The idea of him being hurt or falling into a trap infuriated her. "What does he want, Tobias? Why does he want Alex?"

"To hell if I know. Maybe they pissed each other off in the last century or two. I'm telling you, it's not a matter of if Anthony's going to get what he wants, it's when. Even Kain won't know what's coming," Tobias pleaded with his sister to leave with him.

Tala ground her fangs, turning her back on her brother. "Leave then. I'm not going with you. Alex is my mate, Tobias. I'm staying by his side. You haven't seen what he can do and yes, it's terrifying, but I know he'll be okay."

Tobias sneered, "Fine. If you want to commit suicide, who am I to stop you. I just hope you don't get hurt. I've seen things too and believe me, staying away from Kain is better than experiencing what I've been through."

Pain grew in Tala's heart at the idea of losing her brother. She pleaded with him one last time to ask the pack for help but Tobias didn't listen. The look of terror in his eyes told her all she needed to know. When she inquired more about what Tobias had seen, he quickly shut her down.

"Tobias," Tala sighed as she watched the last remnant of her family shift into his wolf form and disappear into the forest behind the house.

When Kain arrived home from the dinner with Desdemona, he found Tala in the backyard staring out into the woods beyond the back of the house. Glistening tears dripped down her face onto the railing she leaned against. The way she curled her fingers beneath her hand and the trembling in her shoulders showed him how upset she was.

Trying not scare her, Kain carefully approached her, his height allowing him to encase her between his arms and body. Placing a soft kiss on her hair he asked her what was wrong.

At first, Tala appeared apprehensive to tell him. She bit her shaking lower lip before recalling the meeting with her brother and how scared he looked. The warning he gave Tala unnerved Kain. During the late-night visit he'd paid Tobias shortly after finding him, he could tell the young lycan had things he wanted to say but hesitated. Other details like his escape seemed unrealistic as well. With each new piece of information Kain gathered from Tala, he became more certain about his initial theory regarding Anthony.

"He told you nothing about what he saw? No details about his experience?" Kain asked.

Tala shook her head. "He refused to. No matter how much I pleaded with him. Please, Alex. I know he's wrong for running but I can't blame him. Isn't there some way we can find him?"

Kain took a moment to think. On the wind he caught a faint whiff of Tobias. He called to his adopted son. Clint came running out of the house. Kain ordered him to track the scent, reassuring Tala if Tobias could be found, Clint would bring him back. If not, there wasn't much Kain could do.

The two of them stood on the back porch for what seemed like hours. Tala didn't seem like she wanted to talk, and Kain made it a point not to pressure her to do so. Around late afternoon, to take her mind off the meeting with Tobias, Kain offered for them to take some down time since things appeared quiet for the time being.

Breathing hot in his lover's ear, "Come hunting with me. There is nothing more we can do for now, and it has been a while since we hunted together."

A hint of a rose blush fell across Tala's cheeks. She reached up and caressed Kain's face, inhaling a deep breath. She gave a short nod and shoved her butt against Kain's stomach, giggling as she bounded into the back yard. Her movements a graceful dance. She shed her clothes, hanging them on the clothesline.

Once she was naked, she rubbed a hand over her shoulder and glanced back at Kain, licking her fangs.

Kain smirked and shed his own clothes, setting them on one of the nearby chairs. As he descended the stairs, he saw the hungry look in his mate's eyes. It made him happy to see she no longer winced at the sight of his scars and revealed a more sensual side of herself each time they were alone together.

Without shifting, Tala laughed and took off running into the woods. Kain followed suit and sprinted to catch the teasing female. They ran through the trees, leaping effortlessly over the fallen brush and roots.

Joy ignited in Kain's heart each time they crossed one another's path and stole a quick kiss prior to beginning an impromptu game of hide and seek.

Tala hid amongst the trees, giggling and taking off when Kain finally caught her. The scent of his lover lit a wave of desire in Kain. He shifted the tides by hiding.

"Alex?" Tala called out.

Kain covered a laugh. The bush of blackberries he hid in masked his scent perfectly. However, he began to feel bad when Tala looked like she grew more nervous. When she passed by the bush, he leapt out and took her in his arms, his lips meeting her shoulder. He nipped her flesh with his fangs bringing about a gasp exciting him further.

He took them to the forest floor, pinning Tala beneath him. Her breasts brushed his chest as he let his tongue taste the salt of her sweat on her collarbone and neck. A soft moan followed by the light scratching of her nails over his back made it hard to keep from plunging into her.

Kain kissed down Tala's smooth stomach to her inner thigh and back. All thoughts of logic faded into carnal desires the higher his lust became. He wanted nothing more than to fill her belly with his children. The need of the wolf slowly overtook Kain the longer he let his thoughts drift.

Want. Kain's fangs elongated, his nails digging into the soft earth. *Need.* He positioned himself atop Tala and kissed her, invading her mouth with his tongue, catching the spicy taste of mint and cinnamon. *Mate.* He pushed into her, holding her firmly and murmuring in her ear. She moaned and begged him for more; to take her as deep and as hard as he could go. It'd been a while since he'd thought more of mating and less of making love.

When Kain reached his climax, he pushed as deep into Tala as he could go. She cried out as her own climax ran through her body. He could feel her gripping him and taking all he offered.

Exhausted, he let his head drop onto Tala's shoulder, apologizing if he hurt her. She raised up to kiss his shoulder, moving along the parts of his neck she could reach.

"It's okay. You didn't hurt me," she giggled, heaving. "Honestly, I like it when you get rough, baby."

Kain chuckled. He liked to take things slow, but when it came to mating, he preferred things rougher as well. He got up to stretch the pain out of his joints and back. His scars stung though it didn't do much to dull the surge of pleasure he felt.

Tala rolled over and began rubbing against Kain's body. A behavior among the lycans exhibited by females who wanted their bodies to produce pups for their chosen mates. Kain stayed still while Tala rubbed her belly against his thigh, chest, and back.

Every lycan female wants pups, Kain thought to himself, stifling a laugh.

Following their love making, Tala asked Kain to wait for her in his wolf skin while she ran off into the woods after the scent of one of his favorite meals – pheasant. She'd caught the smell during her rubbing session and thought it might be nice to give him a gift.

Her heart pounded. A heat fell across the tips of her triangular ears as she thought about how she'd rubbed against him. The idea of giving him a family had become so strong, she didn't fully understand what happened to her. She caught a rabbit to feed her own hunger before finally catching up to the pheasant.

Leaping, she seized the small bird in her jaws. Holding it in her teeth, she pranced back like a proud pup who'd just caught their first hare. She found Kain sitting and tapping his tail beneath an oak tree.

Lowering her ears, she placed the kill at his feet and backed away, lying low to the ground, whimpering.

Kain almost appeared to smile. He tore into the bird, plucking its feathers with his teeth while Tala waited. To her surprise, he offered her a small piece which she took happily. Once he finished, Kain lay next to Tala and proceeded to lick her face, ears, and neck.

The moon was at her zenith in the sky when clouds moved in and offered the promise of rain. Kain guided Tala to the opening beneath a rotted log, waiting until she went in, following her. They huddled together in the hollow and fell asleep.

In the wee hours of the morning, Kain woke to Damien tugging the recesses of his mind. From the tone of his voice, the young lycan sounded upset about something. The message came across so garbled, Kain had to calm Damien before he could hope to get any indication of what his friend was trying to tell him.

Tyler, a newer and much younger member of the pack had let out a howl to the other pack members after spotting a white limousine with the crest of the Cardoza family on its hood. From the direction, Damien assumed it could only be heading to one place: the pack's house.

Kain's fur bristled. His lips curled over his teeth. *Damien, get Gabriel and Lune. Meet me on the porch.* He waited until Damien confirmed and severed their connection.

CHAPTER FIFTEEN

K ain and Tala arrived home two hours before sunrise. Unfortunately, Tala's clothes had become soaked from the late rains. Kain sent her inside to get dressed and stay there until he told her it was safe. He went through the house after getting dressed to find Damien on the front porch.

"About time," Damien said. "The hell have you been?"

To annoy Damien and tease him, Kain relayed some of the more heated moments of his evening.

Damien cringed. "Okay, next time remind me not to ask."

Kain snickered through his teeth. He knew the severity of the situation but hazing his pack brother always made him smile.

The lycans watched as the limo drove up the gravel driveway and skidded to a crunching stop. It did indeed have the Cardoza crest but more sinister. The figure was bound and blindfolded, bending over like it'd been tortured.

A rather buff man with a shaved head wearing stark black sunglasses got out of the driver's side and made his way to the back doors. From the looks of him, he could have been a bouncer or one of Anthony's hitmen. His bald head and black glasses gave him an almost laughable appearance to Kain. He didn't understand why vampires thought black sunglasses were needed.

Jared emerged followed by Zane. When Kain saw him, the silver-haired vampire offered a subtle nod. Jared smirked at Gabriel the whole time as if daring him to say or do something.

Kain heard from behind him the challenging growl rumbling at the back of Gabriel's throat. "Easy, Gabriel," Kain said quietly. "Watch his body. He is trying to rile you up."

"I know. Still pisses me the fang off," Gabriel snapped in reply.

Following the two, another vampire exited the car. He wore a white business suit and fedora with a black band around it, covering short, curly blonde hair. Unlike the other vampires in his entourage, he sported bright blue eyes. The shoes he wore were high end, branded leather. An ascot the color of blood wrapped around his neck. On his finger, he wore a silver signet ring Kain recognized as the dark god's symbol.

"Is that really him? He's not anything like I imagined," Damien whispered to Kain.

Kain's brows creased as he watched the vampire. Anthony looked much younger than him in his immortal years. "That is what makes him more dangerous. He is nothing like Lilith. She was more into her pride. The look in his eye is nothing short of bloodlust."

Anthony surveyed each of the lycans in front of him before his gaze came to rest on Kain. A smug smirk formed across his lips.

"Ah, there you are. Finally, we meet face to face," Anthony said with an accent closer to that of a formal English gentleman. He adjusted his hat and continued, "I'm a man of few words. I don't care to keep the company of such lowly beasts for long, so I will make this simple. Alexander Kain, surrender yourself and the talon, or I will bring down the full extent of my power on you and all you hold dear."

Damien stepped in front of Kain. His posture threatening. "Wow, you have some balls to demand things like that. I don't give a shit who you are. Kain isn't going anywhere."

Kain saw Zane look away like he hid a hint of being impressed at Damien's boldness. Kain admitted he'd been impressed as well.

Anthony's frustrated eyes strayed to Damien. "I wasn't talking to you. Your youth and inexperience is evident in your lack of respect of those more powerful than you. Be silent and let the adults talk."

Kain had to move quickly to stop Damien from charging at Anthony, warning his friend not to fall for the ploy the vampire was playing on him. "No. This is what he wants. He will kill you, Damien. Make no mistake."

Hesitant, Damien relaxed. He glared at Kain then at Anthony.

Anthony snickered. "That's better. I can see why your reputation precedes you, Kain."

Kain returned his attention to the vampire. He did nothing to hide his own annoyance when he condemned Anthony for ignoring the rules of parlay, refused his offer and promised they would fight if Anthony chose war.

"War? Don't insult me. I'm not as barbaric as my prideful cousin," Anthony replied with disgust. "Oh no, Kain. I'm the type who will hurt you in every way imaginable until you give me what I want. Keep me waiting if you wish to test me, but I always come out on top."

A tense silence lingered as the two glared at one another. The air radiated an atmosphere like there were two titans preparing to battle.

A devilish grin fell across Anthony's face. "I implore you not to keep me waiting, Kain. This isn't like the days where you held dominion over the battlefields and the mere mention of your name made my kind tremble. Here, I am god, and you; you're just another beast."

Kain watched something ghost across Anthony's eyes. He kept his composure but recognized the second pair of eyes staring back at him. The reference of himself as god sent chills down Kain's back.

A feeling he sensed coming from Damien as well. *This is bad.*

Without another word, Anthony got back in the car. Zane dismissed the driver and closed the door for the Don. He went back to the opposite, stopping to offer one last nod and getting inside. Before entering the limo, Jared flipped off Gabriel with a smirk, and then the car drove away.

"Damien, a word, please." Kain stayed where he was, his arms crossed.

"Yeah?" Damien asked after Lune and Gabriel went back inside.

Kain sighed a tense sigh. "Did you see them?"

Damien nodded. "Yeah. What're we going to do? How is this even possible?"

"I am not sure. For now, do what I taught you. Stay diligent and watch for signs. Tell me of any visions or strange dreams immediately. I don't care if I happen to be asleep."

Damien asked Kain how he was, inquiring about his scars and if he still felt as weak as he was when Damien visited him. Kain reassured his friend he no longer felt that weak.

Aside from the damage to the nerves in his hand, Kain felt as good as he could after his deal with the goddess.

"Do not worry about me, brother. There is something I have been meaning to ask you," Kain said. "There is a part of your mind you have gone out of your way to keep from me. Why is that?"

Damien's eyes widened. He clenched and unclenched his fists, glancing anywhere but at the waiting lycan soldier in front of him. "It's. It's nothing, Kain."

The sweat forming on Damien's brow told Kain another story. He reminded Damien about the time he had the dream about the two gods fighting in the meadow near the Circle of Stones.

Again, Damien refused. Despite his greater judgement, Kain let the subject drop. Neither one of them spoke as the faded light of the sun rose over the horizon.

Jill found Tala sitting in the living room reading the fantasy book Kain had been reading on the front porch. She sat next to the young lycan and smiled, asking how Tala was doing.

"I'm fine. Waiting for Alex to get back from the sparring lesson Damien asked him for after they talked." Tala closed the book and set it down on the table beside the couch.

Jill sighed, lowering her eyes. "I heard about the meeting with your brother. It's hard when those we love turn their backs on us during times of hardship."

Tala didn't respond immediately. If anything, she was mad at her brother. "It's okay. Alex sent Clint to go look for him. How did the meeting with Desdemona go?"

Jill told Tala about the events at the dinner with the Cardoza matriarch.

"I don't understand. Why doesn't she just stop him? He's not going to fight his own mother. Especially if she's the one in charge of the Cardoza empire." Tala ground her teeth at what she thought to be cowardice. Desdemona had to have more power than that.

Jill shook her head. "It's not that easy. A war between the Cardozas could shake the state to its core. Desdemona says Anthony doesn't fear going to war with her. Unlike Anthony, Desdemona is a pacifist. Vampires with a peaceful view tend to get attacked by stronger covens. It's the Cardoza name that's protected her."

The explanation didn't make much sense to Tala. She'd never experienced the full brutality of a vampire coven and had only heard stories about Lilith and Demetrius. In comparison with Jill, Gabriel, Damien and Kain, Tala hadn't seen much of the bloodshed of the Blood Wars. Only the elders in her pack knew about it and told stories about the carnage.

Changing the subject, Tala asked how the girls were doing with their grandfather. Saddened, Jill told her she spoke to Charlie almost daily but still missed the pups horribly. Damien warned his father to get them out of the city and into the cabin where they went fishing and hunting during the warmer months. According to Jill, Damien felt they'd be safe there until the fight with Anthony was over.

"Jill, would you tell me about when you and Damien met? I asked Alex, but he said I should ask you if we ever had some time alone."

A blush fell over the female lycan's face. She started from the beginning when she first saw Damien to when she thought she'd killed him by changing him and ending with the Circle of Stones.

Tala's intrigued eyes grew wider the more the tale unfurled. In many ways, it was like how she and Kain met.

The sound of the front door opening and Damien's call to Jill alerted the women to the men's return. She watched as Jill launched herself into Damien's arms. Kain slid behind the two lycans only to get jumped by Tala. His hard, heated body set her heart ablaze with excitement to see him home.

Gabriel cleared his throat. "You think you four can get a den? I'd like to take a shower and get the pain out of my shoulders. Kain isn't exactly a kind sparring partner."

Kain pulled Tala aside, rolling his eyes. "You're out of practice. Seems you have been lazy during my absence."

Gabriel scoffed, flipped Kain off and stormed upstairs.

The private phone Desdemona gave Kain vibrated in the late hours of the night waking Kain from his deep sleep. He answered it to hear Zane's voice.

"I know it's late. I've got a favor to ask you."

Kain ran his hand through his hair and down his face. "What is it?"

"I received something from Magnus a few hours ago. I need you to take it off my hands."

Confused, Kain stood, careful not to jostle Tala who still slept.

Zane requested they meet at the Woods Edge. Kain agreed, promising to meet the vampire in a couple of hours. He hung up and proceeded to get dressed.

The pack's house was silent save for the mumbling voices of Jill and Damien at the end of the hall. To play it safe, Kain requested Lune to accompany him. He didn't want to risk falling into a trap, even if he did trust Zane. Bard still hadn't been caught or seen since Kain last fought with him.

Kain waited for Lune at his car, his eyes locked on the quarter moon in the sky.

"Master," Lune said.

Kain sighed, "Lune, I told you about that title. It is not necessary."

"It is to me. Where're we going?"

"The Woods Edge."

Lune opened the passenger's side door, the look in his puzzled eyes prompted Kain to continue, "I have a feeling you might be needed, old friend. It will not take long."

The two lycans got in Kain's car and began their journey to the Woods Edge.

When they arrived, Zane stood from where he'd rested against the side of his Firebird and opened the door. Kain watched as the vampire leaned in, but the tinted windows hid what went on beyond the door.

Kain got out of his car accompanied by Lune. The two lycans approached Zane in time to see not a vampire but a lycan get out of the back seat.

Beside him, Kain heard Lune gasp. The young lycan kept his eyes towards the ground as he walked up to his fellow lycans.

"This is Joel. Magnus gave him to me earlier this evening." Zane nudged Joel forward. "I believe you've helped one like him before."

Kain watched Joel's submissive behavior with pain in his heart. The familiar scars around Joel's wrists, mouth, neck, and shoulders brought about a sense of nausea. "How long?"

"That I don't know. He won't talk to me. He fought us when we tried to save him. I believe it's been at least since adolescence."

Kain sighed, "I see."

He approached Joel and gently guided the lycan's eyes up. He couldn't have been older than twenty. "Turned from the looks of it."

Zane nodded. "I believe so."

Joel trembled beneath Kain's touch. Kain motioned to Lune to come and help Joel while Kain spoke with Zane. Lune did as he was told, his eyes wide with shock.

With prompting and some struggling, Lune managed to get Joel into Kain's car.

"How bad is it, Zane?" Kain asked, angry.

"Bad," Zane replied. "That isn't all I'm here for, though I thank you for taking him. Desdemona extends a private invitation to talk with you."

Kain tried hard not to focus on Joel's condition. It angered him to learn his kind suffered so badly in the modern day. He shifted his attention to the strange invitation. "What does she want?"

Zane shrugged. "I don't know the details. Only that she wants to meet. Should I tell her you're coming or no?"

Kain affirmed the meeting. Learning more about Anthony and having as many allies as possible, especially in the wake of losing Galeck, was all the lycans had against the Don's power in the human world. He no longer suffered from the vampire's natural aversion to the sun. He could call upon human hitmen at any given moment.

With another thank you, Zane got back in his car and departed.

CHAPTER SIXTEEN

Exhausted and mentally drained after getting Joel comfortable enough to come into the pack's house, Kain trudged up the stairs to his den to find Tala naked on the bed and looking at her phone. All around the room, flickering candles gave off the smell of lavender, vanilla and a hint of cardamom.

He undressed down to his boxer-briefs and laid across the bed on his stomach. Tala's hands rubbing his back helped ease him into a relaxed state. Kain jerked when she smacked his butt and giggled.

"Where'd you go?" she asked as she resumed rubbing his back.

Kain stretched out beneath her hands. He told her about Zane and Joel, leaving out the details to avoid worrying her. The feeling of her fingers tracing the scars on his back felt good despite their origins. It reminded him of what he'd seen in Anthony and how quiet Barghast had been. It took some effort to shove those thoughts away.

Tala crawled on top of her lover, settling into the shape of his body. "I know you aren't telling me everything. It's okay. When I didn't find you next to me, I wanted to welcome you home with something relaxing." She reached beneath Kain's throat, caressing it and kissing his ear and jaw.

Kain relaxed, letting her do what she wanted. The sexual scent of her combined with the movement of her body against his made Kain begin to harden. No one he'd met knew where his pleasure points were, but Tala managed to hit almost all of them every time she touched him.

"Tala." He whispered.

"Shh. When was the last time you let someone pleasure you?" Tala ran her feet over Kain's calves to his feet. One of her hands held his throat, teasing his Adam's apple while the other ran over his shoulder and side.

She wished to pleasure him for as long as she could. They'd been torn apart so many times she wanted to take this time to relish him. To enjoy every part of his gorgeous body.

Tala moved the hand caressing his throat to play with his lips, parting them to pet his fangs and tongue.

Tala whispered into Kain's ear. "That's it, baby."

Unable to take anymore, Kain bucked Tala off him, bringing about a squeak from his mate. He got up and took his underwear off. If his little teasing lover wanted to get erotic, he'd be damned if he left her unsatisfied.

Tala lay on her back with a stunned look on her face as she stared at her lover at the end of the bed. Taking hold of her ankles, Kain pulled Tala until her butt sat against his thighs. "I have something I have longed to do to you," Kain spoke in a low, sensual, almost demanding voice. His eyes full of a darkened passion. "Would it be alright?"

Excitement ran hard into curiosity in Tala's mind at the idea of him exploring her. The thought combined with the hungry look in his eyes sent her into a state of untamed arousal.

She nodded, brushing a lock of her hair behind her ear. Her heart racing.

Smiling and elated at her agreement, Kain glanced over the full length of her slender body. The subtle curves of her hips as she moved her legs in anticipation drew shivers up his spine. Each muscle in her abdomen rippled, glistening with sweat.

A blush lightened Tala's face in the dim candlelight. It surprised Kain when she covered her breasts and closed her legs despite the many times they'd had sex. He assumed it had to do with his revealing a more erotic side to himself. Something he'd tried not to do until he felt she was ready.

Guiding her hands down, Kain smiled reassuringly. "It's alright. I promise I won't hurt you. Should you wish to stop, you have but to say so." He ran his fingertip over the tender skin of her thighs, taking them in his hands. "Open for me."

Slowly, Tala did what he asked. She felt light-headed when he lowered to his knees between her legs.

Kain began his teasing by letting his tongue glide along the slick lips of Tala's sex, venturing up to the nub, flicking it with the tip. Her sexual smell made the wolf in him ache with need to mate. The taste of her was sweeter than the richest honey.

Venturing back down, Kain pressed his tongue into the soft opening, finding it swollen and wet. Tala's sounds pushed him to explore her more.

He breathed hot against her sex.

Tala's belly was on fire. In all the times they'd had sex, she'd experienced a different kind of arousal. What Kain did to her now made her feel nothing short of desired. He took what he wanted, raising her hips so he could access more of her.

The smell of him permeated her nostrils so strong she couldn't help but push into him to let him deeper. She was so wet. She wanted him inside her, filling her to the point of bursting.

A muted chuckle from him was the last straw. Her body convulsed with such intense pleasure she had to fight crying out too loud.

Kain's tongue went deep into her to take as much of her as he could, purring and murmuring for her to give him everything. Gently, Kain set her back down on the bed, licking his lips. His eyes half-lidded with a dark satisfaction.

Tala lay sprawled out, trying to catch her breath against the strongest orgasm she'd ever had.

Kain lay over her, kissing her. She let him kiss down her neck to the dip between her throat and shoulder. "Now, I make love to you."

Kain rolled her over onto her belly, guiding her hips up so he could enter her, finding her still swollen with need. He guided her back down onto her stomach. Holding her close, he made love to her slowly; pushing as deep as he could into her velvet walls.

Tala arched her hips into his, moving with him to help him further inside of her. His lips placed the lightest kisses down her back and up again. His thumb ran along the length of her lips as he spoke tender, loving words in her ear.

The whole feeling mirrored ecstasy.

Kain's breath quickening signaled that he was reaching his own climax. A pulsing followed by the sudden rush of heat inside of her as he filled her made Tala giddy with happiness.

When Kain tried to get up, Tala held him inside of her, his body tight against hers. "Not yet. Please. I want to treasure this moment."

A smile curled across Kain's lips. She rubbed her body against his stomach and chest. Her bottom sitting perfectly in the groove of his hips.

"Wake up, my dearest soldier."

Kain woke to a familiar, yet incredibly unwanted voice in his dreams. A high-pitched ringing in his ears made his head pound.

The room seemed like it was spinning.

Holding his head in his hand, Kain's focus came upon the dark god. A sadistic grin across his fangs. *"Did you think I had neglected you?"*

The pain in Kain's hand hurt worse than the burning scars covering his body.

Barghast walked towards Kain, his claw reaching to take lycan's wounded hand, enraged eyes glowing red amidst the shadows of his mane. He reached for Kain's face, raising it and seeing the light claw marks over his right eye. *"Who has done this, Alexander?"*

Kain jerked his face from the god's claws. The pain in his hand brought about a sense of nausea strong enough to make him vomit if he didn't focus on controlling it.

"Speak!" Barghast's commanding voice boomed in the darkness.

Kain said nothing. He didn't miss Barghast torturing him nor did he appreciate the idea the god was manipulating someone else to get to him.

Someone shaking him while calling his name yanked him from the god's plane and back into a state of consciousness to find Tala over him with a worried look on her face.

Kain rose. The heel of his hand rested against his eye against the headache. "I'm fine, Tala."

"Are you sure? You were holding your hand and flailing."

Kain attempted to smile. "A nightmare. What time is it?"

"It's only 6 a.m."

Raising his injured hand to stare at it, Kain sighed. He wasn't getting anymore sleep not with an angry god wanting answers he wasn't willing to give. Instead, he decided to go downstairs and make some coffee and breakfast.

While the food cooked, Kain decided to check the phone Desdemona gave him. Zane sent a text telling him he was closing in on Stoker and when and where Desdemona wished to meet.

"Don't think I've seen you so down in a while." Gabriel poured a cup of coffee after entering the room. "Something you want to talk about?"

Kain sighed, closing his eyes and imagining his cabin. He missed the quiet routine he had, the sound of the forest and the cool evenings when he sat on his porch to watch the sun set. "I ... am tired, my friend. For five hundred years I stood on the battlefield. I think it might be wearing on me."

Gabriel refilled Kain's coffee and offered him a seat. "I can imagine. You're one of the oldest living among us. In truth, I tried to tell Damien not to go out there. Not because I didn't think he wasn't going to see how you were but because I knew he'd ask you to be his beta."

Kain took a drink of his coffee. "It would not have mattered. With Bard involved, it was only a matter of time. He would have sought me out sooner or later."

"Listen, what happened that day wasn't your fault. You saved many of us by getting us on those boats. Is that why you left? Or was it because of the bane?" Gabriel hesitated to mention the curse.

"I saved many but left a great sin, Gabriel. From that, I cannot escape nor do I expect to. In truth, I do not expect to live through this."

Gabriel's brow raised in disturbing question.

"It does not matter now. Just promise me you will protect and take care of Tala should I not survive."

Reluctant, Gabriel agreed to Kain's request.

The park Kain was to meet Desdemona in smelled of sweet flowers. It was late evening and the breeze helped ease the agitation Kain felt from the conversation with Gabriel before he left for the meeting.

He walked down the cobblestone path until he saw Zane leaning against a willow with his eyes closed. Desdemona sat on a granite bench overlooking the koi pond.

Kain knew the pond well. He'd brought Clint to the park many times as a pup and let him feed the fish and the occasional duck.

Upon seeing him, Desdemona beamed with delight. Only it held underlying tones of sadness. "Welcome, Alexander. Thank you so much for meeting with me."

Turning down the offer to sit, Kain joined Zane in leaning against the willow's trunk. The silver-haired vampire never moved.

"Good evening. I would rather skip the pleasantries, Ms. Cardoza," Kain greeted.

"Desdemona, please," she gently corrected.

"Desdemona. Why have you called this meeting? As things stand, I would rather not be away from my pack for too long," Kain replied. His glare focused intently on both Zane and his mistress.

Desdemona turned her back on Kain, showing an immense trust that he wouldn't strike her down if the opportunity presented itself. "I am aware of Anthony's visit. Zane tried to dissuade him, but he is stubborn and lacks empathy. I asked for your company because there are some things you need to know about me and your father."

Kain tensed at the mention of his father. Especially when the one mentioning him was a vampire. He remained silent, listening.

"Do you recognize this?" Desdemona asked, showing the object she'd been cradling in her hands when Kain walked up to her. She handed it to him and waited.

Kain's eyes opened wide at the necklace in his hands. He recognized the crest of his family the moment he saw the medieval wolf brandishing a shield. It lay in the middle of an ovular pewter pendant. His father had been wearing it when he was killed. Around the edges, Kain saw what looked like dried blood.

"Where did you get this?" he asked.

Desdemona sighed, her eyes diverted towards the swimming fish in the pond. "I removed it from around your father's neck after he passed. He asked me to give it to you when the time came."

A bout of confusion struck Kain so hard it dizzied him. The sensation something he hadn't experienced in many years.

Questions spun in his mind, shrieking like the winds of a hurricane.

Desdemona rose from her seat and drew closer to the lycan. Her ruby eyes shone with tears. "You are truly as handsome as your father. You have his eyes and strong jaw."

Kain's fangs clenched, his lack of trust showing in the threatening way he glared at her. He pushed down the anger enough to maintain some sense of composure. He trusted Zane for reasons he couldn't understand, but Desdemona remained hard to read. She held herself as expressionless as Kain, acting with barely any emotion.

Desdemona once again offered a seat, and this time, Kain took it. He wasn't sure he'd be able to stand if he took another hit as hard as the necklace.

"Alexander, what I have to tell you might not sit well with you. It will leave you with more questions than answers and possibly make you question what you believed about Pentacost. Make no mistake, there was no greater warrior with a heart of gold to many – both vampire and lycan."

Kain listened as Desdemona told him of the first day she met Pentacost and how she fell in love at first sight. She spoke of how she pursued the lycan warrior and how eventually, Pentacost returned her feelings.

The more he heard, the more confused and nauseated Kain became. His adopted mother, Adrianna had been the only female figure he'd ever known. His father never spoke of who his real mother was and typically changed the subject when Kain dared to ask him.

One thing Pentacost did do was look at his son with sadness when Kain asked. It was as if he didn't want to say or perhaps he couldn't for fear of what would happen.

"Why are you telling me this?" Kain questioned.

"When Anthony appeared, I grew more concerned," Desdemona replied.

Kain gripped his hands hard enough to make the skin of his wounded hand ache. "My real mother. Who is she?"

Again, Desdemona sighed, openly regretting she couldn't reveal the full truth out of respect for her former lover's son. She went on to reveal that she never had children with Darius but sent him off to find lovers.

Kain asked if she ever had a child of her own only to learn she had one surviving son she hadn't seen in centuries. The mention of this prodigal child gave Kain a feeling he'd rather ignore. A looming secret he wanted to know but believed he shouldn't ask. He got up from the bench in preparation to leave, thanking his hostess for sharing such difficult information.

His father would be disappointed if he allowed the infamous Kain *reserve* to be shattered in front of anyone. It was something Kain had pounded in his head every day since he came of age to learn what his fate was. In his heart, he always harbored a resentment for his father.

"Alexander," Desdemona's voice stopped him in his tracks, "there is nothing wrong with a lycan and a vampire falling in love. Is your mate not a hybrid whose father was one of my kind? I beg of you not to hate him. He loved you more than his own life."

Kain took a moment to think about Desdemona's words. He remembered the memories he saw of Tala's father and how he looked at Tala with a bright smile and gentle eyes. Kain turned on his heel to head back to his car, leaving the vampiress behind him.

Opening the door, Kain dropped into the seat. He let his forehead fall against his hands on the steering wheel. The very foundations of his mind began fracturing making it hard to hold the reserve. He'd just been told his father was a lover to a member of the vampire equivalent of the mob.

The sudden opening of the passenger's side door followed by Zane's plopping down in the seat dragged Kain back into reality. He glared at the vampire.

Zane appeared to ignore Kain. "I'm guessing by the flames in your eyes, you're wanting to tear me apart for what she said."

Kain didn't respond. He returned his attention to the hood of his car and the music on the radio.

Zane rolled down the window and let his elbow rest on the rim. "Take it from one veteran to another, you don't need to go home with how you're feeling. I know a place we can go to let you cool your head."

The way Zane spoke to him was insulting. He admitted to himself to being on edge but didn't appreciate Zane's assumptions he wouldn't be able to handle the pressure. For centuries, his father trained him to never show emotion and to never crack under any sort of circumstance. It was how Kain lived.

However, Kain's trust in Zane led him to take the vampire's advice. As much as Kain didn't want to admit it, he wouldn't want Tala to worry about him or ask too many questions. He was already tired and needed time to process everything he'd learned.

Surrendering, he asked Zane for directions to the place he mentioned.

CHAPTER SEVENTEEN

Zane gave Kain the directions to a beautiful lake side campsite, informing the lycan of its history as a place Zane and his brother often spent together during their summers as humans. Kain recognized it as not being very far from his old cabin.

Kain walked the edge of the lake, his heart light at the memories it held for him. "I recognize this place. I used to bring Clint here to swim and fish when he was younger."

Zane stood on the embankment, his eyes staring intently at the lake white-capping in the moonlight. "I'd heard you had an adopted son. My brother and I used to come here every summer before we became vampires. I figured it'd be a good place to spend a short time."

Intrigued by Zane's sudden change in behavior, Kain decided to use the opportunity to get to know a bit about this strange soldier. Zane had gone out of his way to help Kain and his pack in ways that could get even the most seasoned warrior killed.

"I'm a former Marine in the United States military. Shortly after completing high school I joined the Corps, leaving my brother, Christian and my mother behind. It wasn't long after I left that Christian disappeared." Zane rolled his hand into a fist at his side.

From his stature, Kain could tell the memory hadn't been a pleasant one. The mention of Christian drew Kain's attention, but he held onto his suspicion to let Zane continue speaking.

"I served almost ten years, receiving letters from my mom about how she couldn't find my older brother. When I came home, I searched for almost two years without even a clue as to where he might be. Eventually, the grief got so bad, my mom died, and I was left to bury her."

"The vampire named Christian. Tala's father. Is he the same one?" Kain asked, receiving a silent nod as an answer.

"I'd appreciate it if you kept this between us. I've provided for Tala for most of her life as nothing short of a monster. A profession I'll never be proud of."

Kain's brow raised in question.

Zane's mouth tightened in a straight line. "Let's just say you and I have history with a certain overly possessive bitch of a vampiress. She's the one who changed me. Against my will, might I add."

Any number of names came to Kain's mind. In five hundred years he'd had encounters with many possessive, bitchy vampiresses. It wasn't until he remembered Joel and how Zane happened to know about the pain the young man went through before a connection was made.

"Emeline." Kain growled.

Zane nodded. "I may not have seen the same level of war you've experienced, Kain, but as a front line Marine, I've seen my fair share of death. Compared to what that bitch is doing, war is nothing. I'd rather be facing down foreign threats."

"War is war, my friend. Thank you for all you have done." Kain extended his hand in friendship to Zane, something he never thought he'd do regarding a vampire.

Zane's shock was evident on his face. With a relaxed smile, he took Kain's outstretched hand and shook it. "This isn't the only reason I brought you here. I wanted to give you an update on Stoker Cromwell and Anthony."

Kain withdrew his hand, joining Zane as he walked onto the pier.

A single lamp with a faded yellow light provided a ghastly light on the surface of the rippling water. The wood creaked under the weight of the two men as they made their way to the end of the pier. The sound of the water and the smell of the fresh pine made Kain smile at remembering the silence of the mountains.

Zane leaned against one of the poles bound together with another by a rusted chain. "As you probably imagined, Cromwell has barricaded himself behind Anthony's strongest thugs. The Don keeps the coward well provided for in exchange for whatever information he can provide regarding you and Damien. It's been impossible to get near him. That being the case, I think I might've found a way. You're not going to like it though."

Kain crossed his arms, his weight supported on his right leg, eyes focused. It didn't surprise him to learn about Stoker's choice to hide amongst stronger vampires. He'd fled after receiving a wound on his arm from Gabriel. The underhanded tactics he used to get a hold of and nearly kill Damien pissed Kain off so bad he almost tore the snake apart. Doing so would've cost Damien his life so Kain held back.

"Stoker knows the inner workings of Ramona's coven here in Big Timber as well. As I'm sure you're aware, she took over after Lilith's downfall. It's another reason Desdemona refuses to act directly. She knows Anthony wouldn't hesitate to attack his sister out of rebellion. You must be careful, Kain."

Kain changed the subject to focus on the way Zane found to get close enough to Stoker to get a hold of him.

From his back pocket, Zane pulled a cream envelope with gold lettering. He handed it to Kain. "This is an invitation to the Don's Masquerade ball on Halloween. He holds it every year to cement his influence in the human world. He's invited you personally."

The decorated letter did indeed have Kain's full name on the front of it. He opened it to read the cordial invitation. A scent of a fine mix of wine and cologne wafted in his nostrils. He wondered why Anthony would bother to invite him. At the bottom, Kain saw he could bring two guests.

Zane waited while Kain looked over the letter. When the lycan finished, Zane cautioned him against ignoring the invitation. If Anthony wanted to talk, it meant he'd grown sick of waiting and no doubt would drop a body until Kain answered the way the Don wanted.

"Tell him I accept. I doubt he would break face in front of so many. About Stoker, Zane."

"Leave him to me. He'll be at the Ball and won't suspect a vampire to be the one to grab him."

Kain offered a half-nod, closing the invitation and putting it in the pocket of his jacket. "What of Bard?"

Zane shook his head.

According to him, Bard vanished after fighting with the Don and hadn't returned. Kain surmised it had something to do with Barghast's wishes over what Bard wanted. The demented lycan was rabid with bloodlust and the desire for vengeance.

If Barghast forbade him from killing Kain or confronting him, it'd be more than Bard could handle. Kain knew how hot-headed Bard could be.

He'd once called Kain insane for not accepting the Shadowed Ones power. This was before Kain tore his forearm from him during the lycans' mass exodus from Europe.

"Emeline and Jared?" Kain asked. He looked over his shoulder. "Magdeline?"

Zane told Kain they'd be at the Ball since the Auberts and the Cardozas held a rather unstable truce between their once-quarreling families. They'd taken advantage of the schism in the Cardoza regime to infiltrate Anthony's territory.

Taking Lune would be out of the question and choosing Damien or Gabriel would be setting them both up as bait for any number of powerful vampires who would want to see them dead. Knowing Damien, he'd demand to go to help Kain in any way he could.

The thought made Kain chuckle under his breath.

Despite what Kain might want, he'd need some powerful lycans to go with him in case things got out of hand. Even with his reputation and strength, trying to escape an entire complex of vampires and their supporters would be fatal.

"I'll have some loyal vampires at the Ball, Kain. Magnus Forge, Dante and Steele will be there. They're some of the strongest vampires in Great Falls and my closest friends."

Kain recalled Magnus' name during a conversation with Lune. He served as an Enforcer for Emeline's enterprise and held a deadly reputation. The mention of Magnus prompted Kain to ask about Zane's involvement with Emeline.

A sigh of remorse came from Zane. "It's not a past I'm proud of. I don't do her dirty work anymore but when I can, I try to free at least one of her unfortunate victims."

"Like Joel."

Zane nodded. "It's another reason I don't want Tala to know who I am. The last thing she needs is to know is how her uncle once tortured people."

Kain agreed.

While they walked back down the pier, Kain made one final request of Zane. He wanted to know what happened to Tala's brother during his time in Anthony's hands.

"I'm not sure what happened to Tobias after he arrived. I was out at the time. What I do know is if the Don released him, he had a reason. No one leaves the Don's custody unless he's damned sure they won't betray him."

"Tala says he's on the run, Zane. Does that not mean he might refuse?"

Zane shook his head. Anyone who made a deal with Anthony Cardoza fulfilled their bargain or they wound up dead.

Hearing Zane's words, Kain realized his instincts regarding Tobias and his interrogation were indeed true.

Clint spent days trying to track Tobias down but ultimately returned empty handed. Somehow, the young lycan outran Clint and managed to cover his tracks and scent.

The two arrived back at Kain's car where Zane's Firebird had mysteriously appeared. "This is where I leave you. I'll see what I can find out about Tobias and tell you at the Ball. Until then, I warn you to be careful. Anthony's a lot of things and I suspect he's becoming more insane."

"What do you mean?" Kain asked.

"He's been talking to someone in his office. I can't figure out if I'm hearing two voices or three. He hasn't acted right in almost four years but recently, he's acted just plain crazy."

Kain didn't reply. It became obvious to him Zane didn't know about Barghast's involvement. The vampire's youth and the fact he'd been changed by Emeline shielded him from knowing about the god's power and presence. Modern times placed many beliefs of superstition or the actions of rogue gods into the category of non-existent.

In a way, Kain was grateful for that. He'd hate for Zane to suffer Barghast's anger. He wished Zane goodnight and the two parted ways.

Kain arrived back at the pack's house in the wee hours of morning. He could hear the birds beginning to rustle in their nests in preparation to start their day. The sound stirred a sense of calmness and sadness simultaneously.

In his pocket, the metal links of his father's necklace jingled. Its weight heavy despite how light it was. Kain sat on the porch, taking out the necklace and running his thumb over the smooth stone. The blood in the grooves of pewter still held the faint smell of his father.

The silence of the night aided in processing the information Kain had received from both Desdemona and Zane. His mind drifted to the memory of the dark night he lost his father to Bard's treachery. He heard the screams of the lycans, the sloshing of the sea, the squeaking of the boats' masts. The smell of salt air renewed in his nose, burning his sensitive nostrils. It soon became replaced with the scent of blood.

Pentacost's roar could be heard over the howling maelstrom adding to the chaos of the escape. Azazel's cries for Kain to focus rang in his ears as if it were happening all over again.

Gabriel's sudden arrival jerked Kain from the vivid memory. He quickly hid the pendant in his jacket. "I wondered when you planned on coming back. Is something wrong, old friend? You seem troubled."

"I am fine. Just some old wounds," Kain replied. "I will tell everyone about the meeting in the morning. Right now, forgive me but I wish to catch some needed sleep. I assume Tala's asleep."

Gabriel nodded. In his eyes, Kain could see his fellow lycan didn't believe him.

Kain got up and went inside, wanting to join Tala but couldn't. He needed to be in the company of someone who understood the deeper part of his soul. Something he guarded from Tala to avoid exposing her to the darkness of the vengeful god. He decided to go down the hall to Damien's room.

The door stood ajar offering enough of a view to see the bed empty. Before Kain could even knock, Damien opened the door. "I knew you'd be coming."

Kain chuckled. "Of course you did. Would it be alright if I stayed in here tonight? I need a place to calm my raging soul."

Damien opened the door to let Kain in the room. "Jill's been sleeping in the nursery recently. She misses the pups horribly. Wherever you want, Kain. I could feel what you felt. I'm guessing you're going to share it later."

Kain offered a tired nod. He elected to crash on the futon in front of the television in the part of the room Damien once called his "man den." Being around Damien's gentle aura always calmed the chaos of Kain's soul.

After the battle with Lilith, Kain requested to be carried on Damien's back during the return to Holt's camp. He didn't fully understand it but welcomed his lycan brother's presence.

It didn't take long before Kain sank into a deep sleep.

Sometime during the night, Kain's dreams shifted to the plane of the dark god. Again, it stood empty.

Kain couldn't understand what was going on.

All around him the red tendrils swayed despite the lack of a breeze. It was the second time he came to the black plane without Barghast's prompting.

An overwhelming sense of dread welled up in Kain's chest. His heart pounded with such force it made him light-headed. It was as though something held onto it and tried to rip it out.

The sound of flapping wings brought his attention to the god's sudden appearance. A look of surprise in his demonic eyes. *"Well, well. I must admit, I had not expected your visit, Alexander. Give me a moment and we can speak since you seem to need my attention."*

The flapping sound stopped, giving way to the clacking of claws against the ground. The dark god stared down at Kain for a moment before kneeling. *"Now, to what do I owe the pleasure of your company?"*

Kain's skin broke out in gooseflesh. "I ... did not come here willingly."

"Is that so? Yet, here you stand before me? It seems very curious to both of us," Barghast made his way around Kain and placed his clawed hands on his shoulders. *"However, my dear soldier, as much as it would please me to be in your company, I have other obligations I must attend to,"*

The dark god took back to hovering above Kain. *"I am preparing the perfect gift to you, favored one. You have my permission to leave this once. Call it a gesture of my generosity."* The god smirked and took off into the gloom.

CHAPTER EIGHTEEN

Two days later was All Hallows' Eve. The time for the Masquerade Ball drew close.

Tala helped her mate get ready, complimenting on how dashing he looked in the costume she purchased for him on an outing with Jill. Noticing the serious look in Kain's eyes, she asked him what was wrong. He'd been acting strange for almost two days.

The strange encounter with Barghast and the mention of the "perfect gift" he prepared for Kain left a lingering feeling of dread. When Damien inquired into the reason behind Kain's behavior, Kain shared the details, leaving nothing out.

As Kain assumed, the young lycan alpha insisted on going with Kain to the Ball and refused to take no as an answer, pulling rank. Hesitant, Kain agreed to take Damien but made him promise to stay out of trouble. Gabriel wanted to go but Kain wouldn't allow it no matter how much Gabriel argued.

Kain tried his hardest to shake the foul feeling something would happen soon and whatever it was would be beyond bad. He elected to take Cade as his second, believing his military training would help alongside his instincts as a lycan. In a rush, Kain knew Cade could get Damien to safety.

Zane arrived promptly at 7pm in a limo to take the lycans to the Ball.

Kain held Tala close, not wanting to let her go. He begged her to stay in the house until he got home.

Tala giggled, "I'll be fine. Gabriel, Scott, Clint and Tyler are all here. Go. I think we're all ready for this to be over." She kissed Kain's lips, holding him close and tasting him before whispering, "I love you."

With one last glance, Kain got into the limo, his soul troubled more than it had been since the Circle of Stones.

The casino hosting the Masquerade Ball was beyond majestic. The grand showroom sported red carpet decorated with gold inlays shaped like flowers.

Tables hosting multiple games like Blackjack, Texas Hold'em, and Craps were spread across the outer perimeter of the room. The middle had been cleared to make room for tables with elegant hors d'oeuvres, champagne, and desserts.

Kain kept close to Zane and Damien. His eyes scanned the room to become aware of every security officer who could be a potential threat to their party.

A vampire with messy, pitch black hair walked up to Zane, standing shoulder to shoulder with him. He greeted Zane warmly.

"Steele. Tell me what's happened so far. Was there any suspicion due to our late arrival?"

Steele shook his head. "It's been quiet. Magnus is by the main stairwell. Are you sure you want to go through with this? You know we're in the middle of something. This could blow our cover."

"Relax. Anthony will behave himself to save face. Besides, he's pulling some serious crap that needs to be dealt with. We need to get a hold of Cromwell."

Steele rolled his ruby eyes. Cromwell hadn't come down from the luxury suite the Don set him up in yet. At Zane's request to keep Emeline blind, Steele strode over to where Emeline stood with Jared and a bleach blonde vampiress with voluptuous breasts.

Kain recognized her immediately as Magdeline. The third Aubert sibling.

Zane took Kain with him and headed over to where Magnus waited by the stairs. "Magnus, where is he?"

"Which one? Weasel-pire or the Don?" Magnus snapped in the voice one might hear in a CEO's office. It held no accent but a hint of sarcasm as thick as Gabriel's.

Zane smacked his head. Apparently, the behavior was normal from Magnus. "We know where Stoker is. Anthony."

Magnus gestured his head up the grand stairs. "Still upstairs. From what I heard he's on the phone with someone. Should be down shortly. This must be Kain." Magnus held out his hand.

Kain was a bit hesitant to take it but his trust in Zane made him reach out and take the vampire's hand.

Magnus laughed, shaking Kain's hand. The lights dimmed, replaced by a spotlight and an announcement telling the room the host had arrived. Magnus, Kain and Zane stared as Anthony descended the stairs with a beautiful woman on his arm. She didn't smell like either a lycan or a vampire.

"Zane. Is that you, my love?" Emeline sashayed over to Zane, wrapping her arms around his waist. "Mask or not, I would recognize this beautiful silver hair anywhere. How've you been? Hadn't seen you around much." She kissed his lips.

Zane tensed at the vampiress' touch. When Emeline pulled away, Kain saw a look of hidden disgust on Zane's face.

"Who's this?" she asked, gesturing her head towards Kain.

Zane pushed her away from him, introducing Kain as a friend.

Emeline's eyes roamed over Kain's body. She licked her nightshade colored lips and fangs. "My, my. Such a gorgeous body. Does this friend have a name?"

Zane glanced at Kain. "My name is Kade. Kade Sinclair."

Emeline ran her finger over Kain's chest. "Well Kade, let me know if you ever want to put this body to work. I'd be more than happy to have you. You two enjoy the party. Zane, I look forward to our meeting later." She winked at Kain and walked away.

Zane's brow raised. He snickered. "Kade?"

"It was a name I used many times in history to avoid conflict. What did she mean by meeting?"

A serious look replaced the jovial mood in Zane's eyes. "It's nothing. Let's focus on getting Cromwell and then getting you three out of here."

A quick motion of his chin sent Steele away from the guest table. He disappeared beyond a door beneath the grand stairwell. Zane's eyes met another vampire in the corner of the room. A younger man with hair the same color as Kain's. He nodded and departed out a fire escape door.

Anthony stopped at a podium set up at the base of the stairs. He greeted his guests, welcoming them to the Ball and offering for them to enjoy themselves. His hand motioned towards the different tables, a smile curling over his lips as the audience broke into applause.

Kain crossed his arms, leaning against the stairs. "I can see why you say he likes to make a grand entrance."

Anthony walked over to Zane and extended his hand. "My most trusted enforcer, how're you enjoying the evening?"

Zane took Anthony's hand, slightly bowing. He introduced Kain after offering a compliment to the Don.

The vampire's bright blue eyes focused on Kain. He reached out his hand. "Welcome, Kade. Any friend of Zane is a friend of mine. I do hope you enjoy yourself tonight. Please come find me if you need anything at all."

Kain's sense of danger warned him Anthony wasn't deceived. The eyes of the black god stared at him from beyond the vampire's gaze. They almost appeared to smile. Kain watched him walk away to go address his guests.

"He doesn't believe it. He knows who I am."

"I know. Stay on your guard. Since Emeline knows I'm here, I'll most likely have to leave you from time to time. Dante and Steele are working on retrieving Stoker. As soon as they text me, I'll come find you. Stay close to Damien."

Zane left Kain to go find Desdemona. The matriarch sat entertaining multiple guests and drinking what looked like champagne. Damien and Cade met Kain at the foot of the stairs.

"Are they looking into getting Stoker?" Damien asked, keeping his back near the wall.

Kain instructed him to be patient. "For now, we can stay here."

"I've got a bad feeling about this, Kain." Damien added.

"As do I," Kain replied.

The night waned on with various awards being given, extravagant dancing and speeches by various high-end representatives—both human and vampire. From their appearance, Kain assumed they were crime lords, drug dealers, corrupt CEOs and government officials. He hadn't personally handled any vampires who dabbled in the human underworld, but he knew many of them knew the existence of lycans.

The Cardozas truly have a magnificent reach. Kain thought back to the words Anthony said in his impromptu visit to the pack's house.

Fighting such power with traditional ways would only bring about the lycans' downfall.

Upon seeing Anthony, Kain asked Cade to take Damien over to where Desdemona and Zane still sat at the table. It was as safe as he could make them amidst such numbers.

"Did you think I wouldn't recognize such a powerful wolf behind the mask?" Anthony's darkened voice whispered from behind Kain. "I'm flattered you accepted my invitation, Kain."

"I already knew you were aware of who I was. Stop the melodrama and tell me why you have been slinking around all night." Kain didn't bother turning around so he could keep his eyes on Damien and Cade.

Anthony burst out laughing, keeping it contained to avoid drawing attention. He invited Kain to his private office, warning Kain against his initial instinct to tell the Don of Great Falls to shove it.

Kain turned to glower at the vampire. Their difference in height dwarfed the noble. "Am I to take that as a threat?"

Anthony took a cup of champagne, placing it Kain's hand with a daring smirk. "A recommendation. Tonight is for both of our races. The night of monsters and myths. Thirty minutes. Don't keep me waiting."

Thirty minutes later, Kain joined Anthony upstairs in his office.

Anthony stood against his mahogany desk. A devilish and prideful smirk played across his face. "Such good breeding. Rather than being late, you're early to our meeting. Nice to see such common courtesies haven't been truly lost in our races."

"Enough, vampire. I doubt you requested my presence to flatter me." Kain snapped.

Anthony moved towards a table with wine glasses and a glass pitcher with what looked like scotch or bourbon in it. "You're as business oriented as the legend says you are. Very well." He poured two glasses and walked back over to Kain to hand him one. "At least let me offer you a drink. We can do business like two respectable creatures of the night."

Kain refused the drink, making Anthony laugh. "Alexander Kain, you insult me. I wouldn't end a life as powerful and iconic as yours with such crude methods as poisoning. Oh no. For you, I would end it as you lived. A figure worth respecting and fearing."

The more Anthony spoke, the more Kain saw of the madness Zane spoke of. His hand shook when he poured the wine.

At the corner of his mouth, Kain saw a slight tremble. It made Kain sick to see what was happening. He'd known the sensation all his life. His hand still stung like shards of ice or the heat of a flame.

The dark god's influence radiated from Anthony like a thick miasma. Its presence slowly devouring him and driving him insane.

Anthony took a drink. "I'll get to the point. So far, I've waited for your stubborn pride to break in response to the threat of delivering body parts to your door."

The vampire got into Kain's face, ignoring the lycan's ability to snap him in two should he wish. "Now, I'm done waiting. Surrender both yourself and the item we both know you have in your possession. If you should refuse or keep me waiting past seven days, I will drop a body at your doorstep every single day it takes you to do what I say."

Kain's fangs grew behind his lips. "Cardoza, do not be a fool. I know what plagues you. What has he promised you? Power? You just declared an open war you will not survive."

Rings of red replaced Anthony's usually blue eyes. "It's you who are the fool, Alexander. Hunting you gives me such a rush. The difference is I hold influence in all three worlds. You will do as I say, or the deaths will start with your fellow pack mate. I believe his name is Nathaniel. Continue and maybe it'll be Damien's children or Damien since you care about him so much.

"I do hope you enjoy the gift I prepared. It gives me chills to know how you will respond."

A wide-eyed look of concern formed in Kain's eyes. Anthony no longer held control of his body. Barghast spoke through him, genuinely anxious. Kain imagined Jillian's face if she lost her children or her mate. He imagined what he would do if he lost Damien or Tala. Anthony could get to any one of them anytime he wanted.

Regaining his composure, Anthony picked Kain's mask up from the chair and handed it to him. "Seems like you're beginning to realize how powerless you really are, Alexander. Seven days. Call it a gesture of my generosity."

Kain took the mask trying to keep his anger under control. He turned and left the room to meet Zane outside of the door. He shoved past the vampire and stormed down the hall with Zane on his heels asking questions.

"Not now. Do you have Stoker?" Kain's voice sounded strained even to him.

"Yes. Magnus and Steele are holding him in the alley behind the casino. Damien and Cade are already there with Dante."

Kain nodded and the two went the back door behind the stairs into the alley.

Kain arrived to find Steele and Magnus with a man in a black Italian suit on his knees with a bag over his head. Damien's face scrunched up into a look of pure rage. He asked the vampires to remove the bag only to be stopped by Kain.

"Not here. We need to go." Kain's tone held no room for argument. The screeching of tires and the headlights of Gabriel's Mustang illuminated the darkness.

Gabriel rolled down the window. "Kain, we have a problem. Get in, I'll fill you in." To the vampires he told them to put Stoker in the trunk after knocking him unconscious.

Zane gladly obliged, cracking his knuckles and knocking the shit out of Stoker. Laughing, Magnus and Steele threw the unconscious vampire into the trunk.

The whole ride home, Gabriel told Damien, Cade and Kain the bad news. Tala was missing and so was the talon.

When Kain demanded to know how it happened, Gabriel's eyes met his friend's. "We ... we don't know."

CHAPTER NINETEEN

T ala opened her eyes to find her hands bound above her head. Her heart sped, making her breathe faster. Sweat dripped down her face from her hairline. She looked down to see a pastel blue dress with a hemline that stopped in the middle of her thighs. Her cheeks heated when she found she wore no panties beneath the thin fabric.

Her head hurt when she tried to remember how she'd gotten there. One moment she was reading and talking to an old friend on her phone, waiting for Kain to return, the next she was here.

Wherever here was.

Terror gripped her.

Alex. She pleaded in her mind, trying to reach out but couldn't due to her pain. The air smelled musty, like a mix of livestock, rust and old blood. All around her, darkness dominated save for the light in small windows high on the walls. It reminded her of the old saw mills her mom used to tell her about. She tried again to reach out to Kain, unable to focus.

"I don't think so," a dark voice echoed in the void.

Tala tried to look around but her limited movement made it hard.

From the corner of the room, the lycan responsible for killing her family emerged, a sick, twisted grin on his face. On his right arm, a vile claw writhed and wriggled as if it had a mind of its own.

"Why're you doing this?" Tears started falling down Tala's cheeks.

The lycan closed the distance between the two of them. He brushed the back of his knuckles over her cheeks. "Shh. None of this is personal, babe.

You should've taken your brother's advice and gotten away from Kain. He's not the virtuous soldier you think he is."

"What do you mean?" Tala's voice trembled.

A deep scowl formed over the lycan's face. "He's a murderer, a liar and a sinner. A monster who hides behind arrogance and pride. He tore my forearm off and left me to die. Now, he's going to face the demons he's run from for centuries."

Tala didn't know what to think. She'd shared blood with Kain and didn't see anything indicating him to be the man she was being told he was. She called the lycan a liar, refusing to believe him.

With a dark snicker, the lycan shrugged. "You can believe what you want. Truth is truth." He moved close, attempting to kiss Tala. She bit down on his lip, drawing blood. "Bitch!" He howled and slapped her with the dark claw.

Pain like she'd never experienced surged through Tala's body. She screamed as a dark voice filled her mind, greeting her and saying it was glad to finally meet her.

Tala found herself ripped from reality and plummeting through stinging red tendrils. Each touch sent renewed senses of flame through her body. She hit something solid, the impact stunning her.

Dazed, she pushed herself up with her hands, flinching when she touched one of the cuts made by the tendrils. The sound of wings resounded in the darkness.

"Finally." A dual toned voice - the same she heard when the claw impacted with her face - invaded her ears.

Tala looked up to see one of the most terrifying creatures she'd ever seen. Its red eyes pierced her soul the longer she stared. The dripping fangs and horrifying talons paralyzed her. She stuttered when trying to ask who he was.

Barghast towered above her. *"Am I to take it Alexander has yet to mention me? How insulting. We have had so many years together. Did you not wonder who gave him those beautiful scars?"*

Too tired to move, Tala could do nothing but listen. Her strength had been sucked away with each touch of the tendrils. She wanted to know about the scars but never got around to it.

It felt too personal.

Something she wanted Kain to tell her when he was ready. He always seemed to have so much on his mind, Tala didn't want to pressure him to tell her.

Barghast began circling Tala. *"Ah, I see. He has kept secrets. That is so like him. Well, allow me the pleasure of introducing myself. I am Barghast, my soldier's dark god."* Barghast tapped a claw on Tala's shoulder, causing her to cry out in pain. *"And you, my little half-breed, will be a god's gift to his fallen angel."*

As he had when he lost Chase, Kain hit his knees upon seeing the empty room. He hadn't waited for Gabriel to stop the car before throwing the door open and sprinting into the house to his room.

An overwhelming sense of loss flooded his heart, his pain threatening to tear his reserve away.

He threw back his head and let out a terrifying roar without bothering to shift into his lycan form. The force of it held such strength, it shook the house to its foundation.

When Damien tried to come in to calm him, Kain shoved past him and went out into the backyard.

He tore the rotted logs and stumps apart and threw them as far as he could.

Damien and Gabriel stood on the porch. Through his fury, Kain made out what they were saying.

"I've … I've never seen him this mad." Damien stuttered. His voice full of shock.

"I have. Only once. I'd hoped I wouldn't see it again." Gabriel's voice remained calm. "I feel sorry for the poor idiots responsible."

With one last slash of his claws against the bark of a tree, Kain fell to his knees in the grass. He let his reserve return then rose to join his fellow lycans on the porch.

Gabriel said nothing, letting the lycan pass unhindered.

Damien remained silent as well but followed his mentor through the house as he shed the Ball clothes and got dressed in a pair of blue jeans, tying the Sherpa jacket around his waist.

In a backpack, he placed a new change of clothes in case he needed them. The whole time Kain prepared, Damien tried to reassure him they'd find who did this and make them pay. Kain never responded. He knew who did it and wouldn't make the mistake of letting him live again.

Jill joined Damien and Kain the foyer while Kain prepared to leave. He'd caught Bard's scent and was damn set on following it.

"Kain," Damien said but Kain interrupted him.

"I want no interferences. Stay out of this, Damien." He could tell Damien wanted to say something but Jill stopped him.

"We will only observe, dear friend," Jill assured Kain.

Kain nodded and walked out of the house.

Shifting into his lycan form, he sprinted towards the scent in the woods. Jill, Damien and Gabriel joined him in their wolf skins, leaving Stoker in the capable hands of Cade, Lune and Scott.

On his way, Kain had to focus to keep from stumbling due to the massive variety of emotions he could feel his mate going through. The most prominent were pain and terror. He could hear her screaming and begging for him in his mind; the thought tearing his heart apart the more she went through.

When they reached the mill at the end of the scent trail, Kain slammed the full weight of his body into the door, shattering it to pieces. His ears flattened against his head when he saw Tala on the floor, her small body trembling and convulsing in pain.

"About time. Not sure how much longer she's going to be with us." Bard smirked, dropping from his seat on a rusted tractor.

Kain's fury filled the room. He looked over his shoulder, making sure none of the other lycans planned on interfering.

This was his fight and he'd be damned if he let it anyone else get hurt. The scars on his body ached and stung in the claw's presence. His hand tingled like it'd fallen asleep. He ignored them all and focused on how angry he was.

"Brought your pack? What's the matter Kain? Too scared to finish off your greatest failure on your own?" Bard mocked Kain. When he didn't receive a response he shifted into his lycan form. *"You always were a stuck-up prick."*

Kain snarled at Bard, preparing to receive the brunt of the lunge the demonic lycan pulled. Kain grabbed Bard by the elbows, careful not to touch the claw. The proximity of the dark god's power began attempting to suck his strength out of him.

Kain shook his head to clear it. If he didn't end the fight quickly, he could wind up getting another serious injury he couldn't heal. He could hear Damien's worried whimpers and shuffling behind him.

Subconsciously, Kain didn't want Damien to see what he could do if he let loose. He knew he'd already scared his friend at the pack house though he didn't mean to.

Tala's pleas became weaker, adding to the strain.

"Enough!" Kain slammed his forehead into Bard's face. The force made Bard howl in agony, gripping his face and stumbling back.

Primal fury overtook reason and Kain let go of his restraint. He roundhouse kicked Bard across the jaw so hard he heard it break. Before the demonic lycan could recover, Kain took a hold of the claw, tearing it from his forearm and throwing it across the room.

As Bard sputtered blood from his broken jaw and yowled at the loss of his arm, Kain sank his fangs into the lycan's neck, spinning him around and throwing him into the remains of a dusty furnace.

Panting from the effect of the claw's power, Kain sank to a knee on the floor. He shifted back into his human form, his reserve replacing the blind fury. With a heavy heart he went to find Bard lying naked amongst the crumbling remains of the furnace. He no longer had the strength to hold the change and choked on the blood draining from the wound in his neck. Bard tried to speak, but the blood halted his words.

Kain dropped to his haunches, his eyes downtrodden. "There was once a time you showed such promise. I want you to know, I never wanted this for you. I tried to warn you."

Bard grew still, his life fading from his eyes. Kain reached to close them, asking Tenebris to forgive his fellow lycan's treachery and to take him into the god's arms.

Kain rose to go to Tala, kneeling to take her trembling form into his arms.

When Damien tried to ask Kain if he was alright, all Kain said was he wanted to go home and get help for his mate.

Back at the pack's house, Mackenzie dressed Kain's wounds while Kyle checked how bad Tala's condition was. When Mackenzie finished, Damien took her place.

"I am fine, Damien. I deeply regret you seeing that." Kain's voice betrayed his fatigue. Bard's death weighed on his heart more than he thought it would.

To Kain's surprise, Damien hugged him. "Shut up, you idiot." A tear dropped onto Kain's arm. "I can feel your pain. I've never felt it like this before. It hurts."

Kain sighed, returning Damien's hug. He reassured his friend he'd be alright.

Kyle came out of the room, closing the door. The look in his eyes told both lycans the prognosis wasn't good.

Tala was in a coma, her body exhibiting signs of some small cuts on her shoulder but otherwise she was physically fine.

Kain pushed by Damien to go into the room. Dropping onto the side of the bed, he took Tala into his arms, rocking her and pleading with her to come back to him. He could feel the mist of tears fogging his eyes. Something he hadn't done since Pentacost died centuries before.

CHAPTER TWENTY

In the days following the encounter with Bard, Kain barely left his mate's side. Zane visited at Kain's request since Tala was his niece and asked what happened. Kain told him which angered the vampire further at the situation. He left to help Damien interrogate Stoker shortly after.

Kyle checked back to make sure Tala's vital signs were okay and to keep her supplied with a steady supply of fluids. "I'm sorry, Kain. I don't know what's wrong. By all medical accounts, she's like Damien was when Jill turned him. She's fine."

"Thank you, Kyle." Was all Kain said, his mind occupied by the mysterious scars on his mate's shoulder. "I need to be alone, please."

Kyle nodded, leaving.

With a sorrowful sigh, Kain touched the small pattern of cuts. His arm ignited in flames, his mind jerked into the black plane where he crashed through what felt like a glass ceiling before hitting a second barrier with a *thud!*

Somehow, he'd been blocked from entering Tala's mind. He tried to break through once he saw her encased in what looked like a wind of miasma. Her face distorted in pain each time a new cut bit her tender skin.

Barghast's sinister laugh broke the screams of the wind. *"Do you like my gift to you, my soldier?"*

Kain's nails raked down the glass. "Let her go. I beg you."

"You beg me? I do not think so." Barghast pushed Kain's face into the glass. *"Look at her. All you had to do was accept my offer. Look!"*

The god slammed Kain's head back down. *"I offered you freedom from pain. You threw it back in my face. Now, she will suffer unless you are willing to make a deal."*

Nausea filled Kain's stomach. He knew any deal he made would damn him after his death but he couldn't let Tala suffer for what he saw as his sins. "What do you want?"

The god laughed, releasing his hold. *"You have strength, Alexander Kain, but even you can be broken if your heart is attacked. I will tell you what I want but first, my servant will call on you and you will answer. Refuse, well. I do not believe I need to explain."*

Tala's screams pierced Kain's heart. "Stop! I will do what you want."

"Good boy. See you soon, dear one."

The following day, Kain requested Damien to accompany him on a visit to see if the packs housed in the motels in the city were doing alright. He'd met Calen, the pup Damien once saved from his friend Chelsea, who had been turned into a vampire. The pup wondered how Kain was doing and why he'd been gone for so long. Kain responded by petting the pup's head, nothing more.

By the time they'd gone to the third motel, Damien inquired about Kain's silence. "Okay, what's the problem? You've been more quiet than usual. It's getting creepy."

A snicker through his nose interrupted Kain's downtrodden mood. "I was thinking."

"Yeah, I got that. What about?" Kain told Damien about the encounter with Barghast, leaving out no details. Damien stopped walking, forcing Kain to do the same. "Like hell are you turning yourself in, Kain. We'll find another way."

"Damien, Tala is suffering. She is not accustomed to the mental strain the dark god can inflict. The longer he has her, the more chance her damage can become permanent." Kain lowered his head, his eyes closed. "She is my mate, brother. What else can I do?"

Damien ran his hand through his hair, down his neck. His eyes enlarged, a devious smile across his face. "We go see a certain bastard of a vampire. Get your interrogation gloves on, Kain."

Kain blinked a few times before displaying a devious smile of his own.

Kain pulled his car up to Ramona's coven during the hour of twilight. He'd called Zane earlier to meet him and Damien to interrogate Stoker.

Upon Kain's request, because of Damien's history with the catacombs, Zane moved Stoker to one of the abandoned servant houses behind the main mansion.

When they arrived, Stoker was on his knees before Magnus. Zane stood against the wall, nodding for Magnus to remove the blindfold they'd put over the former noble's eyes.

Stoker blinked, sneering at Zane. "About damn time. I demand to know why I have been dragged here, thrown into a dingy cell and kept prisoner by my own kind."

When Stoker saw Damien, he rolled his eyes and smiled. He didn't appear to notice Kain who kept to the shadows. "Well, well, Damien Pierce. It's been too long. You look good for a coward who hides amongst the dogs."

Magnus smacked Stoker across the back of the head, sending him to the floor.

Damien shook his head, annoyed. "And you look good for a coward who kisses the ass of the local Don to avoid getting captured. Gotta say, Stoker, you've really fallen. Too much of a chicken to take me on yourself? Gotta beg Anthony to help you finish what Lilith started?"

The exchanges between Damien and Stoker made Kain cover a laugh.

"Fuck off, Pierce! You wouldn't be alive were it not for your little mongrel whore or--" Stoker's words froze in his throat when Kain emerged from behind Damien. Beads of sweat formed on his brow. "Of course. Your boyfriend is here."

Damien looked back at Kain, his brow crooked in confusion. "Seriously? First, you're my man-crush and now boyfriend? What the hell?"

Kain shrugged. He never understood the references either. To him, it made the commenters look more stupid and ignorant.

"Listen vampire, we only want to ask you a few questions. Cooperate and you may yet live. Refuse and I cannot guarantee your fate." Kain refused to let the banter continue in lieu of the life of his mate being on the line.

Stoker guffawed. "Let me guess, you want to know what Anthony's up to, yes? Maybe what he plans to do next." Stoker spat at Damien's feet. "Go fuck yourself, Pierce. You and your has-been enforcer. I'd rather die than give you what you want."

Damien once again looked back at Kain. He made a sarcastic comment about the term "has-been" and then turned his attention back to Stoker. "Alright, your choice. I'd kill you myself but it's not worth my time or energy to do so. Zane, make it painful, okay? He's screwed me over one too many times."

Stoker glanced at Zane, his breath growing quicker as the silver-haired vampire moved from the wall. "Wait, wait." The noble stuttered between words. "Alright. Anthony isn't the one in charge here."

Kain already figured that out. "Tell us something we do not know."

"He hasn't revealed his full plan to me. All I know is he's slowly descending into insanity. He's not making sense." Stoker rambled information Kain already knew.

So far, the noble gave him nothing to go on to find a way to save Tala without offering himself as a shield. "It has something to do with the grand opening of Crimson, his new casino. That much I do know."

Kain's brow creased as he pondered the new name. He'd known Anthony Cardoza owned most of Great Falls and its surrounding land, but this new casino never appeared on the maps within the city.

Angry, Damien demanded Stoker tell him where the new casino was to be built. At first, Stoker declined to tell him but after the lycan slashed him across the face with silver claws, the vampire told him.

The main problem that lie before Kain and the pack was how to go about getting to Anthony and finding out more about his primary plan. If the casino was being built outside the city, it gave Anthony and his vampires more room to move around without destroying his reputation in the human world.

With nothing else to learn from Stoker, Damien left Zane and Magnus to do what they saw fit with the former noble. Behind him, Stoker cried and begged for Damien to spare him, apologizing for all he'd done. The sight disgusted Kain since he knew how much of a coward Stoker Cromwell was.

"Okay, so now we know the location but not much more than that," Damien said, his voice resembling a disappointed sigh.

Kain mulled over their options. There weren't many lying before the lycans. "There is only one way we can learn more, Damien. Zane has said it before. We cannot simply get to the Don through traditional methods. We would be killed on sight."

The same look of revelation dawned over Damien's face. It was the look he had when he devised the plan to defeat the vampires at the Circle of Stones. "That's it, Kain."

Leaning against the open door to his car, Kain stared at his friend, wondering what went through his mind.

"You can't get to Anthony." Damien dropped into the seat of Kain's car. Kain did the same, shutting it and pulling out of the crescent driveway to the main gate.

During the drive home, Damien didn't say much else. At least not that Kain could hear. Everything came out as a mumble or a sudden burst of a mix of "ah-has" and cursing. To avoid breaking Damien's concentration, Kain kept quiet, relying on his mental connection to Damien to try and make sense of his thoughts.

Kain stopped his car, put it into park and looked at his friend. "Mind telling me what this is about?"

Damien grinned and got out of the car without saying anything. When they got to the steps, he stopped Kain. "Get Gabriel, Lune, Cade, Jill, Scott, everyone, including Zane." Damien put his hand on Kain's shoulder. His face looked pained but resigned to do what he felt needed to be done. "Kain, you're going to do what you do best. Be a shield."

For once, Kain was beyond confused. Damien hated it when he did what he was raised to do, argued with him over every time he'd had to. Now, the alpha appeared to want him to deliver himself into the hands of the enemy. "Damien, for the gods' sake, make some sense."

Damien put both of his hands on Kain's shoulders. "You once told Jill she couldn't stop me from doing what a Purifier is supposed to do. All this time, I've interfered with what you were born to do, protect others even at the cost of your own life and body. I'm sorry for that. Now, I need you to do it for all of us."

Kain recalled the conversation with Jill. It'd happened after Chelsea was turned. Damien wanted to try and see if his childhood friend was still capable of being saved.

"Kain," Damien said, his amethyst eyes burrowing into Kain's. "You're going to give yourself up."

CHAPTER TWENTY-ONE

A few hours passed before Damien's small living room became crowded with both lycan and vampire alike. Zane, Steele, Magnus and Dante stayed near the doorway with concerned looks on their faces. Gabriel, Lune, Scott, Cade, Jill, Tyler and Joel all remained spread all over the floor. Their faces mirrored those of their vampire guests.

Damien offered details of the plan he proposed in regards to what Stoker told he and Kain during the interrogation.

Gabriel threw his hands up in frustration. "What you're saying is you want to throw Kain to the vampires in the insane hopes he can do what now?"

Understanding the confusion, Kain offered the details in regards to the dark god's involvement in the whole convoluted scheme.

"What does that mean, Damien? What exactly are you proposing?" Jill asked. Her tone matter-of-fact.

"I don't expect everyone here to understand the minute details. Anthony's going insane because of Barghast's influence. The two are working together but their goals aren't the same. Barghast wants Kain alive for some reason. Anthony wants to kill him to prove a point. We put Kain in the middle, it's like ringing a challenge bell," Damien replied.

Lune scoffed. "You're proposing throwing Kain into a shark feeding frenzy that could land him seriously injured. You realize that, right? What are you hoping to gain?"

Kain took up the conversation when Damien glanced at him as if asking for help. "Anthony is a spoiled brat. My father killed his and now he wants revenge. Barghast will not allow me to be killed over something so petty. I do not know the god's intentions, he has not deemed to share. What I do know, is if I can pit them against one another, it will shatter Anthony's resolve. He will defy Barghast to get what he wants."

Lune lowered angry eyes to the ground.

The question Kain could sense lingering on everyone's mind revolved around the mysterious talon. When Zane requested to know more since he was one of the youngest in the room, Kain told him the talon possessed incredible dark power descending from Barghast himself. It could, in essence, bolster the power of the transformed state of a vampire noble. However, the consequences could be dire.

"I don't like this. We've done some crazy, stupid things, Kain, you know that but throwing yourself in the enemy's hands? Isn't that beyond desperate?" Gabriel growled through his teeth.

Kain scowled at the alpha, his body tense. "I believe the situation has become desperate. The longer my mate remains in the black plane, the larger the chance I could lose her. I will not lose her, Gabriel. You would do the same for any one of us in this room."

Zane sighed. He let everyone know he could get Kain into the Don's personal mansion, but he couldn't guarantee Kain's physical state or what he would have to do to keep from blowing his cover.

Kain took in the scars on his forearms and hand. "Three days, Zane. That is all I need. I do not care what Anthony does. I can guarantee nothing he could do is worse than what Barghast has done."

"Alright. Three days. I'll use the opportunity to find out more regarding what Stoker told us. That should help us get a plan of action," Zane added. "I'll need at least twenty-four hours to set things up in our favor. I'll text you when we're ready, Kain."

Kain nodded. Despite his reserve, his heart grew heavy.

After the meeting, he decided to return to Tala's room to be with her before he turned himself over to an insane vampire.

When Kain opened the door, Tala lay on her back, her eyes closed, twitching from the pain she was experiencing. He breathed out a melancholy sigh, sitting down on the bed.

Reaching out a hand, he stroked his mate's face, bent over and kissed her lips. "Please, forgive me. This is all my fault. He should be hurting me, not you."

Kain gritted his teeth, trying to hold back his emotion. Their connection made the intensity of the feelings she experienced burn in his body. "I cannot lose you. It would destroy what little left of my soul that I have. You gave me back what it means to live a life without war. To see the world beyond death. I beg of you to stay strong. It will be over soon."

With those last words, Kain lay beside his mate, his mind slipping into a sleep he knew wouldn't be restful.

A phone call in the wee hours of the morning woke Kain up from an already restless sleep. He reached over to the bedside table, slowly to avoid shaking Tala.

A number he didn't recognize blinked back at him. "Who is this?"

"Well, aren't you rude?" Anthony's voice chimed from the other side. "Were you not told to expect my phone call?"

Kain gritted his teeth, his eyes squeezed shut.

A laugh came over the speaker. "From your lack of a response, I know the answer."

A squeak of a chair followed by brief shuffling filled Kain's ear. "Listen, I warned you not to disappoint me. Zane and Jared will come and collect you, Kain. I expect you to be a good dog and heel without a fight."

A "tsk" sound went through Kain's teeth. "When?"

"My, my. Antsy. Tomorrow. I look forward to meeting you again." Anthony slammed the phone down on the receiver, ending the call.

Despite how arrogant the vampire sounded, Kain had to keep from smiling. Zane managed to work things out perfectly.

The following afternoon, Kain spent as much time with Tala as he could. He'd be gone for three days and wanted to make sure she had something to remind her of him. He took the metal pendant Desdemona gave him and folded it into her hand, whispering "I love you" in her ear and leaving the room.

Gabriel met him at the foot of the stairs. "Are you sure this is the best way?"

Kain put his hand on Gabriel's shoulder, squeezing it and offering a reassuring smile. "I cannot say if it is best, but it is not the first time I have had to do such a mission either. I will be fine, Gabriel. Anthony will likely want to inflict what pain he can, but you know he can do no worse. Be well, my friend."

Gabriel let Kain pass him. "Kain."

Kain froze.

"I'm not sure why you did what you did but I want to believe you had the best intentions. Doesn't make it hurt less." Gabriel said, disappointed.

Kain didn't respond. He knew Gabriel would find out and eventually speak to him regarding his choice. Without saying anything, he continued walking down to his car.

Damien leaned against the sleek black Charger. The look in his eyes hurt Kain's heart.

Anything Kain would feel, he knew Damien would as well. "Damien, before I do this, may I ask one thing of you?" Kain said.

Damien tilted his head, brow raising.

Kain dangled his car keys in front of his friend. Damien's eyes turned into those of a child who just got released in a toy store. Kain snickered. "Don't wreck my car."

Damien took the keys, rolling his eyes and taking the driver's seat.

Hesitantly, Kain took the passenger's side, focusing his mind during the drive on the mission at hand and remembering why he'd agreed to such madness in the first place.

After dark, Damien pulled Kain's car up under the neon sign of a strip club in Great Falls. The red outline of a scantily clad woman on her knees reflected off the black paint of the car. Kain got out first, followed shortly by Damien.

Zane stood in front of Jared and two other vampires dressed in black suits and sunglasses. Magnus stood in the far rear with Steele, probably in case Jared decided to do something stupid to showboat.

Damien stepped up to Kain's shoulder to whisper. "You sure you want to do this? We might be able to find another way."

"There is no time. Keep a channel open for me, Damien. Trust me, brother." Kain reassured. He walked closer to Zane who took what looked like a silver zip tie out of his pocket and moved around Kain.

Keeping his voice low, Zane applied the zip ties. The silver already burning Kain's skin. "Sorry about this. It was the only way I could get put on this mission. Are you sure about this?"

Kain glared over his shoulder at his fellow soldier. His message clearly understood by the veteran. He heard Damien threaten Zane to keep him safe, or he'd hit Zane really hard.

"Well, well, Alexander Kain." Jared smirked a prideful smirk. Something wood stuck out of his mouth. Kain assumed it to be a toothpick. The other vampires around him appeared excited, almost in anticipation.

Zane's chiding shut the vampire up as he moved him to open the trunk. He apologized to Kain before forcing him to get in and shutting the lid.

Due to his height, Kain struggled not to feel like he was in a can of tuna. The silver tie cut into his wrists, making his skin hiss like it was being burned. He could hear Damien trying to talk to him but the sudden jerking of the car made focusing difficult.

A subtle cold pulled at the back of his consciousness. Barghast's laugh resonated in Kain's thoughts as he fed images of Tala suffering into Kain's mind. It made Kain angry and more determined to shut the arrogant ass up once and for all.

Throughout the ride, Kain kept his eyes closed trying to conserve his energy. He mapped out the route to pass the time, replacing the anger with his composure in the face of Barghast's mocking.

The many stops indicated stop lights until they left the city limits and made their way onto the highway. It seemed like they traveled about an hour before the car pulled off to the right and came to a stop.

It was Jared who opened the trunk, staring down at Kain with the same confident smirk on his face. He reached down to grab Kain only to be stopped by Zane. "Orders, Jared. Step back or I'll kill you."

Jared raised his hands, stepping back and uttering a mocking "Whatever you say, boss" to Zane, barely avoiding Magnus who looked ready to break Jared's neck.

Zane helped Kain out of the car and proceeded to lead him across a parking lot leading up to a building resembling a lavishly decorated casino and hotel.

An automatic rotating door began spinning as the vampires approached. Kain made sure to show Damien what he saw so his fellow lycan could get a layout of the building.

Though beautiful, the décor carried a dark theme. Statues of angels bound in what looked like thorns and blindfolded decorated the grand stairwell, fountains and the columns. All symbols of the cult of the dark god. The floors were a radiant red with purple and gold decorations.

Tables covered in plastic sat arranged in sections while slot machines yet to be activated stood in rows awaiting the moment they could commit carnal deeds of greed.

Further into the structure, Kain found himself led through draping plastic into a wide room with a cement floor. What looked to be chains attached to a single anchor on the floor decorated the middle of the room.

The setup reminded him of darker times during the Blood Wars where lycan generals interrogated their prisoners of both races. He winced at the memories of death screams of vampires pleading to be spared as the sun was let through to burn their bodies. Lycan traitors howled in plain as silver dropped to the floor in bubbling droplets of torture.

To his left he saw what looked to be a table covered with different instruments made of the purest silver. They were meant for him.

"On your knees, Kain." Zane used a demanding tone, shoving down on Kain's shoulder.

From the look of disgust in his eyes, Kain knew Zane had to do some of the things he did to keep the cover he spoke of. Kain knelt to the floor where Zane snapped the silver tie off and replaced it with chains crafted from silver.

Thankfully, the damage done to Kain's right hand kept him from feeling the sultry heat. He could smell the burning flesh from his left wrist.

At Zane's request, Magnus and Steele pushed the other vampires out, taking their places next to the door. Zane informed Kain he was working to get the information regarding Anthony's intentions and would do his best to get Kain out with as little damage as possible.

"Do not worry about me. Find out what we need to know and Zane, can you see what happened to a friend of mine? His name is Nathaniel," Kain requested.

Zane nodded and took his place next to a wall just as Anthony Cardoza appeared in the doorway.

CHAPTER TWENTY-TWO

The smug look on the Don's face betrayed his descent further into insanity. Kain could see the burning slits of Barghast staring back at him. "I hope you like them. I knew regular handcuffs wouldn't hold you."

Anthony puffed out his chest, standing over Kain and staring down at him with pride.

Kain said nothing, keeping his eyes focused on Anthony's and refusing to give him the satisfaction of feeling any kind of dominance.

"Nothing to say? You lost, can't you see that? I own you, Kain. Your life is in my hands!"

The lycan remained silent. He could feel the tension between Anthony and Barghast growing the longer he refused to speak. Anthony's need to have his narcissistic attitude recognized would lead him to eventually slip up and do something to piss Barghast off.

The vampire gripped Kain's hair and held, dropping to his haunches in front of him. Beads of sweat began to form on his brow, the corners of his mouth twitched and his fingers trembled as they held Kain's hair. "Fine, don't speak. Five days from now, I will slit your throat in front of the most powerful vampires in Europe. I will prove I'm stronger than my father ever was."

Kain stared at the second pair of eyes behind Anthony's blue glare. "Do you truly believe the dark god will give you what he promised? In the end, you kill me and walk away from this with false prestige? He is consuming you, vampire."

Anthony threw Kain's head forward and began hitting him repeatedly.

"Silence!" Anthony yelled. "You know nothing! I'm in control. Me! Me alone!"

The hits barely dented Kain's pain threshold. When they stopped suddenly, Kain looked up to see Anthony's arm frozen mid-hit. Fear filled the vampire's eyes like he was fighting against something inside of him.

He didn't know how, but Kain could hear the god's voice. It filled the room like a poltergeist. Behind Anthony, a shadowed ghost appeared, its hand holding the shadow of the vampire. The only other time Kain had seen Barghast take such a form was in his room back at the cabin.

"That is enough, Cardoza. Strike him again and I will tear your soul apart." Barghast's snarling voice didn't seem to resonate with Zane, Steele, or Magnus.

Anthony uttered under his voice and almost fell forward into Kain when he was released, panting.

Kain felt sorry for the young vampire. "Anthony, stop this. I know what his power feels like. It is intoxicating. A drug. You cannot wield the talon any more than you can wield the dark god. Walk away. Please."

Anthony grimaced through his panting. Desdemona made it known to Kain that her "son" wasn't a pureblood. In order to assure Darius left the Cardoza dynasty in the hands of a male heir, he changed Anthony.

Kain wondered what it must've felt like never to have the love of one's father only to have him die in a petty squabble over pride and show. Gods only knew how much he must've experienced all of his life.

Anthony hissed through his teeth. His blonde hair mussed from his struggle against Barghast.

From the table he took a silver blade and, in a rage, stabbed Kain in the shoulder with it. "You know nothing. Not a damned thing, dog. You, who had power. You, who were feared by my kind, know nothing about what it takes to fight to get to where I am."

The silver in Kain's blood bubbled at the entry site. It'd been centuries since he'd been stabbed or cut by anything pure silver.

The sting reminded him of the silver swords and spears used by the vampires in the Blood Wars. During a scuffle, Kain barely avoided being impaled by a noble's silver spear. The excruciating pain brought about a sense of nausea.

At the sight of his blood, Kain saw the whites of Anthony's eyes fill with crimson. His fangs seemed to get larger. He lunged at Kain's face, lashing out with his nails. Had Zane not caught the Don, Kain would have received another scratch across his face.

Confusion filled the eyes of the silver-haired vampire as he stared back at Kain, pulling Anthony, kicking and screaming how much he wanted Kain's blood. The sight of utter bloodlust in the vampire's eyes stunned Kain as well. He didn't understand what caused the sudden change in behavior.

Anthony's mental breakdown left Kain alone in the small room, cut off from the light of the moon. Without some way to get fresh air, the room grew stifling. Sweat dripped from the tip of his nose to the cement floor at his knees. His back ached and complained from being forced to kneel for such a long period of time.

During his training with his father, Kain learned how to put himself in a state of dormancy. The lycan kept his eyes closed, focusing on conserving energy against the wound in his shoulder and the state of the room. He'd succeeded in ticking off Anthony and getting him to question Barghast's loyalty, but the bloodlust was something not even Kain expected.

A slight change in the temperature and the subtle feeling of Luna's energy made Kain aware of what time it was outside. The cold chill climbing up his spine indicated the arrival of the unwanted presence.

Barghast emerged in the blackness. From the sound of it, he was clapping. *"Well done. You managed to shake my pawn and drive him mad."*

Kain remained in his dormant state, tired of the torture, the mind games and the manipulation.

Unwilling to be ignored, Barghast drove the claw of his thumb into Kain's shoulder. When he didn't receive a response, the god laughed. *"I have always admired your ability to do this. However, I have not come to chat. I know you better than even you know yourself. You would not have come here without a means to escape. Let us talk about the reason you are here, shall we?"*

Kain opened his eyes, raising them but keeping his expression emotionless.

"I can see in your eyes that you have many questions. The biggest one being what I want from you, correct?" Barghast ran the blood-soaked claw of his thumb down Kain's jaw. *"I want you, Kain. Well, more simply, your body as my vessel. Anthony was an experiment to see if I could inhabit a physical form. Clearly, things have gone awry."*

Kain's surprised gaze prompted a fanged grin from the dark god. *"Does this surprise you? You have power, Alexander. Much more than any of your predecessors. None of them have lasted so long against me. Now, knowing you, I know I will not be receiving my vessel, so I am willing to take the next best thing."*

A hard knot formed in Kain's throat at what alternative Barghast would propose. For as long as he'd known the Shadowed One, he always hinted at wanting one thing.

"Your soul, Alexander."

Thoughts spun in Kain's mind like a blood-soaked carousel. He kept trying to hold on to the promise the sun goddess made to spare him from Barghast's rage and yet did nothing when it came to Tala being hurt.

If he surrendered his soul, Barghast would be able to torment him even after death in ways worse than in life. On the other hand, Kain thought of Tala. She'd been innocent in this war between Kain and the dark god but he'd targeted her anyway.

"What guarantee do I have you will release her once the bargain is struck?" Kain bluntly asked.

Barghast dropped to one knee. *"A soul such as yours is worth more than that of a mere woman, Kain. Give it to me and I will spare her life."*

Kain clenched his teeth, eyes closed tight. "You must swear any damage will be taken from her."

Barghast gave his word, releasing Kain from the chains binding his wrists. The Shadowed One reached out, asking for Kain to give him his hand.

Barghast burned a mark to seal their bargain. *"So be it. Your woman is now free and you, my dear soldier, are mine once you breathe your last breath."*

The mark felt like a cold fire in the palm of Kain's left hand. He hissed through his teeth, clasping his wrist against the pain.

Kain's eyes shot open to find Zane staring at him.

"I'm getting you out of here. Anthony's been quarantined in his office. He's lost his mind. I'm not sure what happened and in truth, I don't want to know. Dante and Steele will be taking you to a guest house at the coven in Big Timber. Damien has been called and will meet us there."

Shaking his head, Kain looked at the mark on his hand. Again, Barghast manifested in the physical plane. When the experience began, Kain swore he'd been dreaming. A sense of lingering pain stung Kain's hand. "Zane, did you get the remaining information we needed?"

Zane nodded, informing Kain he'd gathered the time the nobles from Europe were set to arrive and the floor plans for Crimson. If the lycans needed to get in unseen, the plans could help them do so.

He led Kain to his waiting car where Steele sat in the driver's side, Dante in passenger's seat. When Kain looked at him with a puzzled look, Zane only smirked, raising his brows and gesturing his head in a nod.

Kain got into the backseat where Zane ordered him to lie down in the floorboard so no one could see him. He went onto to assure his fellow vampires he'd make sure the gate stood clear for them to pass unhindered.

"Keep him safe. Desdemona will have my head if he's hurt," Zane said sarcastically.

Dante and Steele snickered. They rolled up the windows, pulled out and proceeded to drive down to where the automatic gates lie patrolled by guards.

Without turning around, Steele said, "Relax, Zane'll do what he says. Many of the guards are loyal to Desdemona and the old Cardoza regime. It's mostly the human hired hands who serve the Don."

Kain thought about the power Zane had in the Cardoza household. "You trust him greatly."

"With my life," Steele replied.

Steele and Dante's loyalty to Zane reminded Kain of some of the lycans he served with back in the Blood Wars. His command followed him without question even if the mission they were on looked too dangerous.

One of them, a young lycan named William, looked up to Kain like his father. They'd been sent to try and take Demetrius Stone down only to nearly have the whole pack destroyed when Rayes showed up. Had it not been for Jill, Kain would've died that day along with his command.

Images of the bodies of his fallen comrades ran through Kain's mind. He'd argued with the commander of the lycans' pack but lacked the influence his father had in the commander's eyes. The result haunted him well into the centuries.

The lingering fear that Damien and his pack could meet the same fate brought about a feeling of unease. He asked Steele why he agreed to go along with Zane even when it appeared impossible.

Both Dante and Steele laughed which baffled Kain.

"Because sometimes, as soldiers, you have to go on blind faith, even when things don't make sense." Dante commented. "Zane's made mistakes that've gotten some of us killed but he doesn't let it stop him. He's kind of the vampire equivalent of you, in a way."

Dante's reply didn't come as a shock. Despite Zane's youth, his experience as a Marine instilled confidence in those who followed him. In their many times together, Kain could see moments when Zane second-guessed himself, but he did what he needed.

The thought of being compared to a vampire made Kain snicker to himself but it made sense as to why Damien trusted Zane the first time they met. It was Damien's confidence that led to Kain's easy acceptance of the vampire as an ally.

As Zane promised, the guards at the gate opened the opened it without stopping the car or asking any questions.

CHAPTER TWENTY-THREE

As soon as Steele stopped Kain's car in front of an abandoned guest house behind the coven of Big Timber, Kyle met Kain once he stepped out of the back seat. The doctor seemed worried about the damages on Kain's body.

When asked how he knew, Kyle told Kain Zane informed him of the wound in Kain's shoulder and the cuts made by a silver blade on his torso and his wrists.

"I am fine, Kyle. A bit fatigued since I was not allowed to sleep for forty-eight hours and hungry as Sun's hell but fine." Kain assured the doctor as they walked up the front steps to find Jill standing in the doorway.

The female lycan greeted her old friend with a hug. "I'm so relieved to see you're doing well."

"Jillian, Tala?" Was all Kain said in reply.

"She's in the guest room. Damien wishes to see you as soon as you can make time. I can imagine Kyle won't leave you alone until he gives you a check-up." Jill chuckled and made way for Kain to walk through the door.

Ramona led Kain and Kyle to a room they could use so Kain could be examined. As he thought, Kyle quizzed him about how he'd felt while shining a bright light in Kain's eyes. Once the doctor examined and dressed Kain's wounds, Kain demanded Ramona take him to Tala.

The vampiress offered a curt bow and led him through the house to another room and opened the door. Tala sat in the window looking out into the sky. Luna's light brought out the red in her deep locks, giving her an ethereal glow.

Kain's heart almost fell through his stomach. His breath heaved at seeing his mate awake and from the looks of her, unharmed. "Tala."

Tala turned at hearing her name, her eyes enlarged. She got up to run into her mate's open arms, repeating his name over and over as her arms held him tight.

With a swelled heart, Kain kissed Tala's lips, the salt of the streaming tears tasted bitter-sweet on his tongue. One hand gripped her hair while the other traveled down her body. The clearing of a throat at the door drew Kain's attention to Kyle who gestured his head to ask Kain for his attention.

Kain promised Tala he'd be back and left to talk. "What is it?"

Kyle's eyes glanced at Tala then at Kain. They appeared glossy despite the smile he wore. "Kain, she's with pup. You're going to be a father."

Strength left Kain, threatening to send him to his knee. The soft voice of Tenebris reminded him of the god's promise to end the bane with Kain and not travel to his child. It filled Kain with joy knowing his line would be continued but saddened him to think he wouldn't live long enough to see them.

Speechless, Kain nodded a thank you to Kyle and returned to Tala. "Are you alright, my love?"

Tala brushed a lock of hair away from her face, averting confusion-filled eyes. "I..I think so. I don't remember much of what happened. It feels like I've been asleep for a long time, but I don't remember why."

Barghast kept his word.

Petting his face, Tala asked Kain why he looked sad. Kain shook his head, smiling.

"It is nothing, sweetheart. I am overjoyed to see you are safe."

A puzzled look crossed Tala's eyes. To take her attention away from him, Kain took her down to the mattress of the bed, pressing her against the sheets with his kisses. He hadn't been able to make love to his mate and worried he may never get the chance to again. He wasn't going to let Barghast's deal ruin his time with her.

Damien waited for Kain in the main living room of the guest house. Kain arrived in the early morning hours following his love-making with Tala. His body ached, his shoulder hurt, but he focused his mind on what Damien would likely assault him with.

"I take it you saw most of what happened? I did my best to keep our channel open."

Damien nodded. "Yeah. How're you doing?"

"My shoulder aches but I am guessing there are more pressing matters you wish to discuss." Kain wondered if Damien knew about the mark on his hand. He'd done his best to block that part of the encounter off to avoid worrying Damien.

The young lycan clenched his fangs, snarling through them. "I..I have something I haven't told you. I know you know already since you've asked about it multiple times."

Kain did a signature lean against the fireplace, arms crossed, eyes locked on Damien.

A few minutes passed before Damien asked Kain if there was any way his mentor would consider staying away from the final fight. The stern look meeting his amethyst gaze bade Damien to give more information. "I saw your death, Kain. In a vision. I know it's stupid of me to ask but would you consider staying here, please? I don't want you to die."

A sigh escaped Kain's nostrils. He suspected Damien's behavior and the fact he tried so hard to hide a corner of his mind had to do with Kain's death. "In truth, I do not expect to survive this either. I haven't for a while now. However, you cannot ask me to let you go in and fight Anthony without me. You saw only what happened through my eyes. You did not see it all. No, Damien. I will not stand by idly."

Pain filled Damien's eyes. He clenched his fists at his sides, shoulders trembling. He couldn't get another word out before Jill came into the room and informed them that Zane had returned. The vampire requested everyone to meet him in the main meeting hall.

Desdemona and Ramona were all in the room as well as Dante, Steele, Magnus and Zane. Gabriel, Cade, Lune, Scott and Tyler all turned their eyes on the three lycans as they entered the room.

Zane took the center of the room. "The time to end this has arrived. First, I want to lay everyone's fear to rest. Nathaniel is dead. Has been for a while."

Kain watched as Lune lowered his eyes to hide tears. Nathaniel was Lune's younger brother and one of the last surviving members of his pack.

Zane continued. "The Don plans on having the Old Blood visit the grand opening of the casino known as Crimson on the outskirts of Great Falls. His original plans were to execute Kain in front of them as a show of power. However, that isn't what worries me most."

"What is then?" Gabriel snapped.

"The Don has gone insane. We've quarantined him for now, but I don't know how long he'll stay that way. We need to get in, kill him and get out without getting killed by the Old Blood. Many of them will want to kill three of you in this room." Zane concluded, deferring to Desdemona.

The vampiress rose to assure the lycans she would do her best to restore the balance of power in lieu of Anthony's demise. Her family would pay for any damages incurred during the battle. What political influence she had would go to cover the events to avoid superstition in the human world.

Zane resumed the floor, informing everyone of their roles they'll play during the infiltration. Zane would take the guards at the front out due to his previous service as a sniper. A small group of lycans would go with Dante and Steele through the front doors once they're clear. Magnus would let another small group of lycans through the cargo bay and make sure whatever reinforcements Anthony might have would be stopped.

When asked when the plan was to happen, Zane responded by saying two days. He'd make sure Anthony remained under surveillance until then and call if anything changed.

Desdemona offered for the lycans to stay at the guest house since it'd be safer than the pack's house and less likely to come under any unwanted eyes and ears.

The plan was risky. The Old Blood hated the Kain line and had a large hand in the murder of Lucius Wolf. Kain made sure he'd be the one to keep Damien and Gabriel close to him.

Following the meeting, Kain went outside to take in the cool breeze and the rising of the moon. His mind swam with memories of blood ridden battlefields, body parts and the gnashing of angry teeth.

Looking at his hands, he couldn't help but curse under his breath.

"Seems like old times and not the good ones, doesn't it?" Jill walked up to turn and lean against the railing of the elevated balcony.

Kain propped up on the railing, his eyes directed at the wood landing. "Too much so, old friend."

Jill sighed, lowering her head. "Kain, I know what you might think but nothing back then was your fault. We were at war. Casualties, both lycan and vampire, were going to happen."

A "tsk" sounded between Kain's clenched fangs. "I held pups, Jillian. Dead pups still attached to their mothers' wombs. I killed my own people both out of mercy and for desertion. To this day, those images haunt me."

Jill's hand on his shoulder helped the lycan soldier to calm down. "I did things too, Alexander. We'll end Anthony and hopefully finally find some peace."

Kain shook his head. Anthony was only a part of the war. Even if they defeated him, Kain knew of another darker war their people suffered unknown to many. Lycans like Lune and Joel screamed for freedom with silenced voices.

"Kain?" Jill said, concerned.

"It is nothing. Go be with Damien. I wish to be alone for a while."

Jill hugged Kain around the shoulders and left him to his thoughts.

An hour later, Kain left the porch to the back of the house to do some personal training to make sure his skills were still sharp enough to face higher vampires. He'd just finished splintering a stack of cement blocks when Damien walked up to him, asking if he needed a partner.

Kain smiled, breathing heavily. "I'll never say no to having a partner."

Damien took his position in front of Kain, dropping to the stance Kain taught him in the meadow at the Circle of Stones.

Kain remained upright, smirking. "You have not forgotten."

"Not a thing. Even when your sorry ass disappeared, I trained daily. I'm much better than I was when you last saw me, old man." Damien snapped a sarcastic reply, his own defiant smirk on his face.

Kain raised a brow. He'd landed Damien on his ass multiple times after the young lycan called him old. Cracking his knuckles, he smirked. "Guess I still need to put a pup like you in your place."

The two began to spar.

To Kain's surprise, Damien managed to block attacks he otherwise couldn't in the past. He threw a punch so quickly, Kain felt the breeze against his cheek. He praised Damien on improving his speed and reading his opponent.

Kain dropped and slammed his elbow into Damien's stomach, sweeping his foot to take Damien's leg out from underneath him. "You're still too slow, my friend. Anthony will be much faster than Lilith and ten times as deadly."

Damien winced as he pulled himself up from the ground. "Kain, are you doing alright? It seems like you're a bit off. I noticed you looking at each of us at the meeting. Do you know what I saw in your eyes?"

Kain raised a brow in confusion, his arms crossing over his chest as he studied his younger friend.

Damien looked away then returned a glare at Kain. "Fear and uncertainty. I've never seen those feelings before in your eyes. I don't want to ever see that again."

Kain's eyes grew wide. He wasn't aware his reserve revealed anything, but he did admit to himself about feeling uncertain about Zane's plan.

Damien rolled his neck and shoulders. "I can understand how you feel. Hell, I'm scared shitless but it's one thing for me. It's another to see it in you. You always seem so damn calm."

"Damien," Kain said.

"I'm not done," Damien interrupted. "These memories. "What are they?"

Kain cursed himself for not being more aware of the mental blocks he used to keep Damien from seeing things he'd rather kept secret. "I would rather not discuss them. Focus on the upcoming fight. If needed, I can train you more before the final battle as I did before."

Damien patted Kain's shoulder, wishing Kain a good night and looking forward to training with his old teacher.

Kain smiled. "Good night, brother."

CHAPTER TWENTY-FOUR

When Kain got back to the bedroom following his talk with Damien, Tala sat on the edge of the bed wearing a black, lace nightgown. On her face she wore make-up Kain never expected to see including deep purple eye shadow and mascara. Her lips radiated a ruby red which she licked while smiling and arching her body forward, her eyes half-lidded.

Kain looked away a moment then back at her with a coy smile.

Tala reached out her arms, hands open to welcome her lover into her embrace. "Are you going to stand there or join me?"

Kain took his time, removing his shirt and strolling towards her, watching her hungry eyes roam over his body. When he got close enough, his mate's cheek came to rest against the crest of his family on his hip. Her nails traced his abs light enough to bring about chill. They moved up to his chest, tracing the scars, stopping when they met the wounds Kyle dressed.

When she looked up at him, mentally asking him what happened, he promised he'd tell her after they'd made love. For the moment, his words appeared to appease his obviously hungry mate.

Tala's tongue ran a path over his lower stomach down to the deep V of his hip, its wet heat driving him wild. All the previous night's concerns melted away into a lust and need he'd been denied earlier that night. The heat of his body made sweat begin to cause his tan skin to glisten in the faint light.

Breathing heavy, Kain found he couldn't speak. His body shivered beneath his lover's tickling. A small gasp erupted from his mouth when she began to unbutton and unzip his jeans.

He gripped her hair, tangling the deep red strands through his fingers. The other ran over the exposed flesh on her shoulder.

"I wanted your attention, my love." Tala's hands caressed Kain's hips and thighs as she led his jeans to the floor, finding he had nothing beneath them.

As he had earlier, Kain lifted Tala's small body onto the bed and proceeded to pin her down with his weight and firm kisses. Moving to his knees, Kain took the fabric of the dress and pulled it above Tala's head, dropping it to the ground. His muscles flexed and relaxed as he fiddled with the clasps of her bra which he tossed aside.

Kain led her to lie back down on the sheets, leaning in close and speaking hot in her ear. "You will always have my attention, my lady."

After removing her panties, Kain let his hands explore every piece of her body. A soft growl emitted through his fangs at the feeling of Tala's hands as they ran over his chest, back and arms. She raised her leg, to rub his hip, her foot running the length of his thigh to his calf.

While Kain moved his attention to her breasts, Tala took his hair in her hands. He felt her wince when he bit her nipple. The sounds Tala made as her nails dug into his back ignited the same carnal desires as the night the wolf inside took over.

Kain allowed his fangs to roll over the skin of his mate's breasts, down her stomach, eventually returning his attention to her eyes. He smiled as he teased her tender opening only for a moment prior to easing inside of her. His hips moved slow, going as deep as he could with each smooth motion.

Tala's body arched, pushing her pelvis against Kain's. Gentle moans and subtle gasps echoed in the dark room. The sting of her nails on his skin and the murmurs in his ear brought the orgasm ever closer.

He could feel the muscles inside of her growing tighter. Kain closed his eyes, his own pleasure almost unbearable. A growl, more wolf than man, came through elongated, clenched fangs.

Feeling she was close to her orgasm, Kain took Tala's lips with his, wrapping his arms around her as he released into her.

Winded, he lay on his side next to her, his head propped up in his hand.

The petite woman rolled to the opposite side. She scooted back to fit perfectly into her lover's sweat-soaked body.

Kain kissed Tala's hair, his hand rubbing her side down to her lower belly. "Tala, there is something you need to know."

Tala looked over her shoulder, her eyes searching Kain's with creased, worried brows.

Kain told her what Kyle told him when he arrived. He came clean about where he'd been the past two days and assured her he was okay, careful to leave out the deal he made with Barghast. The last thing he told her about was Zane's plan to infiltrate Crimson and kill Anthony.

Kain had to move his face to avoid being elbowed when Tala jerked up and away from him. Her eyes burned with anger. "I don't like this plan."

"Tala."

"No, Alex! I nearly lost you. You're putting yourself in front of a vampire who's been driven mad by bloodlust. Did you ever once think about how terrified this makes me?" She slid from the bed and turned her back on Kain.

Sighing, he got up to go join her, placing his hand on her shoulder only to have it shoved off. "I understand your feelings. I would rather not do this either. This must end for the sake of our people. You and our child."

Tala whirled around, her eyes misty with tears as she yelled at him. "Alex, how many times have you almost died? How much of your blood have you spilled for others? For the love of Luna, it's your life!"

Tears streamed down Tala's eyes.

Kain didn't get angry. How could he when he knew what he asked of her. Instead, he took her in his arms. "I have you, our child, my brother. I need you to understand, I am a soldier. I will make sacrifices to make sure those I love are kept safe."

"But, Alex," Tala began.

Kain raised her eyes to look at him. "I will return to you. One way or the other, I will return to both of you."

Tala bit her lower lip then gritted her teeth, shoving him away. "One way or the other? So dead or alive."

"Tala." Kain tried to keep calm for her sake.

Tala darted passed him to the window and threw it open. She jumped out and shifted, running into the forest. Kain could feel her pain, anger and confusion. He sat on the edge of the bed, resting his forearms on his thighs and dropped his head.

Tears stained Tala's muzzle as she ran to the Overlook, staring out into the sea of trees. The thought of losing someone else to Anthony Cardoza made her angry, but she knew of nothing she could do.

A gentle calling in her mind scared her. The voice felt familiar, but Tala couldn't place it. A chilled wind whipped around her, forcing her to close her eyes. When she opened them, a snowy white barn owl stood on a pure white tree in front of her.

"Who are you?" Tala asked the owl, whimpering and stepping back, not knowing why she felt so afraid.

The owl raised its wings. The tips melting into wisps of stars and sky. Tala soon found herself in an area resembling a vast sea of stars. A thick mist ghosted across a ground made of glass. The moon hung in the distance.

Tala pressed her ears against the back of her head.

A woman more beautiful than any Tala had ever seen appeared within the mist. Her thin dress barely hid her slender form. As she walked, the tail of her dress flowed like water over the glass.

When she drew closer, she held out her arms. *"Do you recognize me, now?"*

Tala drew her eyes away. The shame of her half-blood forced her to avoid the woman's eyes while shaking her head.

Luna took Tala's face, smiling. *"There is no need to avert your eyes. You have done nothing wrong. I am Luna, goddess of the night. Welcome."*

Tala whimpered as Luna stroked her fur.

Luna spoke with a gentle voice. *"Your mind is troubled, dear one. Tell me what is wrong."*

"It's Alex. I'm so scared to lose him. I love him more than anyone I've ever known." Tala found herself rambling.

Luna sat on her knees. *"Ah, yes. My dear Alexander. He is our pride and joy. We too have tried to sway him to rest by his forefathers. You must understand, he is a soldier first and foremost."*

Though she knew the answer, Tala asked Luna if she could find some way to dissuade Kain from going to the final battle.

Luna shook her head. *"That is like asking you not to breathe. Alex was bred for battle. It is difficult for him to find his place in this modern day. It is why we gave you to him to be his mate."*

Tala's eyes widened.

"Find peace, dear one. The child in your womb needs you to. Do not fear for Alexander," Luna lowered her eyes. Tala thought she saw a glistening tear fall down the goddess' cheek. *"He is in good hands. Your mate seeks you. Return to him."*

The fight with Tala left Kain feeling stressed. He reached out to her many times through their bond but received no response. Deciding she needed space, he walked through the guest house until he found the kitchen. Cooking always gave Kain a way to focus his stress into something constructive and he knew the pack had to be getting hungry.

He'd only just begun cooking when Damien sauntered through the door. "It smells delicious in here. What're you cooking?"

"Nothing too fancy. A bit of comfort food to help take the tension off. I saw you on the porch. Were you in deep thought?" Kain answered.

Damien took a seat on one of the barstools overlooking a marble bar where Kain cut vegetables. "This fight with Anthony. Is he really able to use the talon?"

"I cannot be sure. Even I do not know its capabilities. You are the first one I've seen who has been able to touch it without being burned."

Damien sighed, his head dropping. "Kain."

"Yes?"

"Do you think we can win this fight, that I'm strong enough?"

"Yes, my alpha. You've grown much stronger in the short year I've known you."

"Seems all I've been doing lately is failing. You, Jill, the pack. I still don't know what I'm capable of."

Kain placed a hand on Damien's shoulder. "None of us know what you are capable of nor have you failed anyone."

A short silence filled the small kitchen before Damien continued. "Were you able to get fat on pheasants and catch up on football?"

Kain burst out laughing. "Sadly, no. I did go to the bar from time to time to watch the games but otherwise, I enjoyed the silence."

"Wait, you. Alexander Kain, go to bars?" Damien asked with a partial snicker.

"Is it so surprising? I drink on occasion too."

"Wow, think you know a guy."

"Indeed." Kain chopped potatoes in front of Damien. The intense look on the young lycan's face prompted to ask Damien if there was something else.

"Yeah. I wanted to go into more detail about the vision I had."

Kain was unnerved. They'd been interrupted when Damien tried to tell Kain about his vision. "Damien, you know you can tell me anything."

Damien described the dream in great detail. He told Kain of how he saw a decorated ground littered with bodies and smeared with blood.

Kain listened as Damien described seeing Anthony but feeling like someone else was inside the vampire's body. This new presence was faster, stronger and capable of taking on at least five lycans on its own. He saw Gabriel, Cade and Scott getting tossed like they were rag dolls.

A sense of darkness and impending doom brought about a subtle shiver in Kain's spine. He could feel the being Damien described as he described it. It was unlike anything he'd ever felt.

"It almost seems obsessed with you, Kain. Through the whole fight, it constantly focuses on you. I don't know why. I feel dazed as I look up but it's the scream of pain I can hear that really terrifies me." Damien stopped when Gabriel came into the room.

CHAPTER TWENTY-FIVE

Gabriel threw his arm around Kain's shoulders. "You two look like you're attending a funeral. Come on, we're about to go into Hell, might as well enjoy ourselves a bit."

Kain sighed. "Gabriel, you have the worst timing."

Damien scoffed, pissed.

"What's his problem?" Gabriel asked.

"At the moment, dear friend, you are," Kain replied, shoving Gabriel's arm off.

Gabriel held up his hands. "As usual, you're right, Kain. Though you still don't know how to enjoy the finer things in life when they're offered. Fine, I'll settle on getting something for dinner."

Kain finished preparing dinner, asking Damien if he might be willing to join him for another sparring lesson before eating. He needed to keep distracted since Tala hadn't returned and he wanted to teach the younger lycan how to fight higher vampires since Lilith hadn't provided a decent example.

Damien agreed and the two went to change into some workout shorts.

Zane met the two of them in the guest house gym Kain found while looking for the kitchen. Upon seeing him, Damien growled, obviously annoyed at the vampire's presence. He asked Kain what Zane was doing there.

"You will need to know how a true vampire fights. Lilith and Stoker were nothing compared to what you could face when we go to Crimson. They are not like lycans. One hit in the right place can stop your heart." Kain replied.

Kain heard the younger lycan swallow a knot in his throat. "Then how the hell do you fight one? I got lucky as fuck in that fight with Lilith."

Kain positioned himself between Damien and Zane. "Calm yourself. Zane is different than the average vampire. Unlike many, he is a warrior. Read his movements and react accordingly."

Zane fists raised in front of his face and chest. "Damien, I was in the Marines before being turned. Not many of the vampire's today can say that. Anthony's thugs are street brawlers who use more intimidation than actual skill. I'm the ideal opponent."

With one look at Kain, Damien made his way into the ring. It soon became obvious that the younger lycan used more energy than needed.

Kain leaned against the glass of a nearby mirror to analyze each fall to the mat so he could build on the flaws and enhance Damien's defensive skills.

Zane danced around Damien, taking him to the ground and blocking his punches and kicks with little effort. When it was obvious the younger lycan couldn't take anymore, Kain ended the session.

"I've seen enough. Thank you, Zane." Kain said, shaking the vampire's hand.

Zane helped Damien to his feet, glaring at him. "Fight like that and you're dead. I expected more from the legendary Kain's student."

Damien lowered his eyes, grinding his teeth. Kain watched the vampire depart the room.

"Fuck!" Damien slammed his fist in the nearest punching bag.

"Damien, calm yourself. I wanted to see how you would handle a one on one with a vampire."

"Yeah, I fucked it up with Lilith too and almost got you killed. Then there's this damn dream." Damien slid down the mirrors to the floor.

Kain leaned against the mirrors next to his friend. "Finish your dream, then I will train you some more. It is best we are both prepared."

A few hours after sparring with Damien, Kain decided he needed some solitude. His heart felt heavy with the revelation Damien's dream gave him.

He made his way to the small garden behind the house under a tree to keep from getting wet.

"May I join you?" The velvet voice of Desdemona Cardoza filled his ears.

When he didn't answer, she sat next to him on the marble bench and held an umbrella over his head. "You seem cold, Alexander. Something you would like to speak about?"

Kain shook his head. He still didn't trust Desdemona after what she told him about his father.

"Your father would be proud of you. So many look up to you and seek your guidance. I wish my people had someone they could see that way." Desdemona purred.

Kain lowered to rest his elbows on his thighs. "I am nothing like my father. He held a sense of honor more powerful than any lycan soldier. I have broken that honor, defiled it."

Desdemona reached out to take his face. Her slender hands cold against his flesh. "You are more than Pentacost. Yes, you made some mistakes. We all have. Yet, you guide Damien and your pack, train them to stand strong in the face of the strongest foes. You should be proud."

Confused, Kain looked into her ruby eyes to find her looking at him as a mother would her son. She caressed his face and leaned in to kiss his forehead.

"Be proud, Alexander Kain. Be strong and I know you will win this battle." She rose to leave.

"Desdemona," The vampiress turned to look at Kain. "Why did you look at me that way?"

The vampiress only smiled a saddened smile before leaving him to go back inside.

The strange encounter with Desdemona left Kain with more stress. His mind grew weary with everything he asked it to handle. A warm shower over his aching body started sounding really nice.

A sense of cold and darkness crept into the back of his mind indicating the arrival of the dark god. *"I grow eager, Alexander. A day remains. Can you feel it? The finality of it all. So close, my forsaken one. So close."*

Kain refused to entertain him. Instead, he kept his mental blocks up so Barghast had no access to his feelings or his thoughts.

The god laughed. *"I must say, that is something I have always found intriguing about you. Holding that cold pride even when you know the outcome. Remain silent, block your emotions and thoughts from me, it matters not. We will see how you fare when you face my pawn."*

A growl vibrated Kain's fangs. Scrubbing a hand down his face, Kain felt grateful when the god finally left.

The sound of a clock almost seemed to reverberate in his mind.

He turned off the water, dressed in his jeans and made his way back out to the room. A knock on his door caught his attention, confusing him. Tala wouldn't have any need to knock.

Opening the door, Kain was surprised to see who stood at his doorway. "You should get some rest, Cade."

The Silent Soldier didn't move. "I rarely ever sleep on the eve of battle, Kain."

The two soldiers stood in silence for a moment. Surprisingly, it was Cade who ended it. "I want to be honest about something."

"What is it?" Kain asked, closing the door.

Cade propped up a wall. "When I first met you, I didn't understand why so many of our people seemed to be drawn to you. I hated you and wanted nothing more than to find a way to force you down a few rungs."

Kain had to fight back a chuckle. He knew Cade felt threatened by him the moment they met.

Before he could reply, Cade continued, averting his eyes to look into Kain's. "Then I got to know you. It all made sense after that. You guide them, offer them a rock when they don't have one, direction when they get lost.

Holt spoke so highly of you, regarded you with great respect. Looking at them now, 1 understand."

Kain didn't know how to respond. To him, Cade seemed to be as much of a rock as he was.

To hear him say such things about him, Kain offered a slight bow of his head. "It is an honor to hear that from the Silent Soldier. Thank you, Cade."

Cade said nothing else but offered what resembled a smile, opened the door and left the room.

Kain caught her scent, turning to see Tala standing with her hands clasped in front of her naked body. Relief replaced worry when her eyes met his.

"Alex, I--" Kain's arms around her stopped the words Tala wanted to say.

He stroked her hair, making sure she knew he wasn't angry with her. He was grateful to find her safe and glad to be holding her again. He decided he wanted to spend the night next to her, making love when it suited them.

They didn't fall asleep in bed until the wee hours of the morning.

A surprise call from Zane came shortly after Kain finally got his mind quiet enough to get to sleep. Desdemona was moving them into Great Falls the eve of the final plan was to be enacted. Kain would have to tell Tala goodbye and hope she wouldn't get angry at him.

As Zane said, the day before the plan was to be enacted, Zane, Magnus, Steele, and Dante met Kain, Damien, Jill, Gabriel, Lune and Cade in Great Falls. Desdemona arranged for them to stay in one of the hotel rooms set aside for the vampire nobles when they came to visit.

It surprised Kain to see how many humans knew the vampires and welcomed them. He kept close to Damien when his eyes met one of the older vampires he knew would recognize him.

Kain heard Damien ask Zane how often humans chose to willingly serve vampires despite knowing what they were.

Zane replied. "Times are changing. There are those who most likely know what you are as well. This hotel is widely used by the rich, many of who are vampires or lycans. We'll be in Desdemona's suite. As we said, the Cardoza's hold strong presence in Great Falls. Darius ran many of the local casinos or managed hotels like this."

The arrival of Emeline and Magdeline halted Lune in his tracks. Kain could see his body grow rigid the minute he laid eyes on the blonde vampire.

"Easy, Lune. Stay close to me." Kain reassured his fellow lycan.

"Well, well. This is a shock," Emeline smiled, taking Zane's waist and kissing him. "Hey baby. Strange company you're keeping nowadays."

Zane wiped her kiss from his mouth. "They're here as Desdemona's guests. I'm merely showing them her room."

Emeline rolled her eyes, scoffing. "Of course you are. So loyal to your lady aren't you. I couldn't care less. Are you going to greet the nobles at Crimson's grand opening?"

Kain watched Zane, analyzing each movement he made. From the way the vampire acted, he could tell Zane was less than inclined to let Emeline touch him but allowed it regardless.

The dark-haired vampire made her way over to Kain. "Glad to see you're alright, Kain."

Kain turned his head when she leaned into his ear.

Emeline nipped his ear and licked along his jaw. "Miss you, lover."

"Back away, Emeline." Kain warned, careful to keep his body between Lune, Damien and the vampires.

Emeline scoffed. She walked away, pinching Kain's butt to spite him.

Magdeline blew a kiss to Lune and joined her sister.

"Do they know what's going on?" Damien questioned.

"I have no doubt but as you know, Emeline's family despises the Cardozas. Even if she did suspect something, she will not try to stop it. It would please her to see their dynasty in control," Kain replied.

"What's the history between you two?"

Kain refused to reply. He turned his attention to Lune, asking if he was alright.

Lune nodded, taking deep breaths. "Fine. Just need a moment."

The low rumble of thunder in the distance proclaimed the arrival of yet another thunderstorm. In the hallway containing the elevators, Kain couldn't help but stare at Zane and wonder why the vampire seemed so uneasy.

He placed his hand on Zane's shoulder. "Are you alright?"

Zane said nothing but nodded while pressing the button indicating their floor.

The hallway of the hotel was lined with black wallpaper with decorative red rose patterns swirling at the bottom of the paper. The floor held the same pattern only with flecks of silver woven within the petals.

The fresh scent of vampire lingered within the air, its presence making Kain's sense of protection grow stronger. He kept as close to Damien as possible while Gabriel and Cade swiveled their eyes at each room.

"We're here," Zane commented while opening two large double doors to reveal a rather spacious room. "The event isn't until tomorrow night. Try to keep a low profile until then. You have Desdemona's protection but don't assume it keeps you safe from the occasional troublemaker. Room service is available so feel free to order what you want."

"You can count on it," Gabriel said, plopping down on one of the beds. "This is going to be sweet."

Kain could only shake his head at how infantile his friend acted. Cade rolled his eyes and took his place next to the door like some bouncer at a club.

Lune placed himself in the chair next to the window. Jill kept close to Lune.

With nothing more to say, Zane departed the room to leave the lycans to settle in.

"Kain, a minute?" Damien asked in a low voice.

Kain joined the alpha on the far side of the room.

"I have a bad feeling about this."

"About what, Damien?"

"This whole thing. I don't want what happened to you the night before the fight with Lilith to happen again," The young lycan ran his hand through his dark hair, hand on his hip. "I don't want Jill to get hurt again."

Kain looked out of the window at the city lights. The world looked beautiful from the height of the suite. "As I have said to you before, the struggle to survive is the life of both lycan and vampire. I do not know how this will turn out, but I do not believe we will lose. There is too much at stake."

CHAPTER TWENTY-SIX

The night their plan was to be enacted, Kain took a moment to call Tala and check to see how she was doing and to hear her voice for what could be his final time. She spoke highly of how Joel did what he could to take care of her to repay Kain for his kindness.

Kain smiled, shocked at the subtle hint of jealousy he felt to learn another lycan was caring for his mate in his stead. He had to choke back the rising unease he felt in his gut to continue talking to her. "Are you sleeping well?"

"It's been hard. Your scent is so strong I must keep some hint of composure just to relax into your side of the bed. Come home to me, Alex. I don't know if I could handle losing you." Kain could hear the tears she held back on the other side of the speaker.

The desperation in her voice almost made Kain crush the phone. He wanted so badly to tell her he would return to her but the nagging in the back of his mind seemed to indicate the contrary. "I will do my best, my love. Until then, I will try to reach out when I can. Keep your mind open for me."

"Always do. Joel just arrived with dinner."

"Go eat. I will text you when I can."

"Okay. Talk to you soon, babe. Good night."

Kain hung up the phone and looked out at the bright face of his mother peeking through the dark clouds. Her silence left him feeling unnerved at what he knew to be coming.

A familiar, yet unwanted scent invaded his nose, bringing about a low growl from the pit of his throat. The wolf inside of him wanted nothing more than to deal with the newly arrived vampiress.

"What are you doing here, Emeline?" Kain said, keeping angry eyes focused on the sky.

"How rude," Emeline strutted up to him, running her fingers over his butt. "And here I was going to offer my assistance."

The lycan couldn't help but tense at the audacity of her touch. Had this been earlier in the Wars he would've broken her hand and ripped her head off without hesitation.

"You're planning to end Cardoza, isn't it so, Kain?" Emeline whispered, blowing heated air into Kain's ear.

Kain glared at the vampiress, daring her to challenge him. "What of it?"

Emeline held her hands up defensively. "Easy, handsome, I have no intention of getting in your way. I'd love nothing more than to see the Don of Great Falls' reign come to an end. Tell you what, I'll even offer you some additional help, what do you say?"

Caution and years of experience with vampires, kept Kain's suspicion high. "I would assume such information or help would not be free."

She gripped his hips and pulled him to her. "Come to dinner with me. Just a simple outing. It's been so long since we've seen one another. I know you have feelings for me, Kain. I know you enjoyed our night together."

Despite wanting to throw her from him, Kain knew how to be cunning. He'd use Emeline's lust for him against her. His thumb ran the length of her lower lip, stroking her fangs and making her moan. "Just dinner?"

Emeline's scent indicated to him she was indeed aroused at how close he was. Kain backed her against a concrete pillar and leaned in close enough he could kiss her if he so chose.

Her breath hastened as she reached for him just to have him back away.

"Never again, vampire. If you want to help, do so out of your hatred for Cardoza but leave your lust for what never existed out of it." He turned on his heel and walked away with her hissing behind him.

It was three hours before sunset when the lycans met Zane outside of Crimson where Kain had been at only three short days earlier. The drive remained silent with everyone except Damien and Jill riding in Gabriel's car since the guards at the gate would likely recognize Kain's. They pulled the vehicles up behind some construction equipment to avoid detection.

"Take these." Zane handed the lycans each an ear piece like those security details wore to keep in touch.

"Great, now I feel like the equivalent of James Bond," Gabriel commented.

Kain rolled his eyes, inserting the small rubber bud in his ear, making it itch. No doubt his wolf skin would have fun trying to maintain it.

No sooner had he done so that Dante's voice crackled over the small speaker. The vampire warned his comrades something was seriously wrong with the complex.

When Zane asked why, Steele warned them it was too quiet and that no guards patrolled the gate or the outer perimeter.

It didn't take long for Kain to catch the scent of fresh blood over the breeze. From the way his fellow lycans reacted, he could tell each of them caught it too.

Zane instructed Steele to take a quick look to try and get a feel as to what was going on before sending the lycans in. Steele's reply came as a shock when he said he couldn't see anything or anyone from his vantage point in the loading bay. Magnus reported the guards' station at the front gate lay completely empty.

"The plan hasn't changed. We still split into groups. Kain, Damien, Gabriel and I will go in the front. Magnus, Steele, Jill and Cade will enter from the back. Keep in touch and do not shift until we know what's going on." Zane said, his southern drawl making some of the words hard to fathom.

Kain could see Damien didn't like the idea of splitting from his mate. Jill kissed him, assuring him she would be fine. Kain was grateful not to have to kick Damien himself.

They split into their groups and kept close to the ground until they came to the front gate. Magnus had fallen back to his position at Zane's orders. True enough, the guards' station was empty.

Using his elbow, Zane smashed in the window and hit the button to let them inside.

Not a sound echoed from inside the doors despite the line of limos and fancy cars lining the concrete driveway. Zane shouldered the slightly ajar doors open and looked around, nodding to Kain when he saw nothing. Kain went through, his ears, eyes and nose tasting, listening and watching for anything strange.

A heavy scent of blood, both vampire and human invaded his nostrils. He held his arm in front of Damien to stop him while Kain motioned for Gabriel to go around the other side of the slot machines still covered with plastic. Zane remained in the rear in case of an ambush.

"The hell is going on here?" Damien whispered to Kain.

"I cannot be sure. We should have seen something by now." Kain slid down the row of slot machines until he could get a glimpse at the showroom floor.

The sight that met his eyes horrified him.

Bodies of the vampire nobles, the guards, guests and staff lay strewn around the show floor. Each of them appeared to have had their bodies maimed and their throats torn out. Smears of blood lined the once black wallpaper. It looked like a scene out of a slasher movie.

"Okay, I reiterate. What the hell is going on here?" Damien commented, just as surprised as Kain was.

Kain didn't reply. The hairs on the back of his neck prickled at the realization the group was being watched. From the other side of the room, Magnus and his group came out of one of the doors beneath the stairs. Each one had eyes so wide, Kain saw the whites of their eyes.

A whoosh of plastic behind Kain took his attention from the blood bath. He barely had time to bring his arms up in defense before getting slammed by something huge and strong enough to send him through the air and into the bar.

"Kain!" Damien cried out.

A dual-toned, sinister sigh echoed in the room. The sound of claws gripping stone and the skittering of talons across the floor alerted the lycans and vampires to the beast in the large room. *"I can smell your blood. Have I finally found you?"*

Kain got up groaning from the shattered glass on the bar floor. His dazed head made it hard for him to use the bar to help support him as he stood. He reached up to find a small cut, blood dripping down the side of his face. The words the voice spoke didn't remind him of Anthony. They were smoother, like the voice of a vampire with older blood.

Whatever hit him wasn't an average vampire. Its strength and speed hadn't been like anything he'd ever experienced. Another whoosh of air filled the room. Only this time, at the top of the grand show room stairs, Kain could see a fully transformed vampire. Red and black blood coated its fangs and claws.

Damien ran up to Kain as he leapt over the bar. "Are you okay?"

"Fine, Damien. I do not think that is Anthony."

Damien's brows creased. "Neither do I. I sense a deeper malice. Something darker and more powerful. Anthony's shoved the talon in the thumbnail of his wing. Kain, I think something's taken over and it isn't Barghast."

Kain agreed.

The mysterious vampire inhabiting Anthony's body looked bored, almost disappointed as he strolled down the stairs in a manner of the older blood of vampires. *"I have no interest in any of you. I only seek him. His blood is here, and I only want to fight him."*

Him? Kain thought. Nothing this vampire said made any sense. He didn't seem interested in anything going on.

As he suspected, Kain could sense whatever took over Anthony burning through its energy much too fast. At the rate he consumed his host, the fight wouldn't last long.

Kain shifted to his full lycan form and took off into a sprint, sliding across the floor and stopping in front of a newly shifted Gabriel. Damien joined him shortly after.

The vampire looked at all three of them, his eyes moving back to Kain. *"You. It is you. It has been so long."*

In the blink of an eye, the vampire closed the distance between him and Kain, grabbing him by the injured shoulder and hurling him across the room.

Damien and Gabriel latched onto the monster who seemed focused primarily on Kain. They struggled to hold on to him despite them both being in their full lycan form and soon found themselves thrown like paper dolls.

"Leave. I have no quarrel with you." "Anthony" circled around Kain and grabbed him around the arms, raising Kain roaring from the ground in protest.

The vampire's squatty muzzled inhaled Kain's scent. *"Why do you not fight me as you did that day?"* He bit down on the space between Kain's shoulder and throat, using the lycan's body to hurl him, tearing the flesh and bone away.

The excruciating pain threatened to send Kain to his knees. Stars flooded his vision as he tried to ignore the massive blood loss he was enduring. If he fell, he knew none of his pack would survive.

Through the blurring vision, Kain saw Damien and Gabriel struggling against whoever this was. Even Cade, who stood just as large as the creature had a hard time holding onto him, let alone hurt him.

Kain forced himself to his feet just as Zane launched into the beast, forcing it back and tumbling over the stairs amidst the body of the fallen nobles.

Nothing made the vampire angry.

He only seemed annoyed and swatted his enemies away like flies. Kain thought of his father's last moments of life. He began to wonder if the talon held the essence of the monster who killed Pentacost. Anthony had unleashed it when he bonded with the talon.

Kain reached out to his fellow lycans telepathically. *This is not a normal vampire. Do not fight him as one. The talon is burning through his energy. Focus on forcing him to expel it and eventually he will not be able to fight.*

They made sure he knew they understood and shifted their strategy. Each focused on attacking and retreating behind the isles of slot machines.

The change in tactics agitated their opponent.

"Enough!" The vampire screeched at the top of his lungs. He focused his eyes on Damien. *"You. He cares for you."*

Slowed from the wound in his neck and the various injured he'd taken in Damien's place, Kain didn't have time to react to save his friend. He leapt on top of the slot machines, their aluminum tops crunching beneath the weight. The vampire stood with the talons of his feet planted on Damien's head.

"I have had enough. You will fight me, Pentacost or the Purifier dies."

Kain froze. The comments about blood all began to make sense. He'd been mistaken for his own father. *"I am not Pentacost. He died centuries ago. Let Damien go."*

"You lie!" The vampire sneered.

Kain swore he wasn't lying, calling out to Cade and Jill through their link. The lycans lunged at the vampire and held him fast while Kain asked Zane and Magnus to help them.

They held the struggling, screeching beast while Kain scaled the wall and punched it as hard as he could where the cement cracked. He called to the vampires to take shelter as the first light of the morning shone through, striking the monster in the shoulder. Its screeches of pain hurt Kain's sensitive ears.

The monster threw the lycans from his body and on mighty wings took to the air and flew towards Kain.

Seeing him, Kain dropped to the ground, stumbling from fatigue.

Before it could strike, Damien gripped the vampire's claws in glowing silver claws. His lips drew back over his fangs as he stood above Kain, protecting him. *"I won't let you hurt him anymore. I don't care who you are. Leave Kain alone!"*

Burning flesh sizzled from the vampire's claws. He lifted Damien into the air, spun around and threw the lycan into the far wall of the casino.

"Kain, we don't have much fight left in us. Zane and the other vampires can't fight in the sun. We need a plan!" Gabriel yelled over the link as he helped Jill to her paws.

With heavy breath, his own strength failing, Kain gave one more call to Cade. He needed the Silent Soldier to hold the vampire still so Kain could get a hold of it.

As tired as all of them were, he knew their opponent couldn't fight much longer either. Anthony's body was falling apart, he'd been burned by the sun and held off four vampires and four lycans.

Cade did what was asked of him and gripped the vampire in a choke hold. Kain had only seconds to get across the room and grip the creature's top jaw.

What are you doing, Kain?! Damien yelled.

Kain ignored him.

Taking the monster's top and lower jaw in his clawed hands, he pulled the hinges apart as far as he could, spun around until his back was against Cade's, pulling as hard as he could. The top of the vampire's skull came free, its tongue lulling, its body dropping to the ground and turning to ash.

From the ashes, Kain picked up the talon, handing it to Damien who made his way over to them.

Damien took it, his concerned eyes meeting Kain's. "Why are you?"

Kain smiled a weak smile and shifted back. His knees gave way and he fell only to be caught by Damien. "My body is broken. Destroy it so no one else can use it."

"Kain, no!" Damien pleaded.

Gabriel, Jill and Cade joined Damien.

Kain's body began to shiver. "I have..done all I can. You must let me go."

Damien choked. "I can't. I gave you my word. I wanted to save you."

Kain smiled. "You have. The bane is broken. I was the last. My child will be free. Thank you, brother."

With his final breath, the last of the Kain line passed away from his injuries.

CHAPTER TWENTY-SEVEN

Kain opened his eyes to a familiar darkness. The air around him smelled stagnant but felt cold against his skin. It didn't take long for him to realize where he'd fallen. The realm of the dark god lie all around, only this time Kain wouldn't be escaping from it.

Barghast stepped out of the darkness. His large form towering above the lycan who did his best to avoid looking into the searing eyes full of pride. The heat from the ash rising from his thick, black fur caused beads of sweat to form on Kain's brow. *"At last."*

Kain looked back at his family, his eyes saddened to leave them but relieved he'd ended the fight and spared his mate from Barghast's wrath. He walked towards Barghast and scowled at him through tired eyes.

The god grinned. *"There it is, that defiance I adore in you. It will be sweeter when I break you. You look tired, Kain. Let my shadows send you into a deep sleep. My slave for eternity."*

Four months Later
(40 years in the planes of the gods)

"Barghast!" A voice boomed, shattering the black plane like glass. Beams of pure light pierced the void as Solaris walked through the retreating gloom.

Barghast made sure to hide Kain, ordering him to stay silent while he went to deal with the sun goddess. Through shadow-veiled eyes, Kain made out the radiant glow of the goddess who swore to save him from the dark god's vengeance.

"To what do I owe the visit from the Lady of the Sun?" Barghast presented his best face, most likely to avoid further angering the goddess.

"Return to me what you have stolen, Shadow King. You have no claim to him!"

Barghast hissed through his fangs. *"I stole nothing, Sun Queen. He and I made a bargain."*

Solaris chided Barghast, telling him the deal he proposed was undone the moment the dark god asked for the sacrifice of a soul. Surrendering it was an act of the utmost selflessness.

"He shed innocent blood. Blood of his own kind. He blasphemed his gods when he rebelled against a pact made by his family. The Kain line's honor died the moment he forsook it and fled. You know the time of which I speak!"

Kain flinched at the judgmental words. He remembered screaming at his father, telling him he no longer considered the Kain line his family and refused to offer himself up to be butchered like they did. He'd rebelled against lycan law and slept with vampires.

Solaris reached out her hand, ordering silence. *"I have not forgotten. What you fail to recall is who his mother was. Pentacost too defiled lycan law and sired a child from the womb of a vampire."*

The impact of the goddess' words hit Kain like a ton of bricks.

Solaris continued by illuminating the terms of war and how ludicrous Barghast's pact was. She ordered him, again, to give her what rightfully belonged to her.

Barghast growled. *"I will not relinquish what is rightfully mine. Alexander Kain is mine and none of you will take him from my hands."*

The sun goddess shook her head. Her eyes melancholy. *"You have grown so dark. The sun on the lycan's shoulder brands him as my soldier. Be gone or my light will burn away your darkness."*

Despite his anger, Barghast smirked. He raised his claw, raising Kain's chained soul from the depths of the shadows, dropping him onto the floor of the plane.

Solaris gasped.

Making her way to Kain she knelt and brushed his long dirty-blonde hair from his face. A scruffy, unkempt beard covered the lycan's face. His once copper skin now lacked color or firm muscle it once did. She stroked Kain's face.

"It has been forty of our years, Solaris. Did you think a soul could handle being tormented so long and not be damaged?" Barghast laughed in victory.

Solaris took Kain in her arms. *"You will pay for this, Shadow King. I give you my word."*

Tala couldn't hold them back any longer. The pain of seeing her lover's body covered by a blanket and laid to rest in the newly built shed behind the house tore at her heart.

It'd been four months since the fight at the Crimson casino in Great Falls. No one told her any details about how Kain was killed until she begged Jill to tell her.

Downstairs, she heard Gabriel screaming at Damien over why they weren't allowed to give her mate the rest he deserved.

"This is insane, Damien! We should be giving him a proper burial, not leaving him to rot in your dusty shed!" Gabriel yelled.

Damien's voice was less boisterous but still angry. "Gabriel, I told you, we can't. I can't. Dammit, I hate this as much as you do! Don't you think I want to give Kain the rest he deserves?!"

"What I think is you're feeling guilty because once again he got hurt saving your stupid ass! I warned him you would be nothing but trouble!" Gabriel retorted.

Unable to take anymore, Tala stormed down the stairs, her hand on the small bump just barely visible beneath her shirt. "Stop it!" She yelled.

Jill was the first to her feet. "Tala, I'm sorry you heard that."

Tala pushed Jill away. "Damien, please tell me why we can't we give Alex the burial he deserves? I can't see him like that anymore!"

Damien lowered his head, his eyes closed tight. "Because I was told not to."

Everyone in the room gasped.

"The fuck are you saying?" Gabriel snarled.

The younger lycan raised his head, his brow furrowed in frustration as he repeated himself.

"By who?" Tala asked through streaming tears.

"The gods," Damien replied.

Gabriel growled through extended fangs and grabbed Damien by the shirt. "Fuck them! Kain gave everything for them and they turned their back on him! I'm giving my friend the rest he deserves."

Damien positioned his body between Gabriel and the back door. His eyes warned Gabriel he wouldn't let him do what he wanted.

Jill grabbed Tala just as the fight began.

"Damn it, Damien!" Gabriel dropped and gripped Damien around the waist and threw him to the floor. The larger lycan tried swinging at Damien only to have his fist caught and find himself kicked off Damien's chest.

The two brawled throughout the house and eventually out into the yard where they shifted into full lycan form and continued fighting.

Tala and Jill stood on the porch, watching.

Tala wondered if she should try to stop them. Jill stopped her. "No. They both need this. Kain was very dear to them. Losing him is causing the tension to finally surface."

"This is all your fault! I know what he did for you! He was almost dead from all those years he took hell for me!" Gabriel howled, running at the white lycan and slashing across his face.

"So, it was you. You were Kain's original charge." Damien dodged another hit then countered with one of Kain's round house kicks.

"I wasn't only his charge. He dug me out of holes I never thought I could escape from. He got me out of trouble when I thought my father would kill me! You will never know how agonizing this loss is for me!" Gabriel gripped Damien's claws, digging his nails into the dirt.

Tala's heart grew heavier the longer the fight went on, she couldn't watch anymore, left Jill and went into the shed, closing the door. Candlelight flickered in the small space. The only vigil for a fallen soldier.

The heavy scent of her lover's skin filled her nostrils, further deepening the pain she felt.

Suddenly, she screamed, covering her mouth. The commotion ended the fighting in the yard and Damien, Gabriel and Jill all pushed into the shed.

Damien gasped. "This isn't possible. Where's his body?"

Gabriel, a look of shock on his face, shook his head. "I.. I don't know."

Jill looked out of the window. "This makes no sense. There's no blood, clothing or footprints. No scent. Damien, what's going on?"

Damien shook his head. "Jill, I don't know. Who would want to steal his body?"

Gabriel snarled. "He made many enemies. Some blood-sucker might've wanted to dis-honor him."

Joel came in, nearly falling back and catching himself with his back foot. "What in Sun's hell? Where's?"

All three lycans answered "I don't know" at the same time. Tala had her head laid against the empty table, fiddling with the green blanket still permeated with her lover's blood and scent.

The young lycan averted his attention. "I miss him too, but I came up here to let you know Zane is here."

"The hell does that parasite want?" Gabriel barked, crossing his arms over his chest.

"Fang off, Gabriel. Zane did a lot for us against Anthony." Jill snapped.

The vampire walked through the door, stopping with a shocked expression the minute he saw the bed. He took Damien full fisted by the shirt collar, demanding to know where Kain's body was.

When Damien told Zane he didn't know, the vampire's eyes began glowing a burning amber.

Zane's fangs ground against themselves. "First, I get told you refused to honor him with a soldier's burial. Now, I'm hearing you don't know where his body is? Your incompetence is staggering at this point, Pierce!"

Tala took Zane's arm in hers. "Zane, please. No more. I can't take anymore. I'm so upset already."

Calming himself, Zane lowered Damien to the floor. "I'm sorry. You shouldn't be dealing with this much strain in your condition. Who would do this?"

Gabriel scoffed at him. "One of your kind is my guess."

Zane returned Gabriel's sarcasm with some of his own. "Were it one of my kind, I would be able to sense them. I don't smell any foreign lycans either."

A whisper in the back of Tala's mind took her from the room. She followed the voice out into the back yard where a familiar white owl sat upon a branch.

Silver tears fell down its face.

Tala pleaded with the goddess to tell her where her mate was. *"Be patient, dear one. Alexander is in good hands. In three days' time, go to the place in the forest where he found you. Wait for him there."*

Tala attempted to ask Luna what she meant, but the owl took to the sky until Tala could no longer see her small shape.

A cold drop of rain fell from a leaf onto Kain's cheek. He opened his eyes to find himself standing in the same forest he'd been in before. Only this time he wasn't alone.

Pentacost sat on a rock looking down at his son. "It's good to see you again, my son."

Kain greeted his father, holding back none of the frustration he felt after hearing Solaris' words regarding his parents.

Pentacost offered a nod and stood. "I can imagine you have any number of questions but now is not the time."

"Honor me one. You owe me at least one." Kain demanded.

Pentacost sighed. "Is it about your mother?"

"Tell me who she is. Why have you never told me she was a vampire? I have a right to know, father!" Kain could feel the same anger from the time he'd yelled at his father.

"Alexander, leave it alone. What does it matter who your mother was? You are being given a second chance. A life free from the bane."

"Pentacost, tell me who my mother was." Kain growled through elongated fangs.

Pentacost turned around to answer but didn't receive the chance before Solaris arrived. He embraced his son. "Looks like I lack the time. Alexander, let the past rest where it is. I was only to watch over you until she arrived. I am so proud of you. Hold your head high and forgive me for failing you."

Kain's eyes and heart softened. He returned the embrace, forgiving his father and telling him Kain loved him.

Pentacost nodded and walked across the small brook to join the rest of his family in the afterlife.

Solaris held out her hand. *"Are you ready to return home, Alexander?"*

Despite being confused, Kain's heart leapt with joy.

Solaris nodded. *"I will give you a week to get certain promises fulfilled and to be with your mate. Then you are to leave."*

Kain felt like he got hit in the stomach. Nausea nearly took his legs out from under him. "My goddess, have I not given enough? Where am I to go? For what purpose?"

Solaris took his face in her hands. *"There are those who cannot become what they must be with you so near. Others who could use such strength in their darkened hours of need. We have heard their prayers and are sending you to help them."*

Kain mulled the words in his mind. Realization overtook him as to who she meant and what she wanted him to do. He bowed to her in respect. "Yes. I am a soldier, I will go where I am ordered to march."

The goddess' face became stern, her voice demanding. *"Go, Alexander Kain. Your body has been repaired, your soul will find its place. Be with your lover and wait for the dream I will send you."*

CHAPTER TWENTY-EIGHT

Three Days Later

Another drop of rain from the canopy of the forest dropped on Kain's face waking him. The wind felt cool on his skin, causing him to shiver from its gentle kiss. His muscles stitched, his joints popped from the stiffness as he tried to rise.

All around he could hear the soft songs of the woods. The smell of fresh grass and lush green of the forest wafted in his nostrils. He took a deep breath with a smile on his face as he picked up her scent.

He looked around until his blurring vision fell upon the eyes of his lover. Unable to contain his excitement, Kain embraced her thick neck, not caring he had no clothing on. His hands tangled in the strands of deep red fur, caressing its softness.

She returned his affection with gleeful whimpers and licking the side of his face before shifting back and embracing him. Her lips placed tender kisses down the length of his neck to his shoulder, returning to his mouth, tasting him.

Kain broke their kiss when his eyes fell upon his arms to find there were no scars. Confused, Kain let his eyes drift over his bare chest. The crest of his family still adorned his hip but the angry scars once present on his chest and stomach were nowhere to be seen. He felt as though he'd never experienced the curse, his strength full yet foreign to him since he'd been so weak for so long.

For the moment, he relished feeling the strength of his youth over five-hundred years ago. He wanted nothing more than to stay with Tala in the forest.

He found a hollow to serve as a den where they could stay until Solaris called him to leave. It made Kain feel good to once again rely on his survival skills and relish the quiet of the forest.

Tala brought him a backpack full of clothes after Luna appeared to her in a dream to show her where she needed to go to find Kain. It included his favorite Sherpa jacket, a new pair of distressed blue jeans, and the metal necklace Desdemona gave him.

It reminded him he needed to go see the vampiress before he left so he could find the resting place of his father and hopefully learn more about how Pentacost got there.

I guess staying in the forest for the whole week is out of the question. Kain sighed. He served dinner for them and retired to the hollow where Kain spent most of the night making love to his mate, strengthening their bond.

During one of the sessions, Tala asked Kain if he was feeling okay. With a melancholy smile as his only answer, Kain kissed his mate's mouth like she was his only connection to the living world. He let his hands run over her breasts, her belly and sides, returning to splay across her lower belly where he planted a gentle kiss.

Kain rubbed the small mound his mate developed while he was away. "I ask you to come with me tomorrow. I'd like you to meet someone."

Tala ran her hand through Kain's hair, inquiring who he meant.

A sigh escaped Kain, his eyes drawn down to almost closing. "My father. Desdemona brought his remains here to the States and has promised to show me where he's buried."

The following morning, Kain phoned Zane to see if the vampire would mind bringing him his car. Zane greeted his friend, elated and confused how he'd returned.

Kain refused to answer and once again requested his car.

When asked by Zane why Kain hadn't called Damien or Gabriel, Kain informed him he'd contact them when the time was right. He wanted to be with Tala and take care of some things before having to leave.

Zane's voice on the other side of the phone stayed silent briefly before he seemed to understand what Kain meant. Zane would bring Kain's car to the Woods Edge. Kain thanked him and hung up the phone. He packed the backpack with the clothes Tala brought him, his phone and what little breakfast remained, which he gave to Tala.

Through their hike to the Woods Edge, Kain supported Tala when she began to get winded, letting her sit to rest when she needed.

Guilt weighed heavy on his heart at keeping the fact he needed to leave from Damien and Gabriel. They'd be angry and possibly hurt not knowing but Kain wanted to be with Tala and enjoy some time away from pack pressure. He knew Damien would either plead with him to stay as beta or probe him to find out where Kain was going.

As promised, Kain's car waited at the Woods Edge, its engine running and Zane leaning against the pure black finish.

Kain laughed, reaching out to take Zane's paw and shaking it firmly. "You must tell me how you manage this one day. First Anthony's coven, now here."

Zane giggled, returning Kain's handshake and pulling him into a bro hug. "Semper Fi, my friend. Were you ever a Marine, you'd be a damned good one. I wouldn't want anyone else watching my back."

The two veterans smacked each other on the shoulder and parted. Zane got on a deep blue 2017 Kawasaki Concours motorcycle, revved its engine and sped off.

Kain and Tala got into his car and pulled off in the direction of Great Falls. The drive wasn't long but still Kain instructed Tala to try and get some rest. He wanted her at her best when they got to Desdemona's coven.

Desdemona met Kain and Tala as he pulled up the half-moon driveway of her coven. Her smile lit like a beacon across her face when she saw them, welcoming them with open arms.

Kain remained leery since the fight with Anthony ended in his untimely demise but for some reason he trusted Desdemona and her daughter. He walked Tala up the steps, returning Desdemona's greeting.

It stunned him when the vampiress embraced him, forgetting propriety and crying. "When Zane told me of your death, I stood beside myself with grief. Then he told me you had returned. I will not ask how this is possible. Know I am beyond elated, my heart full with happiness to see you safe."

The lycan didn't say anything.

"Come, he is this way." Desdemona gestured to lead them towards the backyard gardens where a lavishly ornate fountain stood in the middle of a cobblestone walkway.

All around, hedges lined with wild berries and blooms sent pleasant smells through the air, adding to the peace of the trickling water. Willow trees blew in the breezes of the night, their long, green tendrils showing signs of budding for the spring.

Beside Kain, Tala sighed happily, nuzzling his arm and winding her fingers through his. He could feel how relaxed she was at the beauty of the gardens.

For once, he too felt completely calm in his soul, away from Damien.

Desdemona led them deep into the gardens until they arrived at a small concrete building decorated with stone wolves. They were rearing on their back legs, chest out with pride, fangs snarling against any enemy who threatened to disturb the fallen soldier sleeping inside. "This is where I had him laid to rest. His remains have been placed in a large stone coffin engraved with his name."

Kain's breath left his lungs in such a way, it seemed he'd been punched. The faint scent of his father seeped through the stone, his influence powerful enough that Kain could almost sense him. "May I go inside?"

Desdemona nodded, producing a golden skeleton key and placing it in the lock, turning it and opening the door. It bore the Kain family crest of the heraldic wolf and shield.

He didn't understand why but when the door opened, Kain hesitated to go inside.

Tala's soft words of reassurance helped nudge him in the direction of the gaping door. Both sides of the crypt displayed flickering candles and the smell of incense.

"I come in here quite often," Desdemona said as she led them through the short corridor.

It didn't take long for Kain's eyes to fall on the stone coffin lying in the center of a small room where all four corners portrayed the same stone wolves as the outside. Tears stung his eyes while he ran his hand over the smooth stone of the coffin.

His father's spirit radiated from it so strongly, Kain could almost hear the clashing of swords. Vivid memories of his father's plated armor forming over strong muscles played in Kain's mind. A roar so intimidating it froze battlefields and sent enemies fleeing echoed in the room.

Kain recalled the moment when he'd seen retreating lycans turn on their heels when his father dawned two shields and sprinted through a line of vampires. The sound of battle cries rallying to Pentacost as he leapt over the head of a horse, tearing it off and taking a vampire noble to the ground made Kain smile.

To Kain, Pentacost appeared untouchable. He had such power, many believed he should have been made king.

Fantasy came crashing down when memories of his father limping towards him replaced the powerful lycan he wanted to remember.

"His sword and armor, do you have them?" Kain asked Desdemona, trying not to stutter.

Desdemona nodded. "I do. They are both buried with his remains."

Kain took the metal necklace out of his pocket. He ran his thumb over the shield shaped pendant, hurting at what he was about to do. "I wish to add this. It is time I let my father's ghost pass into history."

Wide-eyed, Desdemona gestured her head and hand, offering Kain the permission to open the coffin. The stone whined as it was shoved aside to expose the shimmering sword and breastplate. At the top of the coffin, Kain saw the skull of a wolf. He winced, almost floundering until he took a deep breath and set the necklace inside the coffin and closed it.

Pentacost's legacy allowed to pass into legend.

"You may come here anytime you like, Alexander." Desdemona handed Kain a copy of the skeleton key once they exited the building.

Tala stroked her mate's arm. "Are you okay?"

Kain nodded. He felt better than okay. A sensation of true freedom flooded him, joining his renewed strength, scar-free body and eyes no longer clouded by the dark god's influence.

The rest of the week passed quickly. Solaris appeared in Kain's dreams as she said she would, instructing him to say his goodbyes to his mate and child.

"Are you sure you won't see Damien and Gabriel?" Tala asked as they sat on the wood bench at the Woods Edge.

Magnus and Zane pulled up in two different cars.

Kain lowered his head. "Even if I desired to see them, it seems I do not have the time. Magnus will make sure to get you home safely."

Tala embraced him, sobbing. "I can't say goodbye. I won't."

Kain placed his hands on her hips, kissing her and tasting the salt of her tears. "This is not goodbye, sweetheart. Wait for me. I will call you every day, I promise you."

Tala only stared at him. Her anger and pain stabbed his heart, making it hard to keep his resolve on what he knew needed to be done.

Guiding her away from him, he made his way to the passenger's side of Zane's Firebird. He watched as Magnus opened the door to let his mate in and pull away before getting in Zane's car.

"Are you sure you want to do this? I can handle it on my own," Zane asked, his voice stoic.

Kain rolled down the window to let the fresh night air in. "No, you cannot. You know as well as I do I was not brought back without a reason. That was no ordinary vampire. I know the dark god well enough to know he will not let this go easily. Something tells me we have yet to hear the last of the monster wearing Anthony's skin. Which reminds me."

"We found him. It looked like he managed avoiding recapture, but he's malnourished and hurt. Kyle has a request to tell Tala when she's over losing you," Zane replied.

Relieved at having found Tobias, Kain let the cool breeze of the night kiss his face. Tala's voice in his mind made him smile. *I love you too.*

ACKNOWLEDGEMENTS

I would like to start by thanking God for the gifts I've been blessed with. A family that loves me, friends who are there to help me.

My husband, John, for his continued support even though I know this really wasn't his kind of thing. Damien wouldn't be who is without you. You are an inspiration for his quarks and his damage but also his strength in times of trial.

My kids: Amberrose and Grant for putting up with the overtime and sudden deadlines. I know there were tons of hours you wanted my attention but thank you for understanding, even if you are both so young.

My mom, Shannon and dad, Long who are proud of this achievement and for keeping the kids when I needed to pull an all-nighter. Even though you may not like the genre. Lol.

I want to thank Alisha Fisher for being such an inspiration to me and the support system I needed when I wanted to give up.

To Darci Steele for editing the tar out of the manuscript and offering feedback. My beta readers who served as the eyes and ears of the Wolfgods, thank you all. I will definitely be reaching out to all of you.

Kristin Martin and Kim Chance, we may not know each other personally but you two wonderful women have been inspirations and leaders in my life. The positive outlook you have, the passion you show for your books and the world of authors and literature and the overwhelmingly constructive advice you continue to give lit a fire under my rump I have needed for a long time. Thank you for doing what you do.

I want to thank the beta readers who devoted your time to help me get this book finished. Your feedback helped Bane of Tenebris become something it would have taken me a long time to do on my own. You guys are my front lines, without you, I don't think this book would have become what it is.

Finally to my followers and friends on social media. You are more valued than you know.

Thank you all for your support. I hope you will return for part two: Bane of Tenebris.

ABOUT THE AUTHOR

Blaise Ramsay began her creative career in the conceptual art and design industry. For fifteen years, she spent her time crafting characters and worlds for others. Recently she shifted her attention to the world of literature where she writes mostly paranormal romance. Her debut title, *Bane of Tenebris* is the first of four books in the *Wolfgods* series. A portion of the proceeds of her book sales go to charity.

When Blaise isn't busy working with sexy wolf boys, she can be found reviewing books for fellow authors, working for a few book tour companies, holding interviews, and offering guest posts. A professional book blogger, mom, wife, and full blood Texan, Blaise loves nothing more than helping others, meeting new people and coaching folks on Scrivener.

If you would like to get in touch with Blaise, the best way to contact her is through her website Fyresydepublishing.com.

NOTE FROM THE AUTHOR

Word-of-mouth is crucial for any author to succeed. If you enjoyed *Bane of Tenebris*, please leave a review online—anywhere you are able. Even if it's just a sentence or two. It would make all the difference and would be very much appreciated.

Thanks!
Blaise

Want more amazing adventure?

Subscribe to the Newsletter at
FyreSydePublishing.com
to receive:

-FREE Books

-The Latest News

-Exclusive Content

Thank you so much for reading one of Blaise Ramsay's novels.

If you enjoyed the experience, please check out
the beginning of the *Wolfgods* series!

Blessing of Luna by Blaise Ramsay

"A fast-moving story of love, war, and curses."
-Cranky TBC